For all my fellow artist types who walk around with their insides on the outside.

theater lovers

ciara blume

DOLCE VILLA

COPYRIGHT PAGE

Theater Lovers by Ciara Blume

Published by Dolce Villa Press

www.ciarablume.com

Cover Art by Jillian Liota of Blue Moon Creative Studio

acknowledgments

As always, I have to thank my crackerjack editors: Joyce Mochrie, copy editor, owner of One Last Look, and Anya Kagan, developmental editor, of Touchstone Editing.

I'm so grateful to my husband Brian for reading the "dailies" and giving me honest feedback. How many exits on the freeway have we missed while arguing about a character's motivation? I've lost track.

Thanks also to my daughter Marly and her pals Libby and Nicole for reading through the first chapter and indulging me when I needed to discuss and work through Dean and Chelsea's history with someone closer to Chelsea's age. My other three kids; Ani, Fox and Leo have also provided entertaining insight and must be praised for their patience with me always typing away in their midst.

My friend Michelle Price has been a fabulous beta reader and final typo catcher on all three of my books, and I am thankful for this! Jennifer Bob has kindly saved me more than once - catching rogue formatting issues.

Thanks also to my brother Barry Blumenfeld and his wife, Leslie Girmscheid, for enthusiastically reading and being so supportive, and to all my friends mentioned in the first two books in the Lit Lovers series who continue to put up with me while I hole up and write, only surfacing occasionally to check in and throw parties.

My family and friends really are the best. I don't know how I got so lucky.

prologue: chelsea

Fifteen years ago …

I wait with Dean in the wings of the theater. This scene is my favorite part of *Little Shop of Horrors*. It's the moment when Audrey and Seymour finally kiss. But that's not why it's my favorite scene. It's my favorite because it lasts for almost seven minutes. And during those seven minutes, I get Dean all to myself. Just the two of us, alone in the dark.

Seven minutes in heaven.

It's the opening night of the high school theater's limited run, and I've made an important decision. I'm not going to wait around for the cast party. I am finally going to go for it. I'm going to kiss him.

I shift nervously and bounce on my toes in my black jazz shoes, chosen specifically for this occasion. I'm no dancer, though. I wish I had the grace and rhythm of Brittany, the popular senior who is currently standing centerstage, awaiting declarations of passion and a theater-worthy kiss from her costar. Why do things seem to come so easily to the Brittanys of the world? Brittany will probably also be prom queen.

I, Chelsea Porter, on the other hand, am an expert at flying under the radar and blending into the scenery. Hence the black jazz shoes. Perfect for stepping silently during scene changes. My clothing helps to make me invisible as well. I'm wearing black leggings and a baggy, old, oversize, black sweatshirt that used to be my dad's. There's a faded picture of him and his bandmates, all big hair and '80's rocker clothing, reflected by the cracked and peeling tour dates below the image. They hadn't been on the charts for very long, but that one song had been a bona fide hit in '87.

I tug on the black beanie covering my mousy-blonde hair.

Even my underwear is black. Not that it matters what I'm wearing in the near-pitch shadows I'm currently inhabiting with Dean. But it boosts my confidence knowing I've got on something "sexy" underneath my cloak of invisibility. I can feel the itch of stiff, synthetic lace against my recently sprouted boobs. I know Dean has noticed them, as well. I caught him staring at my chest during one of the dress rehearsals. I'd just been wearing a tank and no bra. It was freezing cold in the theater that night, and when the lights came back on? My headlights were definitely on. I was mortified. Dean had handed me his jacket. His *letter* jacket. I hadn't wanted to give it back.

The thong is giving me one hell of a wedgie. I squirm and consider picking it out but ultimately decide against it. It's dark, but Dean still might be able to tell. We use other senses in our inky, velvet-curtained cocoon. I can tell exactly how close he is with my eyes closed. Eight inches at the moment. That's the size of the air pocket behind me, between us. I just have to turn around and lean in.

The audience bursts into laughter, signaling me that I only have two minutes left until the onstage kiss. This is when I'm going to do it. My heart thumps even faster and harder. Can Dean hear it? Can I hear his heart? I'd like to think I can. I close my eyes and listen. Nothing. Just the faint and steady sound of his breath. If I concentrate, I can feel it faintly on the back of my neck. And I can certainly smell him. Dean smells like Old Spice, grass, and sweat. He'd probably been playing football right up to the minute he got to the theater. The smell of him is easy to isolate. It stands out from all the other smells in the theater, as if lit by a spotlight. Somewhere in the background, there's also the dust and must of thrift-store wardrobe items, the cold pizza we hastily snarfed for dinner, and the woodshop and paint smells of the flats we're waiting to swap. But all of that fades to black when Dean steps closer. Six inches?

I can feel the warmth radiating from his skin. Warmth and goodness. Not everybody knows what a good guy Dean Riley is, but I know. I know the real Dean because he's my big brother, Jackson's, best friend. And he's my friend, too, though most people don't really see that. They don't see Dean watching movies with me while Jackson messes around on his PC or Dean helping me pick out the paint colors for the mural in my bedroom. Sometimes I think Dean is more *my* friend than my brother's. Not that I'd say that out loud. Who would believe me?

Dean and Jackson are legends at Ephron High, unarguably the coolest guys in the senior class. Brains and brawn. The most eligible bachelors.

Somehow, they've both managed to remain single almost all the way through the fall term. Not that Dean hasn't hooked up with anyone. From the rumors, he's been hooking up with a different girl every weekend. He even made out with a freshman cheerleader last month. I wanted to hate her, but who could blame anyone for wanting to kiss Dean Riley? Those lips, and the way he smiles at you, like everything is a private joke. Irresistible.

I also can't be jealous. I know that Dean thinks the girl is bonkers. She practically stalked him, asking him for a commitment after the party, and they didn't even make it to third base. This, Jackson says, is why he never makes out with freshmen.

Yuck. I *really* don't want to think about what my brother is up to. My guess, though, is not much. He says he isn't interested in seriously dating anyone till his frontal lobe firms up a bit more.

On the other side of the curtains, an anticipatory hush settles over the audience as they wait to see what happens next. It mirrors my own tension. I feel as taut as a drawn bow.

As I wait for the big moment, I run down the "Perfect Man" checklist in my head. It's like a mantra. Dean checks every box.

My Perfect Man: A List by Chelsea Porter

1. Doesn't put up with bullshit from anyone—check! Dean doesn't care what anyone thinks. He stands up to bullies and calls it like it is.
2. Good with his hands—check! Dean can fix anything. He built the entire Little Shop of Horrors set from scratch.
3. Knows how to ride a motorcycle—check! Dean says it's a life skill.
4. Has piercing, blue eyes—check! Aquamarine, but close enough.
5. Has great hair—check! Thick, wavy, auburn hair, bonus points for the unusual color and shine.

6. Has a great sense of humor—check! Although, I could do without the practical jokes he and Jackson are always playing on me.
7. Good at sports—check! This is mostly because my future kids certainly won't get that from me. I have two left feet.
8. Popular—check!
9. Has a great bod—double check!

I'm just about to do it, when Dean unexpectedly leans forward and wraps his arms around my waist. The audience gasps, and so do I.

He leans his chin on my shoulder and whispers in my ear.

"What do you think, Chels? Should I ask Brit?"

There's no time to spare. I have to do it now. I spin around to face him and reach up to tangle my hands in his hair. Oh, God. It's just as soft as I always imagined.

I pull his lips to mine. Someone in the audience wolf-whistles.

At first, Dean freezes. His hands drop to his sides. But then, something switches on, and he's pulling me closer, kissing me back tenderly and passionately as the orchestra music rises to a touching crescendo.

But just as suddenly, when the music stops and the curtain drops, he shoves me away.

"No!" he asserts. "No. No. No. NO! This cannot happen! What the fuck, Chels? Did Jackson put you up to this? Are you pulling a prank on me?"

All around us, there is motion. Brittany and her costar have rushed off to change, and crew members are wheeling the flats from the last scene offstage, opposite us. It's our job to get the new pieces into place. Now.

"We gotta get this out there. Grab your side," Dean whispers, positioning himself on the far end of the flat, back to the stage. He takes a step back, pulling the huge, unwieldy set with him. He's doing most of the work of moving the large pieces. It's my job to look for the reflective tape marks and guide him.

I'm still buzzing from the kiss, but we've rehearsed this, done it dozens of times.

"Keep going. Left a little. No, right," my voice barely audible in the dark. My hands are shaking. The wooden backdrop wobbles ominously, falling toward me.

"Shit!" Dean says as he scrambles to steady it. I can hear the panic in his voice. It's loud enough for the audience to hear as well, and a small sneaker wave of snickering washes over us.

"It's okay, Chels, you're safe. I got it," he whispers a second later. He stops in exactly the right spot and quickly folds down the braces to secure the set in place. He doesn't look up till he's done, but when he does, he isn't looking at me. He's looking over my shoulder at the backstage area of the wings where Brittany is standing, mid costume change, wearing nothing but a tiny bikini to protect her so-called modesty. There's not a lot of light back there, either, but to our light-starved eyes, she may as well be basking in a ray of golden sun. She wiggles her fingers in a cute, girly wave at Dean, and I watch as he smiles, nodding back at her.

What had he been saying before I kissed him?

"Should I ask Brit—"

Ask Brit. Ask her what?

Oh. Oh? OH! Understanding doesn't dawn gently. It peels off me like a deceptively pleasant, hot wax strip when it's suddenly torn away from your sensitive hairy bits. I want to howl, but I can't.

"You want to ask *Brittany* to prom?" I ask, barely above a whisper, but louder than it should be. Dean's eyes widen, the whites catching the light as his head whips back to my face.

"Shh." He holds a finger over his lips.

But I'm already running away, not paying attention, not watching where I'm going. I trip and slide on my ass, straight into the sets that have just been wheeled offstage. My brand-new, "sexy" thong catches on something, dragging and cutting into my flesh, giving me a rope burn that's only slightly less painful than the blow to my pride.

And then the stacked sets fall like dominos, landing on my left leg, leaving it fractured in two places.

————

After the show has ended and I've been X-rayed, Dean stops by the hospital with a big bunch of roses. He sends my mom and Jackson down to the cafeteria to get some food and sits with me while I wait to get my cast. I still cannot look at him.

"Way to steal the show," he says, laying the roses on the table.

"Sorry I couldn't help with the third act," I say, pretending to be tough.

"I'm sorry I couldn't come sooner." He shrugs. "But you know what they say … 'The show must go on!'"

I snort. "Right. But first, they say, 'Break a leg.'"

"You know you're not literally supposed to break a leg, Kiddo? It's just an expression." Dean attempts to take my hand, and I yank it away. *Kiddo?* He's never called me that before.

He paces around the room, examining rolls of plaster and tape. He fiddles with a frightening pair of oversize scissors.

"Hey, I don't think you're supposed to touch that stuff," I say primly.

"I'm just interested to see how it works. Mind if I watch while they put your cast on? I've never worked with fiberglass before."

"Is that why you're here?" I pout. "Because you're dying to do crafts with medical supplies?"

"No, Chels," he says, putting a hand on my face and turning me to face him. "That's not why I'm here. We should talk about what happened."

"No need. It was just an accident. A stupid accident. Best if we all forget about it," I say. "And the sooner the better."

"I don't know, Chels. I don't think anyone is going to forget tonight's performance," Dean says, barely suppressing that knowing half smile of his. "Especially me."

I fold my arms across my chest, hugging myself protectively, trying to ignore the pain from the uber wedgie between my butt cheeks as I lift my chin higher, attempting to muster whatever scrap of dignity I have left. There's only one thing I need to know.

"Did you ask Brittany to prom?" I ask.

Dean shrugs. "Nah, she asked me first."

"And you said yes?" I ask, incredulously.

"Sure, why not. She's hot." He smiles that rakish smile again, and I feel like smacking him suddenly. Why is he torturing me like this? It's one thing to reject me, but calling me kiddo after he kissed me back and then telling me someone else is hot? What the actual fuck? A fresh wave of outrage crests and breaks over me.

"But you kissed me back!" I spit out, tears starting to collect in the corners of my eyes. "How long after the ambulance left did you wait to make out with her?"

I'm suddenly impatient to get my cast and get out of here. And not just this room. My whole life. Clearly, I can't go back to school for the rest of the year. Perhaps I can apply for an inter-district transfer to another high school. Better yet, maybe I can apply to a fancy Swedish boarding school like Jackson's old best friend, Hudson Holm. Surely there are scholarships for special cases like mine?

Dean uses his thumb to wipe a stray tear from the corner of my eye.

"You're too good for me, and you know it, Chelsea. Also," he says more seriously, "too young."

"I'm not a little girl anymore, Dean," I argue, pushing myself up on my elbows. My oversize hospital gown gaps and slips off my shoulder, revealing the lacy, black bra I'd worn under my sweatshirt just in case.

"I can see that, Chelsea." Dean pulls up the gown, looking away pointedly.

"Then why? Why are you doing this to me?" I whine, realizing a moment too late that I sound exactly like the child I don't want him to see me as.

"Because I don't want to take you out of the oven when you're only half baked." He smiles. "Not to mention my own mushy frontal lobe. Just ask Jackson. We're both still wobbly. Can't be trusted to make good decisions."

"So, kissing me was a bad decision, then?" I narrow my eyes.

"No. I mean, yes. Your friendship means so much to me. It's too special to risk it." Dean's eyes are imploring.

"Or maybe I don't mean enough." I turn my head to face the wall.

"Cut it out, Chelly Belly." Dean sits on the edge of the exam table next to me, calling me by the stupid nickname my mom used to have for me when I was little. I'd made her stop calling me that when I was ten. Right around the time Dean and Jackson started hanging out. They still bust it out from time to time when they want to annoy me, though.

"Fuck off. You cut it out." I attempt to elbow him away, forgetting for a moment that my left leg is broken. Crushing pain shoots through my whole body, making me freeze with pain.

"Shit!" Dean exclaims, jumping up. "Did I hurt you? I'm so sorry. This is all my fault."

"Honestly? My pride hurts a hell of a lot more than my leg, Dean. Maybe you should just go," I say. "I don't want to hear any more bullshit about being a half-baked cake. I get it. You're not into me. Now leave me alone."

"Look at me, Chels." Dean stands patiently by the table and waits. "I mean it, *look* at me."

I know how stubborn he is. He's not leaving till I do it. I force myself to meet his eyes, my tears still streaming.

"There you are," he says. I am surprised to see that his eyes look a bit teary too.

"You know me well enough to know that if I simply wasn't into you, I would say so, right?" he asks.

Slowly, I nod. I do know him well enough. Almost as well as I know my own brother. Possibly better.

"So why can't you believe me when I say it isn't that? Why can't you trust me when I say that if you were my age or, God help me, if you weren't my best friend's little sister ..."

Dean leans over and traces my lower lip with his thumb while staring into my eyes. I feel my lids growing heavy, my eyes beginning to close, as if he's about to kiss me. Which he isn't. In the next instant, he's spinning away and pacing again.

"I tell you what. I just had an idea. Let's make a deal."

It takes me a moment to catch my breath. "You want to make a deal with me?"

"Yes. Here it is—check back in with me when you're my age."

"You want me to 'check in' with you when I'm seventeen? Why? You think we'll be fully baked by then?"

"I don't know how baked we'll be, but the difference between seventeen and twenty isn't nearly as tricky as the difference between fourteen and seventeen, is it? I'm guessing that by the time you're a senior in high school, you'll have a trail of broken hearts in your wake and you won't even remember my last name."

"Probably," I say, thinking *never*.

"If, for some reason, you find yourself single and in need of a prom date for your senior prom," Dean says, "I'll be there. With bells on. Chels bells. Scout's honor," he swears, smiling wryly and performing a Boy Scout salute.

"Deal," I say. "On one condition. We never tell Jackson about any of this." I hold out my hand to shake.

A man walks into the room carrying a clipboard and asks, "Ready to pick a color for your cast?"

"And you have to let me be the first one to sign your cast," Dean says, before grasping my outstretched hand.

We shake on it.

When the cast is done, Dean signs my cast along the top edge, toward the inside, halfway up my thigh. He writes his name, draws a heart, and writes the last two digits of the year I'll be graduating. Then, as if swearing an oath, he kisses his thumb and presses it to the heart he's just drawn. His hand grazes my inner thigh as he strokes his thumb along the top edge of the cast. But then Jackson has to ruin everything by laughing loudly about something in the hallway.

Dean pulls his hand away quickly, just before my mom and Jackson walk back into the room.

Perhaps the night wasn't a total loss after all. Dean Riley just asked me to my senior prom.

chelsea

. . .

I TAKE a sip of my drink, trying to get into the headspace for the Lit Lovers recording session. My brother, Jackson, and I host this podcast, along with a couple of our mutual friends, Emily and Alexis.

It started out as a joke.

Jackson has always poked fun at the rom-coms that my mom and I love, but I know he secretly loves them too. My preference leans toward the sweet stories, but my mom has always had a cringeworthy penchant for spice. Jackson doesn't discriminate. He sees it all the same way. Predictable. A code to be cracked. He likes to act all logical and superior, deconstructing every story like a mad jungle scientist swinging between the branches of pop psychology, human biology, and literary theory. His overly analytical brain tells him that love is nothing more than a numbers game. He's been trying to get the formula right for a few years now and claims everything is research for his new dating app.

The podcast was born after Alexis, who is firmly in the "team spice" camp, pointed out that listening to us all argue was hysterically funny.

There's potentially a lot to unpack here, especially given the lack of romance in both my brother's life and my own. Not to mention the toxic dumpster fire that was our parents' relationship. But by mutual understanding, we don't go there. We keep the conversation light.

It's usually a lot of fun recording the episodes. There's plenty of off-the-cuff banter, poking fun at current movies, TV series, and relationship-themed reality TV shows. We take turns reviewing books and discuss everything from fiction tropes to celebrity gossip. Sometimes we have guests on the show too. Assorted authors and relationship experts have made appearances, along with some of our local pals.

But this week's episode feels loaded. It's all because of the trope of the week. There were only so many times I could juggle the calendar to keep it off the schedule. I know Jackson is going to have a field day with this one.

We're all sitting in Emily's living room on big, comfy sofas, looking off in different directions so we don't accidentally crack each other up.

"Welcome to the Lit Lovers podcast. I'm your host, Jackson," my brother says.

"And I'm Chelsea," I say automatically.

"Emily here, making sure my friends stay out of trouble," Emily introduces herself. You can hear the smile in her words. She has been so much more relaxed and happy lately. I'm a little jealous but happy for her as well. She's had a lot of sad things happen to her in recent years, but ever since a writing assignment took her to Italy last December, things have been looking up. Not only did she and Blaze Smith fall in love while she was covering his book tour, but she's discovered family in Tuscany that she never knew she had. Her hazel eyes are sparkling today, and somehow, she manages to look glamorous, even in an oversize, flannel shirt and her long, curly, brown hair piled in a messy bun on top of her head. I know she's excited about heading back to Italy for Easter.

"And I'm Alexis, here to fan the flames of your literary *desires*," Alexis purrs in her almost comically sexy podcast voice. Alexis is a study in contrasts. She's curvy and athletic, an intellectual who reads tabloids, drinks cocktails mixed with green juice, and wears sequins with sweatshirts. She has shoulder-length, brown hair that's currently overtoned to an unnatural shade of burgundy that only she can pull off. Alexis and Emily have known each other since they were small children and Emily's grandmother watched Alexis after school. Of the four of us, Emily is the only one who didn't grow up in Ephron.

"Today's trope is one that my sister, Chelsea, might want to weigh in on," Jackson announces, predictably. He sounds so smug. "You want to do the honors of revealing the trope, Sis?"

Silence. I bite down on my lip. I won't give him the satisfaction.

"Fine. My sister isn't spilling, so I will. It's not every day that hosting a podcast with your sibling hits paydirt like this, but today is that day! Today is the day we finally dig into the 'your brother's best friend' trope."

"Sounds sexy. I do love me a good, taboo-based trope," Alexis says breathily.

Inwardly, I groan. Why am I even going along with this? And what if the podcast makes its way back to Dean? It's likely it will. Jackson and Dean Riley have stayed in touch.

Who cares? What does it matter if Dean listens to this?

I care. I hate that I still do. But there it is. Jackson may have no idea what really went on between me and his best friend, but Dean knows. I wonder if he still thinks my teenage crush on him was pathetic. Clearly, he'd thought it then. So why should he feel any differently now?

"Easy there, Tiger." Jackson laughs at Alexis, and then he turns his attention back to me. "Seriously, Chels? You have nothing to say about this trope?"

"Nope. Nothing. None of your tech-bro pals are my type." Lamely, I attempt to misdirect the conversation away from Dean. But it's futile.

"You guys, leave Chelsea alone," Emily chides. Emily is so nice. I can always count on her to stick up for me.

"Does the name Dean Riley ring any bells?" Jackson asks.

And here we are. Welcome to Mortificationtown. Population, one.

I cannot show any weakness. You'd think I'd be used to this act. I've been performing it for the better part of a decade. Not constantly, but I still know all the lines by heart.

"Jesus, Jackson, it's been what, fifteen years? You want to give it a rest?" I sigh.

"Not really." He laughs.

"Come on, Chelsea, you're among friends." Alexis attempts to cajole it out of me. "This is a safe space. You can tell us. What's the story?"

Good luck with that, Alexis.

"There's no story. I had a minor crush on one of my brother's friends in high school. Jackson is blowing it all out of proportion now. He'll do anything for ratings."

"Minor crush?" Jackson imitates, mocking me. "You signed up to move theater sets just to be near him. Which, by the way, I just have to share with our listeners, was a colossal *fail*. You know the expression, 'break a leg?' Well, my sister,

Chelsea, took that advice literally. She fell flat on her ass, knocking over half the sets and breaking her leg on opening night. I had to help poor Dean fix everything and do her job for her for the rest of the run."

"Ouch. That must have been traumatic for you, Chelsea," Emily sympathizes. *Two more points for Emily. At least someone has my back. I need to do something nice for her.*

"It was embarrassing," I admit. "I was in a cast for almost three months." *And I still don't wear thongs. Ever.* I do not share that tidbit.

"So, what happened to Dean?" Emily asks. "Is he still in the picture?"

"We still hang out occasionally," Jackson says. "He moved to LA. He's an art director. A super successful and famous one. You might not have heard of his name, but you've definitely seen his work. He won an Oscar for his work on the Titanium Man franchise."

"Wait a minute," Alexis says, and I can sense her scrolling as she says this, going through her tablet for clues. Finally, she hits pay dirt. "Holy shit! This guy?"

We all glance up at the tablet she's holding up. There's a photo of Dean Riley on the red carpet somewhere. And of course, he's not alone.

"Ding, ding, ding!" Jackson goes on to create a picture with his words. "I want our listeners to get the visual, so I will just let you know that Alexis has located a photograph of Dean, and I think that's the inimitable actor Zara Jones on his arm in the picture, a.k.a. Z-Cat the jaguar shifter in the Titanium Man films. Care to comment, Chelsea?"

I do not comment. Nor do I look at the photo. But naturally, he's with Zara. She's one of the most powerful, influential women in Hollywood. Not only is she incredibly gorgeous, but she's a genius as well. In the past few years, she's branched out into directing and producing. And, of course, she's involved in numerous philanthropic ventures. Dean couldn't do better than Zara Jones.

But he could have done a lot worse.

"Holy hotness, Batman!" Alexis whistles. "I mean, I'm not your little sister, Jackson, but I'd take a trip on that trope. You know, for science."

"Yeah, get in line," Jackson teases. "But I don't think good ol' Dean has been hurting for dates."

"Guys! Do we really need to objectify Dean this way? Why can't we just talk about the trope without having to personalize it?" I attempt to steer the conversation away from myself. "Who can name some popular 'brother's best friend' trope examples in film and literature?"

Silence.

"Seriously?" I ask. "There's the one by Tess Bailey, and I think Pippa Grant and Meghan Quinn have both gone there."

"Do tell," Jackson drawls. "If anyone would be up on those titles, it'd be you, right?"

"Emily? Alexis?" I ask.

"I got nothing," Alexis says. "Although I'm definitely inspired now. Makes me wish I had an older brother. Preferably one who was a professional athlete."

"You could always flip it from the brother's best friend trope to the best friend's brother trope," Emily suggests.

"Except then, I would need a new bff, Em. You don't have an older brother."

"Oh please ... take mine!" I say, ducking to avoid the pillow Jackson lobs in my direction.

"Do any of you have stories about embarrassing crushes on your siblings' best friends?" Jackson asks the audience. "Tell us about it on the Facebook page. I'll be sure to tag my old pal, Dean, just in case he wants to weigh in about what it was like to be the object of Chelsea's affection."

Shit. I'm going to have to wait till Jackson posts, then go in and quietly untag him, which means I'm going to have to look at Dean Riley's page.

dean

. . .

I PULL into a roadside café to grab some breakfast and wait for the morning chill to burn off before hitting the road again. It's been a leisurely, four-day trip up the coast from Cali. I wanted to give myself this time to think, to make a proper transition out of this relocation. I've made stops in San Francisco and Portland to visit friends and old haunts. But I'm anxious to get to Ephron now and get to work. After years of dreaming about the possibilities, I can't believe it's finally happening. I'm nervous and excited. I've put my entire nest egg into this passion project, but I'm pretty confident it's going to go well. By June, the amphitheater in Ephron will be fully functional, rivaling the summer stock productions in LA and Ashland, Oregon.

It doesn't have to support me, at least not at first. I'll still take on other projects. But I'll have the luxury to choose when and where I want to work. And in the meantime, I'll be making a difference in my hometown and the creative community in general. I'm finally bringing my worlds together. None of this would have been possible without the support of some of my very influential friends.

Obviously, people back home know that *something's* up. The work going on in downtown Ephron has been impossible to miss. Riley and Son Construction crews have been splitting their time between the renovations to the historic building in Holm Square and fixing up the community center and amphitheater that my production company purchased last fall. The work wasn't just happening indoors. As soon as it was warm enough to work outdoors, they'd started grading the seating areas.

I can't wait to go public with my involvement in this project. There are only three people who know the whole truth right now—my brother, Eli, Zara, and my mom. They've all been amazingly encouraging, but I don't know how everyone else is going to react.

I'll know soon enough.

> Don't forget, we're having dinner with Mom and Dad tonight. I think Mom's already got the champagne chilling.

The text from Eli comes in while I'm mapping my route for this final leg of the trip. A moment later, a second text appears.

> Dad's going to be happy, Dean. I promise. Just like Mom and Brittany are. It's going to be great having you home again.

Make that four people who know. It makes sense that Eli would tell his wife. I can't begrudge him that. Keeping secrets from a spouse is a recipe for disaster. I feel bad for putting my mom in that position, but she agreed that it would be better to wait till I was a little further along before telling him. Less potential for friction that way.

Nearly two decades after I left town and "quit" the family business, things are still tense between my dad and me.

Jackson, of course, is another story. I still haven't told my childhood best friend that I'm the one who has bought and is renovating the property. This is because Jackson cannot keep a secret. He's a genius, but he isn't known for his tact or social skills. I can honestly say I love that guy, but he has zero chill.

And then there's his sister, Chelsea.

She's the person I most wish I could have told sooner. But that would be tough to pull off, considering the fact that she hasn't really spoken to me in ten years.

It hurts when I think about Chelsea. I don't know why she seems to hate me. I'm confused by her, and I'm also a little pissed that she's written me off. Of all the people I would have hoped to impress with my success in Hollywood, would have wanted to be there rooting for me, and would have hoped to dazzle? She was up there. She was sitting in the judgmental stands of my psyche. Right next to my grumpy father. Both of them were checked out, attention elsewhere, ignoring me.

While my dad has openly expressed his disappointment in me, with Chelsea, it's like I don't even exist anymore. I've been ghosted, to put it in very LA terms. I don't even get mass-mailed holiday cards from her.

Jackson hasn't been able to shed any light on the situation. The few times I've mentioned his sister, he's changed the subject, either acting like nothing's up or making insensitive jokes about the time when she was fourteen and she broke her leg because of her so-called "stupid crush" on me. If he knows anything, he's not sharing it. Eventually, I stopped asking and did my best to stop thinking about her. What else am I supposed to do?

I exhale and regroup. I may have tried to put her out of my mind, but I haven't succeeded. There's an unhealed wound in the place where our attachment used to exist. Every so often, I can't resist probing that spot, like working a tender tooth with my tongue, checking in to see if the ache is still there. In a weird way, I'm glad it is. Missing her is such a familiar pain, it's become a part of me.

I wonder what, if anything, she's thought about the work going on in Holm Square.

The waitress, a middle-aged woman in an apron, flirts with me when she comes to the table. But not seriously. She's at least ten years older than me, and I can see she's wearing a wedding ring.

"You look like you just stepped off a movie set," she says, batting her lashes. If she only knew.

"Must be the morning fog," I say. "Keeps my complexion fresh and dewy."

She smiles and takes my order, leaving me to enjoy my coffee in the quiet company of my cell phone.

My life has been so peaceful since the final Titanium Man film wrapped. For the first time in over a decade, I've had time to go surfing and fishing. I finished an entire book series. I've been to the Getty and LACMA, I've slept in, and I've done the *New York Times* Wordle challenge almost every day. All the stuff that my hectic work schedule hasn't left me the time or bandwidth for. It's been glorious.

Zara was right to insist I take some time to myself before diving into this next venture.

The phone lights up with another message from Eli.

> Sorry, Dean. I can't meet you till four now.
> Brit's not feeling well, so I have to take
> Braden to Toddler Hip-Hop.

> No problem. I'll just take a stroll down memory lane & check out Holm Square while you guys get your groove on. Send me pics?

Eli replies with a string of emojis and then sends a GIF of a dancing gorilla. I find myself grinning. For the first time in a very long time, it feels like I'm back in on the joke.

Who would have guessed that I'd ever be close with my brother again? Or that I'd be headed back to Ephron after almost two decades of traveling the world and building my career?

chelsea

. . .

I TAKE a sip of my coffee and wince. I let it get cold again, and it's slightly acrid.

The ancient, drip-style coffeemaker in the teachers' lounge needs replacing, but there's no budget, and we're all playing a game of chicken to see who'll pony up and purchase a pod-style machine, which will only open a whole other can of worms. I can hear it now. "Whose pods are those? Is that coffeemaker eco-friendly? Has anyone seen my refillable pod capsule? It was right here …"

I pop my mug in the microwave, stuff my earphones into my ears, and crank up my music. I have ten minutes until third period starts, and Noah, the honors Lit & Comp teacher, joins me in the lounge for lunch. Noah is my work spouse, and I'm pretty sure he'd like to be more than that. He's made it clear, without making a pest of himself. I don't know what my problem is. He'd be a perfect choice. He checks off every box on my list.

My Perfect Man: A List by Chelsea Porter

1. Is kind and understanding—check! Noah is a

diplomat through and through. He's an expert negotiator and great at getting people to calm down and compromise.

2. Organized—check! Whatever you need done, Noah can create a phenomenal spreadsheet to help you research your options and make a conscientious plan for hiring.

3. Practical/Safety oriented—check! Noah has a lifetime subscription to Consumer Reports. He buys the extended warranty on everything.

4. Has nice eyes—check! Chocolate brown.

5. Has hair—check! Loads of it. He could probably get it cut more regularly, though. The kids sometimes make fun of his wild, frizzy mop.

6. Has a sense of humor—check! Not everyone can appreciate his dry sense of humor, but I think it's just one more sign of his higher intellect.

7. Isn't too into sports—check, if you don't count hiking!

8. Popular—check! Noah is well tolerated by staff and students alike.

9. Takes good care of himself—double check! Noah religiously charts his daily steps and caloric intake and has spreadsheets for all his doctor appointments. I've never met anyone more on top of their health.

And yet … there's no spark. I'm pretty sure it's not him. It's me.

I take my reheated coffee to a round, Formica-topped table, sit down, and flip open my laptop. There's nobody else in here, so it's the perfect time to check the messages on my secret Instagram account.

A couple of years ago, I started posting my trompe l'oeil work to a private account. I have no idea how people are finding it. Hashtags? The point of it isn't marketing. It's more like a journal. A place to record my thoughts and maybe get some feedback from other people in the art world. I only post once or twice a month, which is about the time it takes me to plan and execute my ideas.

Photographing the finished product is the hardest part, sometimes even harder than painting myself into the background. Everything has to be lined up and timed perfectly for me to make my naked self disappear. When everything comes together, it feels like magic—part painting, part performance art.

It looks like there are several new requests to follow, and a gallery has reached out to me about a possible show. I'll wait till I'm at home to respond. Most likely, I'll send a version of the form letter I've sent in the past. Thanks, but no thanks. I only sell my prints on Etsy via a print-on-demand company on the East Coast. Nothing gets traced back to me.

I close the Instagram tab. I know where I'm going next. The Facebook tab is already open. I check if Jackson has tagged Dean yet. There's nothing on the podcast. He must have forgotten. I am relieved.

Unless …

A thought occurs to me. What if he posted something on Dean's profile? That would be so much worse. I might not be able to delete it if he didn't post it from the podcast account.

I'm going to have to search his profile now. It's silly how hard my heart pounds as I consider this. Do I really want to open Pandora's box? I've managed not to look him up once since he left. Sheer stubbornness, wounded pride, and a touch of spite had kept me strong. But some people might say it's time I got over myself. Isn't twelve years long enough to nurse a grudge? So, he left town and never looked back. How can I fault Dean Riley for building a life for himself in LA? He's enjoyed success with a career he is passionate about. That's a good thing, not a crime. It's not like he killed someone.

Success hasn't ruined him, either. He's not like my dad. He looked good in the photo Alexis found of him. Healthy. Fit. The same, but different. I can't get it out of my head. I want to see more.

Quickly, before I lose my nerve, I type in his name.

Of course, Dean doesn't have a normal Facebook profile. He has a public persona page. But at least his avatar isn't a professional headshot. It appears to be a candid photo someone shot of him, studying a set being constructed on a film lot. There's a pencil behind his ear. Old habits die hard.

I scroll through a few more photos. He definitely looks older. But not in a bad way. Sun kissed, and more carved in the right places. His jaw is more defined. He's still lean, athletic, and so damned handsome. More like a leading man than the back-stage visionary type.

But perhaps that's what living in LA, where everyone is attractive and making a fortune in the movie biz, gets you. That and a sex goddess for a girlfriend. Zara Jones, from the look of all their photos together.

Slowly, I scroll farther down through his feed. There are photos from the premiere of the final Titanium Man film a few months ago. There he is, posing with Titanium Man himself, Rafe Barzilay, along with Zara Jones and other members of the cast. Over three hundred likes, loves, and "Wow!" faces. Ninety-three comments, and they're all basically the same.

"Your work blows my mind. You made this franchise!"

"You two are (fire emoji) together! Inquiring minds want to know when you're making it official!"

"What's next, man? You starring in something?"

He certainly is good-looking enough. His aquamarine eyes are as bright and clear as ever, and there are no grays yet in that auburn hair. Not that it would matter. He'd be quite the silver fox. My heart does a little flip into my throat, and I attempt to wash it down with the coffee that's already gone tepid again. I swear there's an evil coffee fairy who's cursed all the cups in this lounge.

I keep scrolling. Two months back. Then four. There's a photo of him in Holm Square. I recognize the gazebo. What the heck? I hadn't even known he was here then. When was that? December? He must have been here to see his folks for Christmas.

The text alludes to some future mystery project he has yet to share.

"Sorry for the vague-booking, but let's just say my next adventure will be the culmination of a lifetime dream of mine. I can't wait to share it with you all!"

The comments don't offer any clues.

"Tease!"

"Any hints?"

"I'm sure whatever it is, it will be AWESOME."

Curious about what it might be, I flick my way farther down his feed, stopping my scroll on a seven-month-old photo of him on a vintage motorcycle on a hilltop somewhere in Croatia, just after the last Titanium Man film wrapped. He's got on a black, leather jacket and sunglasses, and you can tell the wind is blowing gently … just enough, but not too much. His hair is swept back like it's a freaking ad for men's shampoo. The sun is setting, catching his auburn highlights on fire, and the sky behind him is lit with a glorious palette of colors from mango orange to passion fruit purple. There are 736 likes … no, make that *loves*. I hover my cursor over the count, taking note of the reactions, while trying to fight my own. Dammit. Why is he still so freaking hot?

The door to the lounge opens abruptly, startling me and making me jump. I have to fight the urge to slam my laptop shut. As if I've been doing something illicit, and not just checking the feed of an old family friend.

Noah saunters in, swinging his battered bento box. His floppy hair is behaving a little better than usual today. It frames his puppy-dog eyes perfectly.

"Guess who scored fresh, organic hummus from the co-op?" he asks. Then he notices my open laptop and stops. "Oh! Sorry. Were you working? Didn't mean to interrupt!"

I glance down at the screen, locating my cursor over the photo I was just looking at, and my heart drops. Oh no. I didn't just do that, did I? I didn't click *like* on that photo. I couldn't have.

No. No. Nooooooo!

And why? *Why* did Noah have to startle me like that?

There's no other excuse for why I've just accidentally liked the photo of Dean Riley that I was just looking at. The *seven-month-old photo*. Which makes it so much worse. Everyone knows that it's one thing to accidentally like a recent picture. That's normal, polite, checking up on an old friend behavior. But I am balls deep in creepy, scroll troll territory here.

Frantically, I click again, attempting to undo the damage. Maybe he won't notice? His page is relatively active, and he's a busy guy, right? Maybe he doesn't even manage his own page. He probably has a person for that. Some ditzy VA who vapes weed while collecting Titanium Man memes and who doesn't even know my name.

I close the browser tab and lower my screen.

"No worries." I fake a calm smile at Noah. "Tell me more about that hummus." But I don't hear his response. My mind keeps reliving the click and fluttering in panic. Just like a bird repeatedly crashing into its own reflection in the window, tragically hoping for a different result. This can't be for real.

dean

. . .

JUST AS I'M finishing lunch, my phone dings with a Facebook notification, surprising me. I thought I'd had those silenced. Quickly, I flip over to my social media feed. Things have been pretty quiet since the film wrapped, and it's been a few weeks since I've posted anything. I'm not a frequent social poster. I tend to wait till I have something meaningful to share. So, I've been laying low, biding my time till I can post about this new project in Ephron.

Chelsea Porter has liked your photo.

Shut up. Shut the fuck up.

My heart skips a beat as I click on the notification, leading me back to a post I put up months ago. That sunset outside Dubrovnik had been so sick.

I scroll back through the list of likes, looking for her familiar name so I can click on her profile. But I'm not seeing it now. What the heck? Was it a mistake? I click back on the notification, only to be redirected to a blank "This content no longer exists" message.

So, what happened then? Where did her like go? I didn't imagine it, did I? I can still see the notification, and it still has her name on it. She definitely liked the photo. Was it an accident then? Maybe she'd liked it and then *unliked* it. Was she scrolling my feed? It was an old photo.

Is it possible she still thinks about me too?

There I go again. Probing the wound. But dammit, I do still think about her, more often than I like to admit. And once I start, it's hard to stop. It's why I never indulge in Google searches or seek out her social media profiles. I don't need to seek her out, though. She's always in my head when I'm pitching color schemes and when I'm reading scripts, imagining what new worlds would look like. I think it might be her when I'm walking behind a woman with a particular shade of streaky-blonde hair. The memory of her wafts around me like a ghost whenever I smell wet paint and cardboard.

I think about her in the pitch dark. I think about her, and I think about that kiss. I assume everyone must have moments like that from their teen years. Moments that somehow crystallized and froze time. Moments that you remember with your whole body and recall better, stronger, and more clearly than what you were doing ten minutes ago.

The complete surprise of it. And the heat. That's what I remember. That and the way my desire exploded out of nowhere in the dark backstage that night. She was the match, and I was the gasoline. I hadn't even known how volatile I was until her spark ignited me. For a timeless moment, we were both engulfed, bits of us disappearing, transforming, and reforming in the heat. I had to pull away before it consumed us. I *wanted* to consume her.

We were both so young. Too young.

I blamed—still blame—hormones. Raging teenage hormones. Mushy frontal lobes. Those feelings scared me shitless back then. Now I can't help but wonder if anyone will ever make me feel anything like that ever again.

My heart beats faster as I plug her name into the search bar. Now that she's made contact, I feel as if the floodgates have opened. I'm dying to know the grown-up version of Chelsea. Is she still sweet on the outside and salty as hell beneath the surface? Does she still love punk-rock music and sniffing new boxes of crayons? I need to know. Right now.

She started it. She opened the door. I'm going in.

A list pops up, showing me several Chelseas, but there's only one I'm looking for. I scan the list of strangers, relieved when I locate her still-familiar face, framed in a tiny circle. She's still so lovely. Probably even more so now. She's like a blurry polaroid photo that's developed, blooming into full techni-color glory. I click on her photo and suck in my breath.

"Who's the lucky girl?" The nosy waitress looks over my shoulder as she refills my coffee.

"My best friend's little sister." I smile, letting out my breath as the screen populates with the photos she's been tagged in and random status updates. On the surface, there's not a lot here that I don't already know. I know she works at Ephron High School. I know she does a podcast with her brother, Jackson. But in between these stats, there's more. Places she checks in. Things she's baked. The high school plays she's painted the sets for. Thrift store scores.

"Your order should be up any minute." The waitress smiles benevolently at me.

"No rush," I say, diving into my best friend's little sister's feed. "I've got over ten years to catch up on."

chelsea

. . .

NOAH CRACKS OPEN the container of hummus and hands me a paper plate and some napkins. As he arranges an assortment of fresh-cut veggies, he launches into an almost salesman-like description of the Airbnb he's planning on renting over the upcoming spring break. "So, what do you think, Chelsea? Doesn't this place look great? Isn't it perfect for a little getaway? My mom wants to do some hiking and birdwatching with me. She'll love it, right?"

Oh, thank God. He's not telling me about The Shepherds Hut as a prelude to asking me on an "away" date. He's planning a trip with his mom.

Relief swirls with the old sinking sensation that haunts. The one where I wonder what the hell is wrong with me. Would it be so awful if Noah asked me to go on a trip with him? According to the checklist, he's practically perfect for me. Plenty of women would be thrilled to date Noah.

I drag a celery stick through the hummus, still considering my own feelings as I answer. "I don't know. It's still a little cold for camping, don't you think? Is your mom super outdoorsy?"

"Glamping, not camping! There's a fireplace in the shepherd's hut," Noah explains. "And plenty of wood. They say they can even stoke the fire for visitors. We won't have to get our hands dirty."

"Okay," I say. "But don't forget, we promised the prom committee we'd pull out all the old sets and take a look to see what they can use. Some of those sets are going to need to be fixed up and repainted. When were you planning to help me with that?"

Noah and I are "it" when it comes to the high school's current theater department. He's in charge of the casting and directing. I lead the production and design team. We've been limping along together for two years now, despite our difference of opinion about how things "should" be done.

"There's still a couple of months till prom." Noah rolls his eyes. "And I don't understand why they have to make such a fuss. Back in my day, we just hung some streamers in the gym."

"Well, it's not going to be much better than that this year. I feel so bad for the kids."

For the past twenty-plus years, the Ephron prom has been held at the community center near Holm Square. But this past fall, that property was sold. For a while, there was talk of it being a teardown. And then the rumors about a community theater started. That or a mega church. There's been endless speculation, followed by seemingly endless construction. The fencing around the place is doing a fine job of concealing whatever the Riley and Son crew is up to.

In the meantime, the Ephron prom has been relegated to the high school gymnasium—a venue that boasts broken bleachers and the vague perma-stank of sweaty uniforms. Dragging out the old sets is the least Noah and I can do to help. Especially since the theme for this year's prom is "Theater Lovers." The gymnasium transformation is going to be an all-hands-on-deck moment. One that's not going to happen without a lot of prep and planning.

"It just seems like an awful lot of work for one night," Noah says.

"Prom is a really big deal to these kids," I say. "Using the old play sets as the backdrop for prom is a stroke of genius. It's going to look great, and it will save the school a fortune."

Noah crunches a carrot as he considers this.

"Is all that restoration and repainting really a good use of our time, Chelsea? The state of the storeroom is so abysmal. If anything, I'd rather go through and toss all the old sets and props. We don't have to make every show a production. I'm picturing a more minimalistic approach for the theater department. I think we need to tell the prom committee to rent the decor."

"What?" I draw in a deep, garlic-scented breath and push the hummus away. "When were you going to talk to me about this? Or them? They don't have the budget for that."

"I thought you'd be happy to be off the hook," Noah says, giving me a significant look. "And I was sort of hoping that if we had less work to do on this stuff at school, we might have more time for other stuff away from here. Like dating?"

Is he asking me out? Or is he saying he wants more free time so he can date? This is why I can't date Noah. There's nothing less sexy than the passive voice. Just say what you mean already. Unless what you mean is that you have zero sense of production value. Some things are unforgivable. I picture my fist crumpling the list of reasons why I should date him.

You're doing it again, Chelsea. You're being too critical. Finding reasons. Reasons why he doesn't live up to your standards.

"Maybe you're right. But we made a promise," I say.

Noah seems at least partially satisfied with my answer. He leans back and smiles. His eyes are two unreadably muddy pools of melted chocolate as he stares at me.

"You know, I thought about asking *you* to come to The Shepherds Hut with me, Chelsea. I thought maybe we could—"

I freeze. There it is. I'd suspected it was coming, but I hadn't presumed. Good for him for finally spitting it out and for cutting out all the extra set dressing. Because let's face it, an overnight trip together eliminates the need for any sort of prolonged romantic ramp-up. No need to make a whole *production* out of it. It cuts right to the expectation of sex.

It's completely out of the question. There's no way that's happening with Noah any time soon.

It would have been so much simpler if he'd just asked me out. Maybe then I'd have had the time to get to know him better away from school. Maybe something would develop eventually. *Maybe.* But after waiting this long to lose my virginity, there's no way it's happening in a shepherd's hut.

Staring off into the distance, I start to glitch out. All the same old questions. What's wrong with me? I know I'm capable of physical pleasure. I'm not frigid. I just haven't been attracted enough to anyone to want to have sex with them since …

"Hey!" Noah squeezes my hand. "Sorry. Shit, Chelsea, that came out wrong. I didn't mean to pressure you. Whatever. Forget I mentioned it. I enjoy spending time with you. I value your friendship. I just thought it would be nice for the two of us to get away from it all together."

"I've actually put a lot of thought into the sets," I say, choosing not to address the invitation just yet. "You know, a lot of those set pieces have been here since I was in high school. And I was looking forward to restoring them."

I place my laptop into my bag and gather the trash from our lunch.

"I respect your creativity," Noah concedes, "and I'm sure we can come up with a compromise. I'm just not willing to give up my entire break for this."

I crumple my napkin on my empty plate, wishing I had a muffin or something else to eat. I'm still hungry.

"Oof! I gotta run!" Noah suddenly jumps up and piles his plate on top of mine. "Do you mind getting this? My next class is a doozy!" He grabs his bento box and dashes out the door before I can even answer.

As I'm clearing the table, my phone buzzes and vibrates with an incoming message, sending itself dangerously close to the edge. I pivot and lunge, catching it moments before it crashes to the floor.

"Nice save!" Alexis pokes her head into the lounge. She's using a normal speaking voice now, not the hyper-sexual hostess one. Sexy Alexis is a persona reserved for the podcast. Normal Alexis works in admissions at the nearby college. She's frequently here at the high school for interviews and info sessions.

"Hey, Alexis! What are you doing here? I didn't see any assemblies on the schedule."

"I was just dropping off some brochures for the counseling office," she says. "Thought I'd pop by and say hi and leave some of my famous banana bread for you." She places the banana bread on the table next to my mug. "Consider it my apology for ganging up on you with your brother the other day."

"That's okay," I say. Alexis is one of my closest friends. And she knows things about me that nobody else knows. For example, she knows I'm a virgin. But there are other things she doesn't know about. Things like, how I got stood up for prom. And how I shoot images of myself covered in body paint that I sell on Etsy. She doesn't have any idea what Dean really meant to me all those years ago. No more than Jackson does.

The banana bread smells delicious.

"God bless you," I say, taking one last sip of the now thoroughly frigid coffee and wincing. Blech!

"That good?" Alexis raises a brow.

"So bad," I say, taking three steps back to the sink to dump the rest of the undrinkable sludge and wash the mug.

"I can't stay, but I wanted to see if you want to come to The Grumpy Stump tonight? A bunch of us are getting drinks. You never know who might turn up." Alexis waggles her eyebrows. Hope springs eternal for her that she'll be there when I finally meet "the one."

"I dunno," I say, noncommittally. The Grumpy Stump Ax Lodge is a regular hangout and one of our podcast's sponsors. We get our drinks for half price, and on Wednesdays, our listeners receive a discount on ax-throwing lanes. "There's a show I really wanted to watch tonight."

Alexis raises her eyebrows at me. I know that look. It's the "you're no fun" look. The "how do you expect to meet anyone if you won't ever go out anywhere" look.

"You know, Emily and Blaze just left for Italy. That only leaves me and Jackson there to represent the podcast," Alexis pleads.

"Fine." I capitulate. "I'll come. But only if you stop giving me that look. And I don't want to hear anything more about that trope of the week. Ever again. You've had all your fun with me on that one."

"Oh, come on, I've already apologized. And I'm sure you'll get me back," Alexis says. "What goes around comes around. None of us are immune."

"Except my brother," I say. "I'd love to get him back."

"Can't say I blame you," Alexis agrees. "He is a massive know-it-all."

I give my coffee cup a quick rinse and set it on the drying rack next to the sink. On the table, my phone continues to buzz.

"I'll let you answer that." Alexis gestures to my phone. "See you at Grumpy's around eight. Gotta run!"

After she's gone, I look down at the phone in my hand. The texts are all coming in via Facebook Messenger.

> Hey, Chelsea.

> How have you been?

The third one arrives as I'm looking at it.

> It's Dean Riley, btw.

dean

. . .

I LINGER for a few more minutes in the diner, waiting to see if Chelsea responds to my texts. When she doesn't, I pay my bill and get back on my motorcycle. Time to hit the road for the final leg of my journey. Ephron is only a couple of hours away. The mist has burned off, and there are even a few blue breaks between the clouds.

I pull on my Bluetooth helmet, syncing it up with my phone. Usually, I listen to music while I ride, but today I'm going to listen to Jackson and Chelsea's podcast. First of all, because Jackson sent me the link and insisted that I *had* to listen to it. But more than that, I want to hear Chelsea's voice now. I'm curious.

I'm also hoping that hearing the two of them together will spark something and give me an idea for a really good prank to play on Jackson. Pulling pranks on each other is kind of our thing. Or at least it used to be. In recent years, it's been more of a contest to see which one of us can find the most ridiculous mailing lists to sign each other up for. We can do better than that. I've been racking my brain, trying to come up with something to herald my return to town, but I keep drawing a blank.

I pull out onto the winding, two-lane highway, enjoying the burst of speed.

"Today's trope is one that my sister, Chelsea, might want to weigh in on," Jackson says. "You want to do the honors of telling us about it, Sis?"

———

Fifteen minutes in, I pause the podcast.

Holy shit!

How bizarre is this timing? It's weird to hear myself being discussed in this "ancient Ephron history" context on this podcast, but even weirder to hear it now, when I'm on my way to Ephron.

Now it all makes sense. This must be why Chelsea was crawling my profile.

Poor Chels. She didn't sound too happy with her brother, and I don't blame her. It was almost cruel of him to make her relive that episode when she broke her leg. Then again, he didn't know the whole story. He didn't know about the kiss. Not unless she'd told him, and I suspect she hadn't, or I would have heard about it by now. He was just assuming. He was being an ass.

I'll never forget how mortified she was when I came to the hospital. The look on her face when I told her I was going to prom with Brittany. But she'd gotten her revenge for that, hadn't she? One more detail that hadn't come up in the episode.

It still bugs me that Jackson was teasing her like that. Like it was nothing more than ancient sibling BS. Has that been going on for the entire time since I left? Did she think I was in on the joke? At best, Jackson was being terribly insensitive, trying to drum up drama for ratings. At worst, he was being cruel.

I feel a burst of protective anger.

Jackson deserves a taste of his own medicine, I decide. And my mind returns to the prank. Surely, there's got to be some simple but good way to "get" him. I have the element of surprise in my favor. He's not expecting me.

My helmet dings and reads the message from Chelsea aloud as it comes in.

> Hi, Dean. It's been a while. To what do I owe the pleasure?

God, I love my Bluetooth helmet, even though Siri makes Chelsea sound like a robot. I speak out loud to reply,

> I thought I saw you like one of my photos earlier.

> Did you?

> I mean, I thought so. But maybe it was someone else? Still so nice to see your name. What have you been up to?

> Jackson sent you the link to the podcast, didn't he?

I laugh out loud, causing steam to gather momentarily on the inside of my helmet.

> What do you think?

> I think he's an ass. He's my brother, and I love him. But he's also an ass.

> Imagine the stories we could tell about him.

> Right? I'm sorry about that podcast episode. Probably not the PR you wanted.

> You don't need to apologize.

> I'm glad you're not mad.

Messaging with her feels so good.

I pass a bus and remind myself to keep my focus on the road. I should be home by 2:30. Maybe I could ask her out for a drink?

And then it comes to me. Out of nowhere, the perfect prank starts to take shape in my head. There's just enough time to put the plan together before I meet up with Eli. I'll just have to adjust my route slightly to swing by the high school to see her.

> It's really nice to reconnect with you, Chelsea. Talk more soon?

chelsea

. . .

"MS. PORTER, please report to the office."

The speaker in the art studio classroom comes on with a sudden crackle, making me jump.

"Jeez, Ms. Porter, you need to cut back on the caffeine. It was just an announcement," says Donovan, one of my most talented students. He's right. But at least I didn't click-foul this time.

"Ooh. Ms. Porter, what'd you do now?" Madison, a senior cheerleader with a prolific YouTube following for her makeup tutorials, sing-songs. She winks at Donovan. She is currently attempting to paint a sunflower, and it looks like it needs CPR. It's about as lifeless as Van Gogh's amputated ear. Checking out her expertly made-up face, it occurs to me I should try to explain the concept of shading in terms she's more likely to grasp. Highlighting. Contouring. Pop of color.

Next time.

"You can all pack it up for the day," I say, dismissing the class. It's almost 2:30. Most of these kids are seniors, and this seventh block class is their frosting. A chill, low-effort chaser class to finish their day as they sail off into their shiny futures.

34

"Don't forget to bring in three photo examples of natural or weathered texture next time. Use your phones to take the pictures, and be ready to talk about your photos and the emotions that the textures evoke."

I hear one of the football players snickering in the back of the studio, making an off-color comment about the texture of his balls and his girlfriend's emotions.

"If you feel the need to take a picture of your balls, let's make sure they're of the sporting variety and not attached to anybody's undercarriage."

Undercarriage? Did I really just say that word? Who am I? Somebody's eighty-year-old aunt? This is how it happens.

The loudspeaker crackles again, as I am summoned to the office a second time.

"Okay already!" I toss my cell phone in my apron pocket and grab my bag and water bottle before waving at the students.

————

I see Noah standing at the far end of the hallway outside the office, talking to someone, and wonder if he might have something to do with my sudden summoning. Where did I park this morning? I hadn't parked in someone else's spot, had I? No, it couldn't be that. I walked to work today.

If it was anyone but Noah, I would have suspected the summons was a prank, and for a moment, I still wonder if it might be. Unless it's an emergency? I run down the list of all my family and friends, considering the possibilities. What if there's been some kind of accident?

My stomach feels like I've just been dropped a few stories, and I pick up the pace, feeling the familiar surge of adrenaline. It's been a good long while since we've had any sort of news about my dad. But when we do hear something, it's never good. A part of me has been braced for bad news about him for years.

There's no reason to assume it's that, though. I take a deep, cleansing breath. It could just as easily be something good too. A surprise visit from a former student. The principal telling me I am up for an award. No need to make negative assumptions.

"Hey, Noah," I call out as I get closer. "I just got paged. Any idea—"

Noah steps aside as I reach the end of the corridor, where it Ts. A left turn will take me toward the office. As he moves, I can see the back of the person he was just chatting with. They're both looking into the glass case in the hallway outside the office. The one where the sports trophies and photos of all our former football heroes are displayed.

I never look in that case.

The man turns around, but I already know who it is. I know it from the cowlick on the back of his head. And I know it from the way his right foot is tapping, a little impatiently, like his mind is waiting for the rest of his body to catch up with whatever he's thinking.

Dean Riley is standing in the hallway outside the principal's office, wearing the leather motorcycle jacket he had on in that photo I accidentally liked, all of what, three hours ago?

Holy shit! Amazon doesn't even deliver that fast.

I do a double take. Confused, I pat my pocket, feeling for my phone, as if he's somehow jumped out of it and into this hallway.

"Hey there, little Chelly Belly." His aquamarine eyes twinkle. "Look at you, all grown up and ruling the school."

"I'm sorry." I blink at him. "I'd love to chat, but I was just called to the office."

Noah looks from me to Dean and snorts. "Good one, Chelsea!" He elbows Dean like they are old buddies. "We were just talking about you. I bet your ears were ringing."

I cock my head. "No, just the intercom in the studio. Excuse me," I say, attempting to walk around Dean. "I need to see who paged me."

Dean steps to block my path. "I paged you," he says. "I ran into your friend here"—he gestures to Noah—"out in the parking lot, and he offered to walk me in. It was his idea to have you paged."

Noah grins and nods before fawning over Dean a little. "I am such a huge fan of your work. It's so cool that our little town has such an impressive connection to Hollywood."

"Thanks for helping to keep the high school theater tradition alive and well in Ephron, Noah," Dean says. "And thanks for helping me spring Chelsea from her classroom."

There is an awkward pause as both men stand there, smiling at me.

"Anyone want to tell me what's going on? What are you even doing here, Dean?" I ask.

"I'll let you two catch up. I have to get my car in for an oil change. Don't forget about our plans for break, Chelsea … and my invitation." Noah's tone is leading and misleading, all at the same time. His hand lingers on my arm for a beat, then he gives my shoulder a squeeze before striding off.

Dean doesn't miss any of this. He's staring at my shoulder, head cocked, brows raised, question posed. He doesn't really need to ask it out loud. But he asks anyway.

"Your boyfriend?"

"No." I shake my head vehemently. "Just a colleague. We work together a lot. He's kind of like my work husband."

"Interesting." Dean nods. "Not so sure he feels the same way about you that you do about him. Poor guy."

"What are you doing here?" I ask, frowning at him.

Even though I've avoided him like the plague, I've often imagined simply running into Dean. I've thought about it so many times over the years that I have prepared myself for it. I have lines. According to the script, I'm supposed to ask him what the hell happened. Next, I demand explanations. Finally, when he comes up short, it's my cue to shame him. How could he have been so heartless?

But there's no way for that scene to take place in the high school corridor on a Wednesday afternoon in April. This scene is supposed to take place on a stormy night at The Onion, when I'm looking my best, not when I am standing outside the principal's office wearing my work apron. I'm also very aware that the 2:30 bell is about to ring, letting loose a river of teenagers around us.

"I need a moment," Dean smiles, and I notice the way his eyes crinkle a bit at the corners now, softening the effect of his laser-like stare. "It's really weird being back here with you!"

"You might have said you were in town when you messaged earlier," I say, swimming upstream through the cognitive dissonance. I'm still confused.

"I wasn't in town then. I was on my way. And I had to cut the chat short. I needed to keep my eyes on the road. You were a real distraction."

He's looking at me with those sea-glass eyes, and I have temporarily lost the ability to respond with words. Or maybe there aren't any perfect words for the bright flashes I'm experiencing. Attraction, affection, betrayal, pain. Red, pink, purple, green. Each feeling captures a version of me for a split second like a colored camera strobe. This happens when I get emotional. I literally see red.

The bell rings, bringing me back to the present. It's just Dean. It's been a really long time, but he's still Dean. We're both adults now, and it's been a really long time. I'm over it. This doesn't have to be a big deal.

I gesture to the front doors. "Let's take it outside? It's about to get super crowded."

"God, it's good to see you, Chels."

Dean draws me to him in a quick hug before taking my hand and pulling me through the door.

"Hey, look," he says, pointing at the sky, "a rainbow! Make a wish."

"You don't wish on rainbows, Dean. You follow them to your destiny."

This is crazy. We've slipped right into a conversation we might have had fifteen years ago, and it's like no time has passed.

"My destiny must be back here in Ephron, then." Dean's sparkling, aquamarine eyes rival the sky. "Anyway, I was on my way home, listening to that podcast, when I had a crazy idea. I didn't want to crash my bike, so I thought I'd just swing by and ask you in person."

I raise an eyebrow. "You were texting me from a motorcycle? Are you insane?"

"Bluetooth helmet." Dean shakes his head. "Although yes, I am a little insane." Students are starting to stream out of the building now, and some of them are looking at us, and whispering.

"Can we get out of here? I want to run my idea by you." His fingers wrap back around mine, and he tugs me gently toward the parking lot. "Want to come for a ride?" Dean asks hopefully, gesturing toward his motorcycle. "I've got a spare helmet."

I shake my head.

"How about we take a walk instead?" I suggest.

Dean shrugs and squeezes my hand. "Sure. You lead the way."

dean

. . .

"DOES Jackson know you're here in town?" Chelsea asks me.

I'm still holding her hand as we walk toward the park down the street from the high school. I remember it well. There's a playground there. That was where everyone used to sneak off to in order to make out. But it has changed. No more tunnel-of-love slide or swings. It's all been replaced with toddler-friendly, eco-themed equipment. The slides have been swapped for climbing webs, and the swings have been removed to make way for bouncing mushrooms mounted on springs. I pity the kids today.

"No. I haven't spoken to Jackson yet. I wanted to chat with you first. Care to sit?" I give her hand a squeeze, reluctant to release it, and gesture at the bench beside the tragic, not so magic mushrooms.

Chelsea is peering at me suspiciously, but she sits. I have to take a moment to admire her. Same old Chelsea, and then some. The Facebook photo hardly did her justice.

Her thick, blonde hair is streaked with a dozen shades of blonde from pale to caramel. Currently, she has it twisted up into a bubble-shaped bun on the top of her head. No contact lenses for her. She's wearing teal-framed, cat-eye glasses and a dress-like artist's apron in a vintage floral print over faded jeans and a lavender sweater. Everything about her is neat, tidy, tucked in, and perfectly controlled, save for the stray wisps of hair that have escaped her bun and one small smudge of light-blue paint smeared on her jawline. I'm tempted to wipe the paint away with my thumb.

"It's so weird to be here," I admit. "And so awesome to see you."

Chelsea shifts in her seat. "You said that before. It's certainly a surprise to see you. You here to visit your family?"

"Nope." I take a deep breath, deciding, on the spur of the moment, to tell her the truth. The whole truth. "I'm here to stay. My production company bought the community center and the amphitheater. I'm opening a seasonal outdoor theater."

"What?" Chelsea's eyes widen and she sits up straight, staring at me in disbelief. "*You* bought the community center? That was you?" I watch her face as she processes. "Wait, is this the big secret you vague-booked about?"

"Aha! You totally were creeping on my profile!" I laugh. "Busted. I knew it!"

Chelsea turns a bright shade of red.

"I was not creeping. After we recorded the podcast, I was naturally curious about what you were up to." Her voice holds just the faintest hint of defensiveness.

"Sure, sure." I let it go.

Isn't it enough that she responded when I reached out? Best to let bygones be bygones. I'm not going to ask her to explain the reasons for her decade-long cold shoulder right now. I'm just going to live in the moment, happy to finally be spending time with her again. It's like no time has passed.

Chelsea shakes her head. She's still blushing, staring down at her shoes.

"I have so many questions," she says, turning back to stare at me with those intense, almost violet, gray eyes. "Who knows about this? How do you expect a theater here to make any money? And why didn't you tell me you were on your way back to Ephron when you messaged earlier?"

"That is a lot of questions," I agree. "Let me see … first of all, nobody knows about my involvement in the theater. Well, nobody except my mom, my brother, and my business partner."

"Wow," she says, staring at me. I can see the follow-up questions forming in her brain. Twice she starts to say something, and stops.

"You're the very first friend I'm telling," I offer, holding her gaze and reading all the questions in her eyes.

"What about your dad?" She raises her brows.

"I'm telling him tonight."

"Are you nervous about that?" she asks, kicking at the dirt.

"It's going to be fine," I say, repeating Eli's words. "Right now, I want to know what you think."

She blinks at me a few times. "I mean, I'd heard some rumors about the old community center being turned into a theater. But I didn't think it was true. But honestly? You're telling me first? Why?"

"I don't know."

We both notice my leg nervously tapping a beat on the pavement beneath the bench, and I jump up to pace around the mushroom patch.

"I guess I was thinking that you, of all people, might understand what all this means to me," I say.

"Which is?" Chelsea asks. "I'm sorry, Dean, but it's been a minute. I'm not sure I know you so well anymore."

She's right to ask, of course. Perfectly reasonable.

"No. You still know me, Chels. I've had a great run in LA, but it's always been live theater that makes my heart race. No CGI. No movie magic. You only get one chance to tell the story and create the experience. And to do that *here*? To create a storytelling stage that will draw crowds to Ephron?" I exhale dramatically.

"Wasn't that old place practically falling down?"

"It wasn't as bad as it looked. Mostly cosmetic stuff on the building and the amphitheater just needed some love and upgrades. It's going to be magical."

Chelsea crosses her long legs, balancing a loose clog on the top foot. I can tell she's starting to play out the possibilities. "Okay, tell me more." She leans back on the bench seat, watching me.

Suddenly, it feels very important, critical even, that I sell the idea to Chelsea. Even more important than it had been to explain it all to Zara when I'd first pitched the idea to her. If Chelsea gets it, everyone in Ephron will get it.

"You know how Ashland does Shakespearean dramas every summer?" I ask. Chelsea nods.

"And they have big-name, famous actors who travel to participate? There are a few theaters in LA that do this in the summer as well, but most of the actors I know want out of LA

44

every summer. They want a break from the traffic and the whole scene, you know? They want to get away, go to camp like so many of them did as kids. They're nostalgic for places like Stagedoor and Interlochen."

I can see her eyes glazing over. Shit. I've lost her by droning on about Hollywood and rich kid summers. I bring it back to Ephron.

"Anyway, the winters here in Ephron may suck, but as we both well know, the summertime is glorious. There are the long days, the great weather, lots of fun things to do, wineries to tour, an up-and-coming food and music scene." I tick all these points off on my fingers. "We've done extensive viability studies, and considering the growth of summer tourism in the area, we're in a sweet spot here. Plus the amphitheater and grounds are perfect for shoulder season events —music festivals, concerts, etc. People are looking for more cultural experiences and things to do."

"Are you opening a theater or applying for a job with the Ephron Tourism Department?" Chelsea quirks a brow.

"Both!" I enthuse. "I've been so fortunate in LA. I've made a lot of good friends in the movie industry."

A shadow of doubt flits across Chelsea's face and disappears almost as quickly.

"No really, I know it seems crazy and frivolous, but I have met some truly amazing artists who are also good people. Good people, like Rafe Barzilay. He's signed on for an inaugural production of *A Midsummer Night's Dream* this summer. It's going to blow everyone out of the water. The sets, the lighting, the talent."

"Hold up. You're telling me that Rafe Barzilay, Titanium Man, is spending the summer in Ephron? No way." She looks at me in disbelief.

"Way," I argue. "And that's just for starters. There are more people coming on board. I can't talk about them all yet. And you can't discuss any of this, okay? Give me a day or two to break it to my dad and make the news public?"

"I won't tell anyone, I swear," Chelsea promises. "Thanks for sharing this with me." She takes a breath, as if considering something, then she asks, "What about Zara Jones? How does she feel about this project?"

Her tone is totally casual. Too casual. I know what she's really asking.

I look at her sideways, raising my eyebrows. "Is this you trying to figure out if me and Zara Jones are a thing? Because get in line, Chels. The tabloids have been hounding us for years."

She blushes again.

"Well, you said Rafe was coming to town, and that made me wonder if the rest of the Titanium Man cast was also on board. I'm not sure Ephron is ready for that much A-lister action. Ephron folks might not be prepared for that level of fancy. Anyway, why be so secretive about who you are dating?"

She's still not making eye contact when she takes a long swig of her water.

"What do you think?" I ask.

"About the theater or the celeb sightings?" She slowly screws the cap back on her water bottle.

"All of it!" I say, grabbing the handles of one of the bouncy mushrooms and pulling it back. I let the mushroom go. "Except maybe not the Zara Jones part. I'll just put that to rest now. Zara won't be acting in *Midsummer*. She can't commit to anything at the moment."

"And by commit, you mean?" She raises her brows.

"We're very close, but we're not a couple," I say, keeping it simple. Zara doesn't want anyone to know about her involvement in the theater just yet. She doesn't want her celebrity to hijack the story.

The ride-on mushroom is still bouncing around wildly, making me question whether these fungi are really safe for children. I steady it with my foot.

"Okay, Dean." Chelsea sits up again and claps her hands together decisively before holding her hand out to shake mine. "I have to hand it to you. I think the theater is a brilliant idea. Fantastic. Life-changing. I mean really, I can see this changing lives. I honestly don't know what else to say."

"Is that a Paul Hollywood handshake?" I reference the *The Great British Bake Off* and slap her hand before shaking it. "I'm not sure how to feel about a handshake from you."

"Paul's a total handshake whore compared to me." She laughs at the reference. "I can't believe you watch that."

"Are you kidding?" I shake my head. "There is nothing about that show I do not love."

"Anyway, I'm honored you told me about it before anyone else. Even before Jackson." She pauses there again, as if she wants to say more. Then doesn't.

"Crew buddies for *Little Shop*, crew buddies for life!" I say, dropping back down onto the bench. "But that's not the only reason I came to see you today. There's something else I wanted to run by you."

"Something else?" She looks wary.

"You know how Jackson and I used to play pranks on each other? I've been racking my brain for a prank to surprise him with when I came home. And it just dawned on me while I was listening to the podcast earlier. But I can't pull it off without your help."

Chelsea looks doubtful. Uncomfortable even. Maybe this wasn't the best idea. Maybe I'm being too familiar with her. Like she said, it's been a long time. I study her face. She's so damn pretty. I don't think she's even wearing any makeup. Her face is bare, aside from some lip gloss and that paint smear. I've dated dozens of women in LA who spend a lot of money on cosmetics and workouts and trendy boutique clothing, trying to achieve something like Chelsea's natural look. They're all missing the mark.

There's still a certain tension between us. I don't think I'm imagining it. But there's other stuff too. Stuff we should probably talk about.

Later.

She's staring at me, suspicion clearly doing battle with her curiosity. I can see glimpses of her younger self, the little sister who got left out and left behind. And then got even.

"Go ahead," she says, sitting up straighter and lifting her chin. "Tell me what you were thinking."

I smile slowly, conspiratorially, at her. "Just hear me out, Chelsea. I really hate the way Jackson was goading you on that podcast. He was totally out of line. I'd be happy to punch him in the face, for both of us. But if you're game, I think we can do a much better job of putting him in his place."

chelsea

. . .

SHIT!

Shit! Shit! Shit! Shit! Shit!

I'm sitting on a bench in make-out park with Dean. My brain is having a hard time processing this. I'm still flashing through time and emotions. I'm fourteen, and I'm freaking out. I'm eighteen, and I'm pissed off. I'm twenty-nine.

Calm down, childhood version of Chelsea. We're all adults here now.

He's still so distractingly good-looking. I want to reach out and touch him. I need to confirm that he's really here. My brain zooms in on seemingly random details. Like the stitching on his jacket. The smooth and even machine stitching on top of the chaotically distressed and weathered surface of the leather is so calming to look at. My eyes keep going back to the stitching until I realize I'm staring awkwardly at his torso. But if he notices, he doesn't say anything. In fact, he's acting like everything's normal. Like nothing ever happened. Which is weird. But also reassuring. Like that stitching.

Hold it together. My cup of wtf runneth over.

It's embarrassing the way my head is popping off right now. I focus on the things Dean is telling me and organize them into a list of bite-size facts.

Just the Facts: A List by Chelsea Porter

1. Dean Riley is back in Ephron.

2. He's opening a theater.

3. With celebrities.

4. This is going to mean jobs, tourists, and more.

5. Ephron will never be the same again.

Increased tourism is not the part that I keep coming back to, of course.

Dean Riley is coming home to Ephron. He's going to be here now. All the time. This means I could run into him any time at the grocery store or in a bar.

He sits back down next to me, closer this time. Close enough to smell him. He smells nice. Like fresh air and sandalwood soap. Different than teenage Dean used to smell. But recognizable. He's still in there. The base notes of how he smells remain the same. Achingly familiar. It gives me goose bumps. It makes me wish he'd wrap his arms around me and put his chin on my shoulder and whisper in my ear.

This is just an emotional echo.

It's such a clear one. The kind you usually only get when a certain song plays. I remember *exactly* how I felt, standing backstage next to him, like it was just last week. Like some sort of emotional wormhole just opened up, sucking me back fifteen years.

"Imagine Jackson's face when we start making out in front of him and casually tell him that we're madly in love."

I forget to breathe. This might be the exact fantasy I played out in my mind sixteen thousand times. Complete and total wish fulfillment. A decade late and three hundred dollars on a wasted prom dress short.

When my biological responses finally kick in, making sucking in air an immediate priority, I end up choking on my own spit and bend over in a fit of coughing. My shoe goes sailing. Smooth.

I really need someone to smack me on the back.

"Shit! You okay, Chels?" Dean pauses to pat my back and retrieve the clog that's popped off my foot. Without comment, he pops the shoe back onto my foot. It's weirdly awkward that this seemingly intimate gesture *wasn't* awkward.

I suck in a deep breath, grateful for the oxygen. "Sorry. I just swallowed wrong." I stall a moment, taking a swig from my water bottle. Dean continues to pat and rub my back gently, and I don't do anything about that. It feels so nice.

"Come on, Chelsea. This is a perfect prank. No setup, no props. We just have to plant ourselves in Jackson's path and, you know, pretend we're into each other for a few minutes." Dean leans back and smiles wickedly. "Jackson's head is going to explode."

My head is already exploding.

"He's not going to buy it," I argue. "Jackson knows we haven't talked in years. And how do you know I'm not seeing anyone?"

Dean frowns. "I assumed if Noah was chasing you, you were available. But just for the record, are you currently dating anyone?"

I shake my head and swallow again. No point in lying, it's a small town and he'd figure it out. I answer truthfully. "No. I'm not seeing anyone at the moment."

"Good." Dean weighs this info. "Then we're both unattached at present. Makes it much simpler. Speaking of Noah, he actually gave me an idea for where we can pull the prank on your brother."

"Wait. You told Noah about this plan?" I can feel my eyes bugging.

"Only in *very* general terms," Dean says. "No particulars. I told him I was enlisting your help in playing a joke on your brother. He mentioned something about an ax-throwing place that sponsors the podcast? He said Jackson would probably be there tonight."

"You sure you want to pull a prank on my brother at a bar where there are axes?"

"I like to live dangerously." Dean's eyes sparkle with the challenge. "All we have to do is make out a little. How bad can that be?"

"Pretty bad," I say, feeling my heart thumping hard.

"You didn't seem to mind kissing me backstage on the *Little Shop* set," Dean murmurs.

Oh, shit! So, he did remember that kiss.

"I'm not sure I want to repeat that performance," I say. "I'm lucky I don't still walk with a limp."

Dean momentarily looks like I've let the air out of his tires.

"Fine," he sighs. "I'm just being stupid. I don't know what I was thinking. You don't need my help with your brother. There's no reason for Jackson and I to keep playing pranks on each other. It was a dumb idea. I've just missed you guys, and I was excited to spend more time here. I was really hoping …

I don't know, that we'd all kind of find our way back to each other." He sighs again. "God, that sounds sappy. Never mind."

He leans forward, placing his elbows on his knees and resting his head in his hands pensively.

"Did you ever tell Jackson that I kissed you backstage that night?" I ask him.

"God, no." Dean shakes his head vehemently. Then he cocks one eyebrow. "How about you? Did you tell him that I kissed you back?"

I feel weirdly vindicated. I hadn't imagined it. He *had* kissed me back. I don't know why it surprises me so much to hear him admit it now.

"No, no way." I shake my head. "I never told anyone, least of all my brother."

"Why not?" Dean asks. "Especially if he was teasing you like that. I bet it would have shut him right up."

"Maybe." I sigh. "If he believed me. Which he probably wouldn't have. But it was none of his business, you know?"

"Yeah." Dean nods in agreement. "I do know. Totally. But I'm not the one who had to live with him being such an ass. Honestly, Chelsea, I had no idea he was making fun of you like that, or I would have set him straight a long time ago about what went down the night you broke your leg."

"It's not really a big deal. It just came up because of the stupid trope," I say.

Dean nods. "I get it. It's not like you talk about me all the time. I just hate that that's the discussion you have when you do."

He looks so earnest and apologetic that it makes me reconsider. His plan is actually pretty solid. The prank would definitely get Jackson off my case, once and for all. But more than that … maybe it would help us both move on from the awkward situation I created all those years ago when I threw myself at him.

Dean Riley doesn't have to be the guy who broke my heart anymore. He can be the old friend who helped me get back at my obnoxious big brother. Doesn't everyone always say that laughter is the best medicine?

"You know what, Dean? It is a stupid idea, but just stupid enough that it might work. I can't wait to see the look on Jackson's face." I close my eyes and take a deep breath. "So, I'll do it."

With this proclamation, I stand up and stretch, rolling my neck and shoulders like a responsible stretcher who's just completed an athletic event, instead of a dork on a park bench who's struggling not to lose her shit. I cannot wait to cram my earbuds into my ears and turn my NSFW music up to dangerous levels and go for a jog. I need to process.

Dean is looking at me incredulously, and he's smiling that same smile. It still slays me.

"I'm going to go now"—I back away before I say or do anything stupid—"but I'll text you my address. You can pick me up at 7:30."

dean

. . .

ELI'S not due to meet me till four, but I head over to the property—my property—early.

I call Zara on FaceTime to let her know I've arrived.

"This is it," I tell her, turning on the phone's camera so she can see the work that's been done on the place. But she's more interested in hearing how I'm doing.

"You ready?" she asks me. "How do you feel?"

"I feel pretty damn good, actually," I say. "I ran into some old friends, and I'm going out with Chelsea and Jackson tonight. Remember I told you about my old friends, the ones with the podcast?" I don't mention the prank. I'm sure she wouldn't approve.

"That's great. What about your dad?" Zara asks.

"We're having dinner. I'm going to tell him everything then," I say.

"Good." Zara sounds satisfied. "I trust everything is still on track for this summer, then?"

"It is." I smile. "Rafe's manager is sending back the contract, and we've got Lorelei on board now too. Not too late for you to change your mind. You'd be an awesome Titania for *Midsummer Night*."

"Not this time. You know I've got other plans."

"I know. Keep me posted on that." I grin. "But you still have to make time to come and visit. This is your baby too."

The community center is one of a handful of historic buildings that flank Holm Square. The building itself is large and sparse. Before it was the community center, it was the town's original church. There's a Gothic-feeling central tower with an old clock face. Above that sits the bell tower. The bells in the bell tower haven't rung since I was a toddler. I'm not even sure they still can ring, though I intend to find out today.

Thanks to my dad and Eli and their crew's work over the last few months, the building has been lovingly restored and refreshed. They just finished replacing the roof and repairing the original, stained-glass windows. Everything, I've been assured, is in working order. I'm excited to get inside and check things out.

But as compelling as the historic building is, it isn't the main reason I bought this property.

The land that comes with the community center is over five acres. It's the largest piece of undeveloped property in downtown Ephron. Over the years, it's been used as a fairground and Christmas tree lot. It has hosted antique car shows and flea markets. Nobody has developed it, however, due to grading issues. A hundred yards back from the building, the land starts to slope off gently, down toward the industrial district.

The original residents took advantage of this, turning it into a feature. They turned the slope into an outdoor theater. There are records of outdoor church services being held here not long after the church was built, and even some photos in the archives of a brief theatrical run in the 1930s. We can thank the residents of Ephron during that era for carving out the hillside and stacking stones to create seating areas.

The stage itself is simple, backed by a thick grove of trees.

It's perfect.

I walk the perimeter of the fenced-off lot, checking the progress on the areas that we plan to use for parking, concessions, and equipment.

I've had a bee in my bonnet about this place since I was in college. I spent the summer interning at the outdoor theater in Ashland, Oregon, and it occurred to me that we could do something similar up here. But then I forgot about it. I got swept up with the work I was doing on the Titanium Man films. It wasn't till we were about to wrap—and I paid a quick visit home and saw the property was for sale—that I began to think about it again. This time in earnest.

My colleagues were intrigued as well. But especially Zara.

"It won't be easy to get all the work done and the permits in place for this summer," Eli had warned me last fall. He'd seemed skeptical. But from the looks of things now, it appears we're right on track.

I can't help but wonder what my dad thinks about all the work they've been doing the past few months. As far as he knows, he's working for "Turning Table Productions," the name Zara and I incorporated under. Eli and I thought it best not to tell him until we were closer to being finished, due to the strained relationship my father and I have had since I left town. My father might not have been as enthusiastic about the project if he'd known I was involved. He's never gotten over my defection from the family business.

I see the Riley and Son truck go by and note the stroller in the back. Eli must have brought Braden. Great! I'm excited to spend more time with my nephew, but I also think having him around when we break the big news to my father can't hurt. It might help my dad temper his reaction.

Best case scenario, my dad recognizes this is a good thing—good for the town and good for me. Worst case, he loses his shit over the fact we hid my involvement from him. But what does he expect? He's hardly been the biggest supporter of my career.

I make my way back toward the community center, texting my brother as I walk back up the hill.

> I'm just down the hill. Be there in a few minutes!

By the time I finally get up there, Eli's on his way in. He spins the jogging stroller around and steps it backward up the stairs. The door to the community center is already standing open.

Braden eyes me suspiciously as I pretend to steal one of his goldfish crackers. When I make a silly face at him, he giggles and sticks his tongue out at me. I'm not usually a jealous guy, but when I look at Braden, I do feel jealous of my brother. All that joy and wonder. I want that. Someday.

Ever since Eli and Brittany had him, my social life has taken a hit. Partying has lost its luster. What's the point of going out with a different woman every night when there's no one I'm interested in staying home with? It feels like I'm running in place.

"This place brings back so many memories," Eli says, gesturing at the building. "All those Scout meetings and parties we came to here."

He's so right. I first met Jackson in this building. My dad signed up to be a Boy Scout troop leader not long after we moved to town. Jackson had been in our troop. And Chelsea had always been waiting on the bench in the hallway when we came out after our meetings. She'd be sketching in her sketchbook, anxious to show us what she'd dreamed up.

"How was hip-hop?" I ask Eli. It's hard to picture my six-foot-two brother busting a move with a bunch of toddlers.

"Hopping." Eli huffs. "I tried to convince Britt to sign him up for Pop Warner football, but apparently, they don't take them till they're three."

"Everyone ready to do this walk-through?" My dad walks out the front door, holding a clipboard.

I don't know who's more surprised, him or me. Eli might have let me know our dad was already there.

"Surprise!" Eli says.

"What's going on?" My dad looks from my brother to me. "I thought we were doing the walk-through with Turning Table. Not that I'm not happy to see your brother." He frowns, looking anything but pleased to see me. "To what do we owe the pleasure, Dean?"

"Seriously, Eli?" I glance at my brother, who is biting back a smile. "You think this is funny?" It's not funny. It's nerves. Eli always laughs when he's nervous. That's how my mom could always tell which one of us was responsible for the damage.

"Gaaaaaaammmpa! Up! Up!" Braden strains at the straps of his stroller, reaching out to my dad.

"Eli?" My dad looks suspicious, and in that moment, I see the resemblance between him and Braden. Same red hair and wild smattering of freckles, although my dad's hair has faded some. And there's also something about the eyebrows.

"Nice to meet you, Sir. I'm Dean Riley, the CEO of Turning Table Productions." I hold out my hand to shake his.

"Up! Up!" Braden demands. But my dad appears frozen to the spot. Shocked.

Finally, he turns to Eli. "Oh, this is rich. You've known about this the whole time, haven't you?"

Eli shrugs. "I mean, yeah."

"And Mom too?" My father narrows his eyes at both of us now. I swallow and glance over at Eli, who is squinting up at the eaves of the building like he's searching for swallows' nests.

"I see." My dad nods and bends to unstrap Braden. "Come here, Buddy. There's my little guy."

Braden curls into my father happily, staring almost smugly at Eli and me. Good call bringing him. Adorable toddlers are the kryptonite of grumpy grandpas.

"Fair warning. He's ready for a diaper change," Eli comments.

"Nothing I haven't seen." My dad shrugs. "You two have always been full of shit. Come on, then."

With that, he turns to walk into the building.

"See? That went well," Eli whispers.

"You could have warned me," I shake my head at him.

My dad starts the tour in the spacious, tiled foyer. There's not much he needs to show me that I'm not already familiar with. I spent almost as much time here growing up as I spent in my own backyard.

"We've rebuilt the benches by the door. There's storage inside." He points at a paneled Dutch door to one side. "Most of the coatroom is still original. We put in a drying rack for umbrellas. And as you can see, we've repainted everything." He pauses. "When were you planning to tell me? Is there a reason you thought you had to keep me in the dark?"

"We can talk about that over dinner," Eli says.

"So that's why your mom made me smoke that brisket last weekend," my father grumbles, walking into the area that was once used as a chapel. The massive room boasts a balcony on both sides, a stage, and windows that extend most of the way up to the three-story-high ceilings. The pews are long gone, but it's easy enough to set up seating or tables, making it a perfect location for weddings, receptions, and community events.

This room is where my senior prom was held.

Quickly, we tour the two wings that are divided into classrooms, storage, and the meeting rooms that we used for Scouts. Finally, we end up in the glassed-in atrium area, which provides additional event space. This space has always been popular for fall events when rain is a real threat. At the moment, it's sitting empty, but I can imagine it decked out for Halloween or a winter wonderland.

"So, what exactly are your plans for this building?" my dad asks while Eli changes Braden's diaper. There's an edge to his voice, an unmistakable challenge.

"Seriously, Dad, weren't you just saying that the buyer could do whatever he damn well pleased with the place?" Eli notes.

"That was before I knew the buyer was a Riley. This place has a lot of meaning to this town and the people who live here."

"Don't you think I know that?" I ask.

"You've been gone for a while. For all I know, you're planning on turning this place into some kind of escape room/Pilates studio/selfie museum."

"That might do really well," Eli jokes.

"I'm not doing any of that," I say. "For the most part, I don't want to change the use case of this building. I want it to remain a community asset."

"He's more interested in the amphitheater," Eli says.

"Great. You planning on turning this place into the next Coachella?" My dad raises his brows. "Let me know so I can invest in a better security system. Those summer festivals bring all kinds of unsavory types to town."

"If, by festivals, you include Shakespeare, then yeah." I roll my eyes. "Fans of the bard party hard."

My dad levels a hardened look at me. "Listen, son, I'm just trying to look out for this place. It's my hometown, and I'm a hometown kinda guy."

"Well, I guess that makes two of us now," I say. "I bought a place here. I'll be moving into a loft in the warehouse district. I think your teams did some work on that renovation?"

My dad raises his brows incredulously. "You bought a place in Ephron? You do know that we don't even have valet parking here, let alone a Whole Foods?"

"Enough, Dad. Dean grew up in Ephron, same as me," Eli says.

"Yeah, but this place wasn't good enough for Dean," my father scoffs. "We'll see if he sticks around. Have you told anyone else about this big move you're making?"

"I wanted to tell you before making it public," I say. This gives me an idea. "But now that you know, we can let the cat out of the bag, no?" I walk over to my nephew, who is back in the stroller and not looking especially pleased about it. "Hey Braden, you want to help Uncle Dean ring those giant bells in the tower?"

"They might not work," warns Eli. "Plus, it might not be safe."

"But they might," I say. "Don't you want to find out?"

"They'll work just fine," my dad says gruffly. "Don't you think we had a structural engineer up there to make sure everything was in working order? What kind of operation do you think this is? Honestly, Eli!"

"Well, it might scare the shit out of people," Eli warns.

My father rolls his eyes at my brother. "It's a church bell, Eli, not an air raid siren."

"I'm just saying, people haven't heard the bells ring here in decades," Eli defends.

"Well then, it's about time they heard them again," I say, scooping up my tiny nephew and his bag of crackers too. "Because the Rileys are about to shake things up in Ephron."

chelsea

. . .

I COULD SWEAR I hear a bell ringing while I'm drying off from my post-jog shower. I open the window of my apartment and stick my head out into the spring air. I can't quite hear it anymore, but the air still feels like it's vibrating, buzzing with something.

It's been such a weird day.

I text Alexis.

> Firming up our plans to meet at The Grumpy Stump. Is Jackson coming?

> He said he'd be there. Hudson, Georgia, and Xander are in. Not sure abt anyone else.

Alexis ticks off the names of most the members of our close friend group. Perfect. It sounds like it'll be a pretty decent turnout for the prank. For a moment, I consider telling Alexis about Dean, bringing her in on the joke, but I immediately dismiss the idea. It's better if it's kept a secret between me and Dean and nobody else knows.

The plan is for Dean to meet me here at 7:30. We'll head right over to The Grumpy Stump together. This way, we'll arrive before the others and get a booth. We've worked out a cover story for our so-called relationship. Nothing complicated. We'll just say we reconnected on Facebook.

It's delightfully simple. We just have to get there first and wait.

I breathe into my hand, checking for garlic. Why did Noah have to bring that hummus earlier?

What to wear?

Whatever you were planning on wearing, you don't have to dress up for him.

I could tell myself I'm not dressing up for Dean, but I'd be lying. It's not exactly *for* him so much as because of him. Him and my relentless pursuit of symmetry. I don't want to look out of place next to him. But he's just so good-looking, so effortlessly cool.

He's always been that way, but now, in his expensive clothing, with his So Cal tan and Hollywood haircut, it seems even more exaggerated.

I assess myself in the hall mirror.

My hair is no longer mousy, thanks to my brilliant hairdresser's excellent understanding of color theory. Her highlights and lowlights and expert cutting skills have turned my hair into the one thing I feel fairly confident about.

Other than that? Meh. I'm still best at disappearing into the background. Average height, size 8, C-cup bra. There's not too much to comment on about my stats. I'm living smack dab in the unremarkable territory of being neither thin nor fat, neither busty nor flat-chested, neither short nor tall. Flying under the radar is my specialty. I could have pursued a job with the CIA. There's nothing wrong with me. But there's also nothing noteworthy about my appearance. And normally, I'm okay with that.

I'm a blank canvas.

It might take a little more effort than I'm used to making for a night out if I want to sell my "relationship" with Hollywood Dean.

I head to my bedroom and dig in the back of my closet for the skintight, shiny, black bodysuit I bought to wear under my costume at the town's Halloween masquerade. I went as a web crawler—half spider, half bot. I don't think anybody besides Jackson really got it, but whatever. That's art. Sometimes your ideas work, and sometimes your protracted explanation sounds a lot like "you had to be there."

The bodysuit is low cut and cleavage-giving. Just the sort of thing that I imagine the type of girl who dated Dean would wear. Maybe I could layer it under a jacket? Craft a smoky eye? Toss on some chunky jewelry?

I try it on and immediately rule it out as too thirsty. It isn't my style.

But then it dawns on me that it doesn't matter what I wear. In fact, the *less* effort I make, the better. I have to dress normal for this prank to work. The best costume is no costume. If I show up in something totally out of character, people are going to figure out that something's up right away. We're not going to be able to pull it off.

And I really want to pull it off, for reasons I'm not entirely clear about. I mean, I don't actually want him anymore, do I? That ship sailed a long time ago. He's totally wrong for me, and always was.

Guys like Dean Riley are dangerous. They seem so perfect, but they can't be relied upon to follow through. It's all flash, dazzle, and a whiff of cologne. Guys like him make promises with the best of intentions and promptly forget. And guys like Dean are always leaving. Dean is too fancy for this tiny town.

Best thing you can do is set that kind of man free. Toss them back. Release and walk away. I ought to know.

Once upon a time, my father also couldn't wait to get the hell out of Ephron. He played in a band, and he was really good. Plus, he was really lucky. But then he knocked up my mom and got stuck here. We know how that story plays out. It ends with Jackson and I dragging our dad off the front lawn and our mom making up stories after every bender. It ends tragically, when our dad drives the family car over an embankment with our elderly golden retriever, Murphy, in the back seat.

Spoiler alert—our dad made it. The dog and the station wagon didn't.

This is why I make lists. My lists keep me from disappointing people like my father did or from getting disappointed like my mother. So I don't drive myself crazy like Jackson, trying to find the holy grail in some kind of algorithmic compatibility code. My lists keep me honest. I am in control of my own destiny. I call the shots.

I make good, responsible decisions.

I pick up my journal and settle down in the window seat to capture my thoughts and reaffirm what this means, while I eat my perfectly healthy dinner salad.

10 Things Chelsea Doesn't Do: A List by Chelsea Porter

1. Date guys who drive motorcycles.
2. Get drunk.
3. Make her private life public.
4. Overshare.
5. Break her promises.

6. Use people.

7. Lie.

8. Burden others with her problems.

9. Have one-night stands.

10. Leave.

11. Get what she really wants because life is totally unfair

Where did #11 come from?

Frustrated, I tear out the page and crumple it up. Why do I suddenly feel like crying? There are still two hours to go until Dean picks me up. I should have gone for a longer run.

dean

. . .

"TELL GRANDMA WHAT YOU DID, BRADEN." Eli walks into my mom's kitchen, holding his pink-cheeked son.

Braden imitates pulling the rope and yells "Bong! Bong!" at the top of his lungs.

Mom praises Braden and gives me a long, hard hug. She smells like apples and cinnamon.

"You look good, Mom," I say. "I love the silver!" She's let the silver streak in her dark hair grow out, and I think it's kind of cool. It gives her an edge.

"I have a book I saved for you to read. Remind me to grab it before you go. It's so good. You have to read it."

"What's it called?" I smile. My mom loves to read almost anything, but her favorites are cozy mysteries.

"Oh, I can't recall it now. Something with a cat? A bird? Maybe a bell? We just read it in our book club last month."

"Did you hear the bells?" My dad enters the kitchen from the back, coming in through the mudroom off the garage. He kisses my mom on the lips.

"I think the whole town heard the bells. Are you kidding me?" my mother asks. She looks from me to my father. "So, are we all good here? Shall I get some champagne?"

"Hold up a moment," my dad says. "I'd like to go over why everyone thought it was a good idea to keep me in the dark first."

"Here we go," Eli mouths at me.

"It's my fault." I take the blame. "I didn't want them to tell you because I wasn't ready for you to know."

"Why the hell not?" My dad sounds angry, but he actually looks hurt. His brows are furrowed. He crosses his arms across his broad chest.

He's still got at least fifty pounds and four inches on me. The man's a giant. He's the kind of guy you definitely want on your side. As a little kid, it would always give me a thrill of pride to point him out to people, to say "That's my dad!" Eli and I would argue over whose turn it was to sit on his shoulders on the Fourth of July. Sitting up there, surrounded by fireworks, was better than being in a spaceship. And now, after all these years, he's still intimidating. Especially when he's not on your side.

"I didn't tell you because I didn't want to be talked out of it. I didn't want to hear all the reasons why you think my ideas are stupid, and too fancy for Ephron, and how nobody here wants a theater. I didn't want to hear it from anyone. Least of all, my own father."

"Well, what if that's what you needed to hear? You'd rather hear it from a stranger?"

"This isn't a decision I made on a whim, Dad. I based my plans on market research and experience. I have investors and advisers who have reviewed the plans. I don't need your opinion about the viability of the project," I say, speaking firmly, despite the narrowing of his eyes and reddening of his face.

"But you needed my help getting the work done, didn't you?"

"Damn straight," I say. "There's nobody else I would have considered working with on the construction. There's nobody better. But it wasn't a favor, Dad. It was a contract. That's another reason I didn't want you or the rest of the crews to know. I didn't want preferential treatment."

"But your brother knew. And your mom." My dad takes his seat at the head of the table.

I'm not going to apologize for telling my mother and Eli. My mom has always had impeccable taste, and I'd relied on her to make some of the design decisions for the community center renovation. And I'd needed Eli to keep an eye on things while I was wrapping everything up in LA.

"Mom and Eli were supportive of me." I shrug. "I needed help from someone I could trust."

"Kevin." My mom walks to my dad and puts a hand on his shoulder. "I think what Dean is trying to say is that he wanted to make sure his ducks were all in a row before he shared his big news. Aren't you glad your son is finally coming home? Isn't this what we've always wanted? Both of our sons close by?"

My father slams a fist on the table, making the silverware shake and the glasses tremble. "No, Jenny. This isn't what I always dreamed of."

Out of the corner of my eye, I see Eli taking Braden outside. My dad continues his speech.

"I haven't always dreamed of having Mr. Hollywood Fancy-pants and his floozy du jour putting on shows in my back-yard. You know what I always dreamed of and what I

71

worked so hard for. I built Riley and Sons for you, and for my boys, and little Braden." My dad looks around, only just registering that Eli and Braden have left the building.

"I think you mean 'Riley and Son,'" I say, thinking that he should have had a funeral for that lopped off letter when I left for UCLA.

"Enough already," my mom says, "you're being ridiculous. Maybe we shouldn't have kept it from you. But can't you just be happy now? This is good news." She looks over at me imploringly, but I'm not sure what she expects me to say. I can't change the past and make this better.

"You know what? I don't want to ruin your dinner, and anyway, I've got plans. I'm meeting some friends for drinks," I say.

"Nice," my dad says. "See his priorities? He's been home for less than twenty-four hours, and he's already headed out to party. What are you, Dean, thirty-three? When I was your age, I'd been married for a decade, and both you boys were in grade school. Are you ever gonna grow up?"

My mom has tears in her eyes, but I'm not going to stick around for another minute of this.

I don't know what I was expecting. Somehow, she and Eli had convinced me it would be different. And stupidly, I'd believed her. I'd allowed myself to hope.

My dad still hasn't congratulated me on winning an Academy Award. So why was I expecting him to congratulate me on opening a community theater?

———

I use my keycard to pull into the parking garage of the loft building and look for my assigned space. There's not much to carry upstairs. I just have a few things in my bike that I packed for the journey.

The elevator dings and opens up on the top level. These lofts are all penthouse units, built on the roof of the original Hearth and Holm warehouses. I pause for a moment in the breezeway, taking in the incredible view of the river. It's a crisp night, but not too cold. The air is so fresh, and it is crystal clear—no smog. Someone's cooking dinner on the communal patio. I hear people laughing and smell barbecue wafting from the far end of the long, open corridor.

I can't stop thinking about my dad's words, "Mr. Hollywood Fancy-pants and his floozy du jour." Is that what he really thinks of me? I've barely dated anyone at all for the last couple of years.

But you certainly earned the reputation before that. You worked hard to foster it.

In my younger years, I leaned in hard on a negative attention model. People say that negative attention is better than no attention. My dad hated flashy cars? I'd rent a Ferrari when I came home for Thanksgiving, with a model as my date. With every success, I'd taken the opportunity to rub his nose in it, sending lavish holiday gifts and booking first-class plane tickets and hotel rooms to attend every premiere. But it was just Mom and Eli who came.

I just want to take a long, hot shower and hit reset.

I let myself into the loft, not even sure what exactly to expect inside. I've seen photos, but the place was staged, and it's not the same as doing your own walk-though. I'd purchased the place solely on my brother's recommendation and Jackson's praise for the project his old buddy Hudson pulled off here.

Hudson Holm. For decades, I've heard about this guy. When I first moved here, Jackson talked about his grade school best buddy so much, I'd started to hate him. I felt a little jealous even. Hudson was super smart—he got straight A's and was in math club with Jackson. Like me, Hudson recently came back to Ephron. I wonder whether his transition has gone more smoothly than mine seems to be going. Maybe I'll get the chance to ask him if I meet him tonight.

The loft interior is minimalist and modern. Polished, concrete floors and Venetian plaster walls punctuated by the odd, reclaimed beam. Floor-to-ceiling windows run the length of the two-story apartment, and I can tell it will be flooded with sunshine during the day, thanks to the southwest-facing exposure.

There's a box on the kitchen counter, along with a bag of bed linens. The box contains an inflatable mattress that Eli and Brittany dropped off earlier. At least I won't have to sleep on the floor till my furniture gets delivered. I peek in the bag, amused that the linens are Titanium Man themed. I'll have to save these for Rafe when he comes to visit. Someone, possibly Britt and possibly Braden, has thoughtfully included a bag of goldfish crackers.

The six-pack of beer on the counter is definitely from Eli. I pop one of the bottles open and reach for my phone just as it's lighting up with a text from my brother.

> Sorry about Dad. Don't worry, he'll come around. He's only like this because he misses you so much.

Is Mom ok?

> She's pretty pissed off at Dad. But she'll be ok. She wants you to know that she saved some brisket for you if you want to stop by for lunch tomorrow.

Darkness is descending quickly, so I look around for the light switch. I locate a bank of them on the wall behind the kitchen counter and flick them on and off, one by one.

Nothing.

Frustrated, I turn on the flashlight on my phone and go in search of a working light switch. There are bulbs in the canisters, so that's not the issue. I test the switch by the door. Nothing. The ones by the stairs don't appear to be working, either.

Finally, I locate the fuse box outside in the breezeway and check to see if maybe something got thrown. And that's when I see the yellow service notice hanging next to the meter. The electricity isn't scheduled to be turned on for another twenty-four hours.

Shit! How had I managed to get the dates wrong?

I go back inside and test the tap. Tepid at best. No hot shower for me. It's going to have to be frosty and fast if I'm going to make it to Chelsea's on time.

Somehow, despite everything, I'm still looking forward to seeing Chelsea again.

chelsea

. . .

DEAN IS LATE. Only five minutes, but still …

I do the *New York Times* Wordle challenge while waiting and try not to stress. With every passing moment, I'm questioning this decision to go along with the prank. Is he going to expect me to ride on his motorcycle with him? It's just two miles, but I'm super anxious about it. I haven't been on the back of a bike since I was seventeen, and I'm not sure tonight's the night. Maybe he won't show up at all. Maybe he changed his mind. It wouldn't be the first time. My phone dings.

> Sorry. Had a problem with the electricity at my place. Be there in five.

So, it is still happening. I check my breath one last time. I think I'm good. Just the same, I pop a stick of spearmint gum in my mouth.

"TENSE." I finally solve the puzzle in five tries that should have been three, and a second later, I hear the buzzer.

"Be right down!" I say into the intercom. I toss on my fur-lined, leather jacket. It might be overkill for the weather tonight, but the temperature is falling fast.

"Sorry I'm late." Dean shivers.

I do a double take.

"What the hell happened to you?" I ask. Honestly, he looks like a drowned rat. His hair is soaking wet and plastered to his head from wearing the helmet. He's only dressed in a thin tee under his motorcycle jacket. He appears to have goose bumps on his goose bumps. I could offer him a sweater, but I'm not sure I have anything that would fit him. Maybe an oversize sweatshirt from the fun run?

"Cold shower," he says, gritting his chattering teeth. "No electricity. And this was my only clean shirt. I'll be fine. I'll warm up when we get there."

"You should be dressed warmer," I say. "You're going to catch pneumonia."

"Don't be silly, I'll be fine." He scowls. "Hop on." Dean reaches back for the purple helmet. It has a Z on it.

"Whose helmet is that?" I ask.

"What do you mean?" Dean looks confused. "It's a spare."

"It's got a Z on it, though."

"So?"

"So, I feel weird wearing someone else's helmet. How about you leave your bike in my parking spot, and I drive instead?" I reach in my pocket and pull out my keys.

I wasn't actually expecting this ploy of driving to Grumpy's instead of riding the bike to actually work, but seeing how cold he is has given me hope.

"Do you think Zara has lice or something? That's a little rude, don't you think?" Dean balances on the bike, looking vaguely annoyed.

"Of course I don't think that!" I blanch at the thought that I've somehow suggested that one of the most powerful women in film might have cooties. "The opposite, actually. I was thinking she probably wouldn't appreciate ME wearing HER helmet."

God, I'm awkward.

"Honestly? Zara could give a crap. She's never even worn this thing. I got it thinking I could convince her to go for a ride sometime, but she said she's not interested in being an organ donor, so whatever."

"I'm liking her more and more," I mumble.

"You two would probably get along great." Dean nods, still subtly shaking. "Wanna get going?"

"I have butt warmers in my Mazda," I say, still trying to lure him off the motorcycle.

Dean heaves a sigh, and I can see him capitulating. But he's not going down without a fight.

"Fine, Chelsea. You win. We don't have to go on my bike tonight, so long as you promise to give me a rain check on coming for a ride with me. When was the last time you were on a motorcycle?"

"Probably the last time you picked me up in Holm Square on one."

"This baby is so much better. She's so smooth, she purrs." He runs a reverential hand over the chassis, stroking it.

"That said"—he smiles charmingly, finally relenting—"I'm not going to say no to a woman who's offering to toast my buns."

―――――

On the drive over, Dean can't resist messing with the seat controls and the radio, checking out which satellite radio stations I have hot listed.

"Classic Rock, very good." He taps the station and "Baba O'Riley" by The Who comes on.

"We're all wasted!" Dean hums along and sing-shouts a verse, impersonating a tortured artist.

I could sing along, too. I know all the words. But I hold my tongue.

"God, I loved this album in high school." Dean laughs. "Such a cliché."

Me too. I loved it because he did. Any time Dean mentioned a song, a movie, a television show that he liked, I was in. I studied his picks like I was his disciple, preparing to worship at his temple.

Some of it stuck. I still like The Who.

"I don't know, it could have been a lot worse, all things considered. I think The Who is still relevant. Much more so than your famous make-out song by Robin Thicke," I say.

"Oh, God, I can't believe you remember that. But it never failed me, I'm telling you. Mind if we listen to it now? You have Bluetooth, right? I can probably pull it up on my phone."

"Trying to get me in the mood?" I laugh.

By the time we park down the street from The Grumpy Stump, Dean seems to have thawed out. His hair is drying, and I notice the way it curls at his temples and by the back of his neck. His presence seems to fill my car, that signature Dean scent, wafting off him in the heater's blast.

"Thanks for being such a great sport, Chelsea." Dean places a hand on my knee as I cut the ignition. "Seriously, you have still got to be one of the coolest women I have ever met."

"How so?" I ask, trying to act nonchalant while simultaneously worrying about how I am going to get the smell of him out of my car. His scent is just distracting enough that it might be a safety hazard.

"Well, for starters, you've never compromised. You're doing exactly what you love—teaching art, staging plays."

"Still in Ephron. Rub it in, why don't you?" I give him a look.

"What?" He looks hurt. "I mean it. I think it's cool that you're still here and still doing the things you love. You've always known yourself perfectly. No compromises."

"I guess this is the point in the conversation where I'm supposed to congratulate you for your Academy Award, right?" I wrinkle my nose. I don't have to be a stalker to know that fact. I just have to be a normal person who watches the Academy Awards. He looks wounded by my tone, and I instantly regret being salty. "Sorry, Dean. I didn't mean that to sound so bitter. Honestly, it's incredible. Very intimidating."

Dean shrugs. "Well, it shouldn't be. I didn't do it alone. Plus, it's a trap. It's not like you get to win one award and you're good, you're done. Turns out, there's always a newer or bigger award to chase. It's a vicious, never-ending cycle. Trust me. It's not all it's cracked up to be."

I have the feeling he's not just talking about his Oscar.

Dean stares out his window, rubbing his hands together and blowing on them. "Anyway, I'm here now, aren't I? I'm here too."

"True," I say, "but you know what's funny? When you had me paged to the office earlier, for a second, I thought maybe it was a setup for some kind of teacher award or something. And I was excited about it. You won an Oscar, Dean. A freaking Oscar. I've never won anything."

"I won for creating a pretend world. You've got a real one."

Dean reaches out to tenderly chuck my cheek, and I feel my face flush. Suddenly, the car feels too close, and I realize we've only got about ten minutes before the others start to arrive.

"There's already a crowd outside. We better get inside, or we'll never get a booth," I say.

"Already phoned ahead and reserved one," Dean assures me.

I didn't even know that was a thing you could do at The Grumpy Stump.

"Here's how I think it should go down." He speaks like he's giving stage directions. "You and I will walk in, holding hands. We'll slide into the booth and order ourselves some drinks, and then ... *you know*."

"Then we wait for Jackson to show up?" I ask.

"I think to be convincing, we need to already be in character when he shows up." Dean gets out of the car before I can respond, rushing to my side to hold the door and take my arm.

As we walk in, Dean slips a bill to the hostess, who nods as if she's been expecting him. She escorts us straight to the one and only VIP booth in the place. It's not VIP in the traditional sense. There are no velvet ropes or plaques. But Grumpy's table is as VIP as a booth can get at a stump-themed bar with ax-throwing lanes.

The centrally located round table is made out of resin, into which a massive slice of tree has been submerged. The horse-shoe-shaped booth is upholstered in sparkly, black vinyl. It's perfectly situated, facing the front door.

"Our podcast crew is kind of a big deal at this place, but I have to admit, I've never sat at Grumpy's table before," I remark as I ease into the booth. Dean slides in right behind me.

"There's a first time for everything." Dean winks, pulling me closer. And then he kisses me. No preamble. No asking permission. Just—pow!

My brain goes purple and fuzzy, and I'm not sure if it's the neon sign in the window or if I'm flashing and seeing feelings again. What were we just talking about? First time? No. This would be the second.

Dean's lips move against mine, and he places a hand on my face. Frosty! His fingers are still cold, but it doesn't feel bad. It feels good because his lips are like fire and my face is burn-ing, and then he does something with the tip of his tongue, and I forget about gravity.

Don't get me wrong, it's not like I've never been kissed. Or like I don't know how to kiss. In fact, as a twenty-nine-year-old virgin, I've become rather expert at kissing … and several other things that don't involve *the actual act* that I've put off so embarrassingly long. Why have I put it off so long again? I seem to have amnesia because, God help me, I want him. The pull is achingly familiar. It's low and slow and deep and even more insistent than it was all those years ago, if that's even possible.

This guy.

The kiss feels dangerous. Like I'm a little drunk and suddenly thinking about riding a mechanical bull. It can't be safe. It's definitely a bad idea. But I won't stop. I can't. Instead, I *lean in*, dragging my teeth against his lower lip and then sucking it. His hand moves to my waist, pulling me closer, and before I even know what I'm doing, I am turning toward him and crossing my outside leg over his. Any closer and I'd be straddling him.

I open one eye, cautiously peeking, expecting to see his eyes closed. But Dean's eyes are both wide open, looking at me with an expression of shock and admiration. I pull back.

"Damn, Chels. That escalated fast!" he says, breathless.

"Too much?" I ask.

"You always were an excellent kisser." He traces my lower lip with one warming finger.

"How would you know?" I ask. "You only kissed me that one time."

"It was a memorable kiss," he admits. "Probably one of the most memorable ones I got in high school." Then he pauses to consider. "Or since." He smiles wryly.

"Bullshit!" I shake my head at him. "That is such a lousy line. I was beyond awkward, and we both knew it."

"Well, then, you'll just have to wipe that memory from my mind and replace it with a new one." Dean places a hand on the back of my head and pulls my face back toward his. This time, he closes his eyes. And just before his lips touch mine, he whispers, "Incoming."

I don't fully process his words immediately. I'm too busy processing the feeling of his lips moving under mine. Hard and somehow soft at the same time, like a really good mattress. Like something you can sink into and feel supported by. I could lose myself to dreams in these lips.

Incoming. As in, coming in for the kiss?

By all means, welcome. Let me roll out the red carpet. Let me take your coat. I slide my hands inside his leather jacket. His T-shirt is soft and so thin that I can feel every ridge of his hard, muscled chest underneath it. Just enough muscle, not too much.

Incoming. His tongue sneaks between my lips, and I don't hesitate before sucking it. I'm even closer to sitting on his lap now, and I think that he might actually be getting a little bit aroused because, if I'm not mistaken, that definitely feels like …

Incoming.

Behind me, Jackson clears his throat. Loudly. Rudely. Get lost, Jackson! I've completely forgotten the whole reason we're here and doing this.

"Dean? Dude! What the hell are you doing here? Why didn't you say you were coming to town this week," my brother exclaims. "If I'd known, I would have—"

Dean hasn't stopped kissing me, but something is different. He's pushing me away. Ever so slightly. I pull back, and our lips come apart with a wet, smacking sound. I turn around to look at my brother, and Jackson gasps. Full-on, *little girlie* gasps.

Like someone just put a rubber snake in his underwear drawer.

Or a plastic spider in his box of cornflakes.

Or a bucket of ice water over the bathroom door.

Payback is a bitch.

Behind Jackson, standing wide-eyed in the doorway and also staring at me with disbelief, are my friends Georgia, Hudson, Xander and Alexis.

"Whaaaat the fuck is happening here?" Jackson speaks slowly, suggesting that he may, in fact, be glitching out.

Dean and I burst into giggles. We can't stop laughing as we make room at Grumpy's table for the rest of our party. We laugh so hard, we cry, and then we keep laughing a little more, which is the point when everyone starts to look at us like we've really lost it.

"The thing is ..." Dean finally manages to speak when someone brings over a glass of water. "We have big news. We're actually a couple."

He gestures between himself and me.

"Mazel tov?" Hudson says.

"No," Jackson says. "No fucking way." He slaps the table.

"What? You didn't think your little sister was cool enough for your best friend?" I raise an eyebrow at my brother and fold my arms across my chest. My ribs are still aching from laughing so hard.

"No ... that's not it," Jackson insists, a little sulkily. "It's just that ... just that ..."

Dean and Jackson speak at the exact same moment then, making it almost difficult to make out what either of them is saying.

"Gotcha!" shouts Dean.

"I knew it!" yells Jackson.

dean

. . .

"DON'T BE RIDICULOUS," Chelsea says. "I'm not going to let you sleep on the cement floor of a freezing-cold loft."

I try to explain to her that I've stayed in worse places, but she won't take no for an answer.

"I have a pullout couch that's actually pretty comfy," she insists. "And hot water if you want to take another shower in the morning."

"That depends," I say. "If you kiss me again like you did earlier, I might be more grateful for a cold shower."

"Cut it out, Dean." She bites her lips, staving off more laughter. "Butt warmer?"

"Yes, please." I nod emphatically. And then I feel myself staving off a wave of laughter again too.

"His FACE." I snicker.

"His gasp!" Chelsea agrees.

"We got him so good." I chuckle.

"So, so, so good," Chelsea agrees. "So much better than I could have imagined. In fact, I think you made a little girl's dreams come true tonight, Dean."

We both stop laughing when she says this.

"Oh, my God." Chelsea slams on the brakes at the yellow light, waiting for it to turn red. "I didn't mean it that way. I meant it in the 'being the prankster instead of the prankee' way because you know I was always on the receiving end of Jackson's pranks, and a few of yours, too, you know, and it was just so great to finally—"

"I know," I interrupt. "I remember." Her face is lit by the red light, so it's impossible to tell how much she's blushing, but I'd put good money on a royal flush. The red light shining on the two of us is practically pulsing. I file away this visual for dramatic use in a film or on stage.

"Honestly, I'm surprised you still remember," she says.

"Of course I remember you kissing me. I wasn't lying. It was a pretty spectacular kiss. One that I beat myself up for stealing from you."

The light turns green, and she drives.

"Stealing?" she says in disbelief. "How do you figure? I am the one who threw herself at you."

"You tossed the ball, but I sure as shit caught it and ran with it. I shouldn't have taken advantage of you like that."

"Dean, don't be ridiculous."

"You were a kid." I groan. I'm genuinely embarrassed when I think about it now.

Before I kissed Chelsea, during my senior year, I'd made out with plenty of other freshman girls. Nothing serious. Just kissing. I knew when to call it quits.

87

But with Chelsea, it had been different. I can't explain it. I just didn't feel like I would be able to stop. Not that I couldn't control myself, or that I was going to overpower her or anything. Just that if *she* didn't want me to stop, if she'd asked me to keep going, I wasn't entirely confident I'd be able to say no to her.

We were both young, but she was definitely too young. Even if she wasn't my best friend's little sister, it would have been wrong.

We drive on a few more miles, sliding silently past several green lights before she speaks again.

"Do you remember the promise that you made me?" she asks.

Of course I remember. But I'm not sure why she is bringing it up now.

"At the hospital," she says quietly, as we pass through Holm Square and past the community center. "Ring any bells?"

"Funny you should mention bells." I glance up at the bell tower in an attempt to change the subject. I don't really want to talk about this right now. I don't want to hear her apology. I'd rather forget about it. Move on. Live in the present.

"I thought I heard a bell earlier!" Chelsea says. "Huh. It's been so long since I heard those bells, I thought maybe I was imagining it. Anyway, the hospital …"

"The hospital you say?" I ask.

Of course I remember that promise. I remember signing her cast. Touching her leg. The sweet, soft flesh of her thigh. I remember thinking how all that pain was really my fault.

"It was more of a prompromise than a promise, don't you think?" I ask, rhyming prompromise with compromise. It was over a decade ago. Best to let bygones be bygones. No need to hold a grudge. No need to discuss how hopeful I'd been

88

when I came home that spring. How ready I'd been to honor my prom promise. And how she'd put me firmly in my place. Her revenge for my earlier rejection was served up cold. Ice cold.

"So, you do remember." She sighs and parks the car in front of her building. I wonder if she regrets it. If she ever wonders.

I do.

"So, who'd you end up going to prom with?" I ask.

"Really, Dean?" Chelsea cuts the ignition. "You were home the month before my senior prom. I told you who I was going with."

"No, you didn't," I reply. What she'd told me was that she was going with me. And that had been a lie.

"Nobody." Chelsea gives me a strange look. "I didn't go to senior prom."

chelsea

. . .

TWELVE YEARS AGO …

It's a warm spring evening. I'm sitting and reading in Holm Square when I hear the motorcycle. It's loud and annoying, pulling me out of Forks and away from the delicious love triangle that is Bella, Edward, and Jacob. *Rude.*

I've taken to sketching and reading on a park bench after school most days. It's better than going home. The house is too quiet, and the chores, on top of my homework, seem endless. Dad hasn't checked in or sent any money in almost two years, ever since the accident. Mom is juggling two shitty jobs to make ends meet, so she's too tired to do all the things she's always done, like clean the house, do laundry, and make dinner. I never realized how much she did till she stopped doing it.

But she's not too tired to date. She goes out an awful lot. And sometimes, she doesn't come home till the next morning. This annoys me less than it annoys Jackson. At least she isn't crying all the time anymore, and she's not on my case. I'm practically the only one of my friends without a curfew. Not that I go anywhere or do anything. But the point is, I could. If I wanted to. If I had an Edward.

As hard as things are, it's still better than when my parents argued all the time. Back then, I never knew what to expect. What an idiot I'd been to believe my dad would get better. For blaming my mom for his drinking. I'd been so sure everything was her fault. Right up until my dad killed Murphy.

Oh, God. I can't even think about the dog. I still miss him so much. Poor, ancient Murphy. We'd had him since I was four. I don't even know what he was doing in the car with my dad that night. Where were they going? Of course, my dad had been fine. The drunk drivers are never the ones who die, right? I hate him so much now. For Murphy. For fucking up our family. For not getting better. For leaving. Why couldn't he just get better? Do better?

I don't wish him dead. I just wish him … I don't even know what. Different? But that's impossible. We are better. Better without him in our lives. I'm never going to put up with the kind of fucked-up shit my mom did. My eyes fill with tears as I try to get back into the story. If only I had an Edward. Or a Jacob.

If only. If only my life were more like a book. On the surface, this town is just like Forks, the town in *Twilight*. Minus the cool vampires and wolf shifters. The mix here is so predictable, it's almost reassuring. You've got your jocks, nerds, goths, and churchies. And then there's me, the crazy boho chick. That's what Bryce Holm called me. Like that shithead was doing me a favor, offering to take me to prom, despite what a "weirdo" I am.

But I'm not going to prom with anyone if I'm not going with Dean Riley. Least of all, Bryce Holm. I don't want to go to prom that badly.

Last week, my mom asked me if I'm having sex with anyone. When I said no, she seemed surprised. Almost disappointed. She was probably super excited to be that cool mom she never had. She recovered quickly, though. After I told her I didn't want to talk about it, she offered to buy me a vibrator so I could "explore my sexuality" on my own and "avoid making the same mistakes" she did. I can only assume she's referring to getting knocked up with Jackson when she was the same age I am now.

It got worse.

She also tried to tell me about this guy she's dating. Something about his big-dick energy waking up her chakras. You'd think I'd be used to it by now. And I kind of am. It doesn't shock me. I just really don't need to know about my mom's chakras. Thank God Jackson wasn't home. His head would have exploded. He hates when Mom gets like this.

As annoying as my brother can be, I've been counting down the days till he gets home for the summer. Even if it means I've got to clean the whole house. I can't wait to have Jackson and Dean around again. They'll be here in time for prom. And I will be holding Dean to his promise.

I attempt to get back into my book. Thank goodness I don't have to choose between Edward and Jacob because I'm not sure I could handle that. But no worries about that. For me, there's always only been one guy.

For a while, I was worried Dean would forget. That he wouldn't honor the deal we'd made and take me to prom. But Dean's not like that. When Dean makes a commitment, he sees it through.

Last Christmas, when Jackson was in the kitchen popping popcorn for our movie fest, I brought it up again. I tested it out, mentioning it casually, like I was joking, but Dean hadn't hesitated. He'd pinned me with those intense eyes, bringing back all the feels, leaving me breathless.

"I haven't forgotten. Just say the word, Chels. I got you."

"You better," I said.

Of course, Jackson had walked in at that moment.

After that, I went ahead and bought the tickets. I started shopping for a dress. And I made another decision. A really big one. After prom, I'm planning to sleep with him. All of my friends have already had sex. So why shouldn't I? Even my mom thinks it's time. I can't think of anyone else I'd even consider losing my virginity to. I've been in love with Dean since I was twelve years old.

I'm not stupid. I know we're both still young, and it's not like we're getting married or anything. He's still got another year at UCLA, and I'm starting college here in Ephron this fall. All the more reason to lose my virginity now, and with someone who really matters to me. I don't want to be one of those sad girls who gets drunk and loses it at a frat party.

And maybe, just maybe? Maybe what? It's silly to think that Dean and I are meant to be like Bella and Edward. Or Jacob. Whichever one she ends up with. I haven't even finished the series yet.

I'm not a child. I don't believe in fairy tales. I have no idea what the future holds, but what I do know is that I love Dean now.

The motorcycle revs again. Closer. Louder. I close my eyes. If I didn't know better, I'd think it was Dean. But he's not supposed to be home for a few more weeks.

dean

. . .

WE PARK ON THE STREET, and I follow Chelsea up to her apartment. I would be lying if I said I wasn't curious to see what it looks like. What her world looks like. Telling stories with spaces is the essence of my job. I can still picture the mural Jackson and I helped her paint on her bedroom wall when she was thirteen. Not many teenaged girls would want a sunset effect, pulling in colors from an Indian Sari and layering on a block-printed paisley in faux gold leaf. Jackson had lost patience when we were still blending colors and left us to our ways while he worked on a bit of code.

I want to get a read on grown-up Chelsea. I'm dying to see what her bedroom looks like now.

The apartment building isn't far from Holm Square. Close enough to walk to the center of town. It's also not too far from the residential area where she and Jackson grew up. It's hard to picture her living anywhere else. But I recall her mom sold the house the summer after Chelsea graduated from high school.

"You don't have to rescue me," I say, breaking the silence on the way upstairs. "I'd be fine camping in the loft for the night." There's no way I want to crash with my parents, but I could get a hotel. Or even call Jackson, for that matter. *But I don't want to do either of those things, do I?*

Chelsea opens the door and flips on the lights.

This old building has great bones. High ceilings and casement windows. Crown molding and wide baseboards. The entry and connected living room are painted a supersaturated teal. It feels homey. Warm and cool at the same time. But what hits me more than the way it looks is the way the place smells.

Vanilla, roses, and paint. Did she always smell that way? So good, and so familiar and foreign at the same time.

So *sexy*.

"The bathroom is through there, and the kitchen is here, obviously." Chelsea waves toward the open-plan kitchen with gleaming, quartz countertops and sleek, teak cabinets that coordinate with the living room furniture.

"I love midcentury modern," I tell her. "Where did you get all this great stuff?"

"Thrift shops, mostly," Chelsea says. "That sofa bed is from a friend of my mom. She got it from her mom, who brought it here from Denmark. I had to have the mattress custom made. It's comfy."

"Can I see the rest of the place?" I ask.

"It's kind of a mess," Chelsea says.

"Oh, come on, it's me." I roll my eyes. "And it looks pretty clean to me, anyway."

Growing up, Chelsea's house was always on the chaotic end of the spectrum, and it was part of what made me love it there. My own mom was a neat freak.

"Love this piece." I stop to admire one of the prints in the hallway. From a distance, it looks like an aerial photo of bathers floating in the ocean. But as you get closer, you realize this is a trick of light, color, and texture. It's not an aerial photo at all. It's a painting, and what's more, it's a painting that's been painted on a human body. The curve of a hip defines the water line.

"Wow. So cool! I love this." I gesture at the painting. I look again, examining the golden signature on the piece, wondering who did it. It's a mere squiggle. Indecipherable. I can't make out the name. "It's amazing. I don't think I've seen this artist before."

"Thanks." She straightens, watching me. "It's probably no one you're familiar with."

I take a couple of steps down the hallway to look at the next one, my brain already playing the game, looking for the trompe l'oeil trick.

The second piece is more surreal and whimsical, like the illustration from a children's storybook. At first glance, it appears to be a bedroom without walls. Like *Where the Wild Things Are*. The floor is a lush landscape of grass and flowers. The backdrop is a vibrant sunset sky, just on the brink of turning to night. The light of a full moon is shining down, pooling around the unmade, wrought iron bed. There's something about the winking face of the moon. I look again. And that's when I see it. It's so clever. The pupil is formed by the point of an erect nipple. I squint in an attempt to separate the carefully hidden person from the background. Her knee forms part of the vine-covered headboard. Her toes are the tassels of a rumpled bedspread.

"Holy shit," I say, turning back to her. "This is *you*. You painted this."

Chelsea freezes. "Don't be silly," she says. "I got it on the internet."

What gives it away is the paisley pattern on the pillow. I know that print. It's just like the paisley we repeated all over the walls of her childhood bedroom. And the sunset colors too.

"Okay, but I know it's you," I say gently, seeking out her eyes. Why is she denying it? Looking more closely at the image, I can faintly see a scar that I know she has on her elbow. I was there when she fell off her bike.

"No, it's not." She pulls me back toward the living room. "Come on. There's nothing else to see. It's just my studio and my bedroom down there." She points at the two doorways at the end of the hall. One of the doors is closed, but through the open door, I get an enticing peek at another dark-walled room with a *wrought iron* bed. I take a step toward the bedroom. I want to check it out. I find myself wondering what color her sheets are. And what she looks like when the moonlight shines down on her sleeping there.

"Can I get you a cup of tea, maybe?" Chelsea tugs on my arm again. "I have some gingersnaps that I made yesterday. They came out pretty good. Not quite *British Bake Off* good, but they do have a nice snap!"

What reason could she possibly have for denying her own work? She's so incredibly talented. I just don't get it. There's so much about her that I don't get. Everything that's familiar about her is flanked by something secretive and unknown. It's maddening.

"Fine." I capitulate, deciding not to push for now. "If you'll have a cup with me."

I settle on the couch and watch her as she puts up the water and moves to gather items for me. She pulls a quilt from a compartment under an ottoman and dashes off to her bedroom to retrieve a pillow and sheets.

"There's a new toothbrush and some toothpaste in the bathroom," she says. "I try to keep a spare for when my mom visits. She always forgets stuff."

"How is your mom?" I ask. "She's in Oregon now, right?" I recall Jackson telling me excitedly, after he sold his startup, that the very first thing he was planning to do was buy his mom a place near the ocean. Somewhere she could start fresh and wake up and write every day. He bought her house before he built his own.

Chelsea answers my question, "My mom is doing great! She's in Oregon, and I don't know if Jackson told you, but she runs a coffee shop/bookstore there. They do events a few times a year. She's had her poetry published in a few anthologies, and she's dating this author. He's a really nice guy ..." Her voice trails off, hopeful and wistful.

"That's so cool." I smile. "Your mom deserves some happiness. I'd love to take a trip down there to see her sometime."

"That would be interesting," Chelsea says.

"Why?" I ask.

"She's not your biggest fan, is all." Chelsea keeps talking as she returns to the kitchen to put together a tray with the mugs of hot water, some teabags, and a plate of cookies.

"Really?" I can't tell if she is joking. Jackson and Chelsea's mom was always like a second mom to me. Or maybe a cool aunt. She loved to try and shock us.

Chelsea shrugs. Finally, she brings the tray to the surfboard-shaped coffee table and places it on top of a stack of art books before sitting down beside me on the couch.

"It's just so weird that you're here," she says. "I'm still struggling with the context of you being here versus in a magazine or on a screen."

"I am originally from here, and you've known me forever, Chels. It shouldn't be so weird," I object. But I'm struggling as well. I'm having a hard time reconciling this cool, sexy, talented woman with the sweet, sassy kid from my memory.

"It's been such a long time since you've been back in Ephron, though," she says quietly.

She's wrong, but she's right. I've been here plenty of times, at least a couple times a year. But I haven't *really* been here for much more than a four-hour layover on those occasions. My appearances have all been cameos. I show up for the party, and then I hightail it to Seattle. No overnights. That's been my motto for over a decade.

"Have you missed me?" I ask, trailing my fingers over her arm. It's a loaded question, and we both know it. The chemistry between us is insane. It's intoxicating. I am dying to lift that curtain of hair and kiss her neck. If only there was a plausible reason to extend our performance from earlier. I would like an encore.

Chelsea glances down at my hand and holds her breath. Then she sits up straighter and leans forward to pour the tea.

"Well, you know, the high school hasn't had a decent set since you left." She lifts her cup to her mouth, takes a tiny sip, and then puckers her lips to blow on the steaming liquid. This does nothing to cool me down.

"We did *Guys and Dolls* last year. It was so sad. And for next fall, Noah is trying to convince me we should go minimalist with *Grease*, like it's some kind of mash-up of Ibsen and musical."

"You can't go minimalist with *Grease*," I object. "That would be a crime against musical theater!"

"I know! I have been gathering props and vintage clothes from local thrift shops ever since we decided on it," Chelsea enthuses. "I found the most perfect plastic hair rollers."

"I can't wait to see it all." I love the light in her eyes when she talks about props.

"Noah is so determined to scale back on our productions. I'm not sure why I'm fighting him on it so." She sighs and takes a sip of her drink.

"So, you and Noah must see a lot of each other, working together," I say. "How long have you known him?"

"He's been teaching at Ephron High for a couple of years." Chelsea snaps a biscuit in half but doesn't eat it.

"And he hasn't made his move yet?" I ask.

"He's kind of asked me about asking me out a few times, but given the fact that we have to work together, and there are all sorts of weird policies about teachers dating, I haven't encouraged him. I wouldn't want to rush into anything."

"So, it's not happening then?" I ask, reaching out to tuck her hair behind her ear. My fingers linger against the soft skin of her neck.

"I ... uh ... I don't know, maybe?" Chelsea says. Then she narrows her eyes at me. "Why?"

I shift closer toward her. This might be a terrible idea. One of the worst ideas ever. Or it might be one of the best. And there's no other way to know. *Plus, she invited me up.*

"I think you know why." I stare into her eyes, wide pools of smoky gray that remind me of all the colors mixed together. "I think we have some unfinished business here."

She shivers, but she doesn't move away or break eye contact. "It was just a prank, Dean. We both only did it to get Jackson back. And it was delicious, but—"

"It may have started out as a prank," I say, "but it didn't feel like a joke when we were kissing earlier tonight, did it? You were delicious, Chelsea."

I lean forward and tentatively brush her mouth with mine. I'm so hungry for her, it's crazy. I want to smash faces and crush her, and at the same time, I want to put her on a pedestal, safe from any sort of harm.

Chelsea makes a noise, somewhere between a moan and a whimper, and then her hands are behind me, reaching up under my shirt. Her back arches as I lean her back, lifting her shirt, cupping her breasts. I can feel her nipples hardening through the thin fabric and I pinch them, making her squirm. In return, she bites my lower lip. Her lips press kisses from my jawline down to the hollow of my throat. Then she flicks her tongue against my Adam's apple.

I place a knee between her legs and reach for the button on her jeans, my need growing more and more intolerable with each passing moment. It's almost painful how much I want her.

Suddenly, Chelsea sits bolt upright, knocking me in the chin and coming so close to kneeing me in the balls that the sudden spasm of evasive action is almost as painful as if she made contact. I taste metal and realize I've bitten my tongue.

For a moment, I'm stuck, still leaning forward on my fore-arms, knees pulled protectively in.

"No!" Chelsea jumps to her feet and pulls down her shirt. "No, no, no! You don't get to do this to me now. I am not the stupid teenager who worshipped the ground you walked on. This isn't fair. I am a grown woman. I have a life."

I'm still not able to speak, but I attempt to nod as I drop sideways into a semi-seated position and gently probe at my tongue. Not too bad.

"I'm sorry, Chelsea," I finally manage to say. "I didn't mean any disrespect toward you. And I think it's more than obvious that I'm aware you are a grown woman now. Grown and gorgeous."

"Oh, please. I am aware I can't hold a candle to the likes of Zara and all the arm candy that came before her, but I'm actually okay with that, Dean. I'm okay with it because I don't date men like you."

"Men like me, meaning what, exactly?" It's my turn to narrow my eyes at her. She is glowing, as if lit by the stoplight again, but I have no idea what is making her so angry.

"Men who make promises they can't, or won't, keep. Men who leave." Chelsea's hands are on her hips, and there are tears in her eyes.

I flinch. What the fuck. This sounds ridiculously familiar. She sounds like my dad.

"I'm here now," I say.

"Well, congratulations for coming back to Ephron after all these years. But don't expect a parade or anything. You're a little late. We've all moved on."

Chelsea spins on her heel and retreats to her bedroom, slamming the door.

I consider leaving, finding a hotel, or braving the cold cement floors of the loft. But a moment later, she's back with a hand-knit afghan and some thick socks.

"Here," she says. "It gets cold in here. And it's raining again outside. So don't even think about leaving. I don't want to hear about anyone scraping you off the road. I'll see you in the morning. I have to be out of here by 7:30."

———

I creep out of Chelsea's apartment at dark o'clock, before she wakes, and head back to my loft to regroup, but it's so cold and dim, and there's no place to sit. So, I make my way back into town to set up shop with my laptop at the Ephron Diner. I'm the first one there when they open.

"I know you," the curly haired, blonde woman in the barista apron that reads 'Coffee Witch' says.

"No, you probably don't." I shake my head.

"Aren't you that guy from that show?" She tilts her head sideways and narrows her eyes at me.

"Nope. Just a regular Joe."

"Huh." She pauses for a second, like she's about to say something, then she reconsiders. Her lips twitch a little, and she looks skyward like she's consulting her oracle, before looking back at me. "You know what? I think you really are a regular Joe. Possibly the first one I've ever met. Cream, no sugar?"

"That's me." I nod.

"Wow," she says. "I feel like I should get your autograph."

"Don't mind my niece," says the burly, older man behind the counter. I remember him as one of the owners of the diner. He's got just the slightest hint of a Greek accent. "She thinks she is a coffee witch. She likes to tell people what to drink. Much better when she tells them they are something fancy that doesn't come with free refills!" He winks at me and smiles affectionately at the woman.

103

"Hey, I don't do the choosing. I am merely the messenger," the woman says. "I'm Kenna, by the way. Are you new in town or just passing through?"

"Dean Riley," I say. "I've just moved back to Ephron. I'm from here originally, but I haven't lived here for ages. You'll probably get sick of me. I'm a terrible cook."

"Riley as in Riley Construction?" Kenna asks curiously. "They've been doing a lot of work on our building."

I nod. "My dad and my brother."

"That's why you look so familiar!"

There's something so familiar about Kenna as well, but I can't put my finger on it. She seems a bit younger than me, so I don't think we'd have been in school together. But her face gives me the feeling that I know her well. It's the same kind of feeling I used to get all the time when I first moved to LA. I'd see someone walking down the street and swear I must know them from high school. But in LA, it usually meant that they played the brother's friend or the crazy neighbor on some sitcom I watched years ago. Funny trick of the brain.

I take my first sip of coffee and let the caffeine filter through my bloodstream as I plan my first full day in my new, old hometown. Things aren't exactly going as I'd envisioned. For starters, I sure hadn't expected to wake up in Chelsea Porter's living room today. And the fight with my dad? Frosting on the shit cake.

Nobody tells you that no matter how many awards you win, or how much money you make, you will still feel like a confused adolescent when you go home, back to the place where you grew up. Forget about the wisdom of age and your briefcase full of insight. Your baggage, whatever it is, will be waiting for you. Feelings you thought you wrote off years ago have a way of showing up on your doorstep. I just hadn't expected Chelsea Porter to deliver my bags. Bags of regret?

Guilt? Resentment? So much to sort through. Twenty-two years' worth.

When my family first moved to Ephron, I was in middle school. My brother, Eli, was in high school. As a football prodigy, he had no problems making friends. He stepped right into stardom —the beloved quarterback/sports hero this town had been waiting for. Kevin Riley's pride and joy. Dad never missed a game and got up early to drive my brother to the gym, no matter the weather. They worked out together.

It had been harder for me. Even though I played football and was pretty decent enough at it, I didn't love it. Academics weren't my thing either. Not that this mattered to my dad. He would have been fine with my following a trade school trajectory, swapping out shop for trigonometry. It would have made more sense, given the expectation that I'd go into the family business. And Lord knows, I was handy. Kevin Riley made sure his boys knew how to use power tools properly by the age of twelve. Even the dangerous ones.

But making functional things was far less fun than pulling off pranks and building fantasy forts. By seventh grade, I had perfected my recipes for fake poop and fake barf. A perfect day for me involved using all the tinfoil in the house to line my closet and turn it into my take on a Tardis. My mom, normally a fan of my creativity, was not amused when I helped myself to every lid of every jar and bottle in the fridge as the console knobs.

Both of my parents decided I needed to get outdoors more. That had been the excuse for my dad to sign me up for scouting. It hadn't been all bad. The troop was how I met Jackson.

My instant bond with Jackson had a lot to do with the fact that both of us were occupying the territory on the social fringe of Ephron. I was new in town and his best friend had just moved away. We didn't have to hide our eccentricities around each other or pretend to be someone we weren't.

Jackson didn't give a shit about football, and I had no clue how motherboards worked, but we both loved building tree forts, playing video games, creating elaborate fictional worlds, and complaining about our stupid, annoying parents. I had it much better than Jackson, though. At least my parents got along. My dad might have had unrealistic expectations of me, but at least he genuinely thought about me. Jackson's dad worried more about the whereabouts of his stash than he did about his son.

My father's expectations were non-negotiable. Riley Construction Co. is Kevin Riley's biggest accomplishment. He built the company "from nothing" so that we could all have a secure and predictable future. We could dabble in whatever hobbies we wanted in our free time, but working for the family company was a foregone conclusion.

Eli fell in line, barely finishing junior college here in Ephron before taking a full-time position alongside our dad, helping to run the company. Naturally, everyone assumed I would do the same. If anything, they had even more faith in me. I actually liked making things. I was always building something. I took scrap materials to create scale models and skate ramps. I loved learning about materials, from drywall to concrete. And I didn't have to be asked twice to learn how all the specialty tools worked.

In retrospect, that might have been what broke my dad's heart the most. He didn't see my betrayal coming. I applied to UCLA's School of Film and Television secretly, using my own money. I told nobody. I didn't think I'd get in. I'd never expected to win a coveted scholarship.

Nobody forbade me from going to UCLA. They didn't even ask me nicely not to go.

"I'll just try it for a year," I told my parents. "It would be rude to just say no. Do you know how many people tried to win this scholarship? It's an honor!" I was desperate for their approval, wildly and willfully hopeful they would find it in their hearts to be proud. But the opposite was true. It was as if I had signed onto the crew of a pirate ship or joined a cult. They were hurt. Confused. Angry. My father called me "fancy." I still hate that word.

Mrs. Porter was the only person who congratulated me. She baked cupcakes for Jackson and I in the colors of our future alma maters.

"I'll come home and work every summer," I promised.

"You want to waste your life with this nonsense, I'm not going to stop you. But don't expect me to rescue you when your big dreams fall flat," my dad said, shaking his head sadly.

"Are you sure you want to waste your time on a theater degree?" my mom asked. "I know you enjoy working on plays, but what exactly are you going to do with a degree in that? How's that going to help you build houses?"

"Good luck, loser," my brother said. "Try not to catch an STD."

At the end of the first year of college, summer came, but I didn't come home for long. I took an internship instead, rationalizing that I was building my portfolio and would be of more use to my family with a successful career.

When my brother finished college and went to work for my dad full time, my father changed the name of the company from Riley and Sons to Riley and Son. So, I was off the hook. But I wasn't sure I wanted to be, if it meant being such a disappointment.

I shoot a text to Zara.

> 33-year-old Oscar award winner, and I can't get a date or a single pat on my back in this town.

107

She has a point, of course. I didn't come back to Ephron for my dad, or Chelsea, or anyone else. I came back for the chance to make something magical happen for this community, and the sooner I get back my focus on it, the better.

"Can I get you anything else?" Kenna asks, refilling my coffee.

"No." I shake my head. "I'm good. You know, you look so familiar. I wasn't rude to you in high school or anything, was I?"

"People sometimes tell me I look like that actress Lorelei Dupont. She was in the last Titanium Man film." Kenna strikes a pose, imitating the dramatic villain played by her doppelgänger. It's downright uncanny, and it's funny because even though Lorelei is a goth "Wednesday Adams" type and Kenna is blonde and sunny, their faces are eerily similar.

"That's IT!" I snap my fingers. "I gotta take a selfie with you and send it to her."

"You know Lorelei Dupont?" Her eyes widen, then narrow to a squint as she scrutinizes me. "Wait a minute. You're *that* Dean, aren't you? The one from the Lit Lovers episode whom Chelsea had the crush on, and who works with Rafe Barzilay, and oh my god. OMG. I have to sit down."

Kenna plunks the coffeepot on the table and sits down in the booth opposite me.

"Ephron keeps getting more and more interesting. Ever since Hudson Holm came back to town last fall," she says.

"Just wait till this summer." I wink. I'm not going to give Chelsea and my dad another thought. I'm ready to get to work.

chelsea

. . .

"DID you have fun at the ax-throwing place last night?" Noah settles into the seat next to me in the teacher's lounge.

"We definitely shocked Jackson." I smile.

"Good," Noah says. "He had it coming. That will teach him to make fun of you!"

I start to defend my brother but change my mind.

"You listened to the episode?" I ask.

"Oh, yeah. You know, I had a crush in high school too," Noah confesses. "Of course, I was an only child, but this girl went to my band camp, and our moms hated each other. Something about a parking spot. I don't know. All I know is that the more my mom said I shouldn't talk to her, the more I wanted to offer to carry her clarinet."

He shakes his head, lost in thought.

"So, I've been thinking about the theater sets the prom committee requested," I say, pulling out a list. "We don't have to refurbish *all* of the sets. We can stick to the most iconic shows. I know that there are set pieces from all of these shows back there somewhere. It shouldn't be too much work to get them out and fixed up. But I think we need to get started right away if we want to finish the work in the next week. That should leave enough days at the end of the break to go hiking. I've cleared my schedule."

"Really?" Noah perks up like a puppy whose owner has just grabbed the leash and shook it near the door. "You'd do that for me?"

"Sure, for you, and the kids, and *your mom*," I say. Wait a minute. Did he think I was saying that I wanted to go on the hiking trip with him? "Do you need to go online and reserve the hut for you and your mom?" I clarify.

"Oh. I already grabbed the reservation," Noah sheepishly admits. "I didn't want to take any chances of losing it. It's going to be so special!"

"What is going to be so special?" Alexis shoves the lounge door open with her shoulder, carrying a green-wrapped sandwich in a clear, clamshell container in one hand, and a take-out cup in the other.

"Hey! What are you doing back here?" I ask. It's not unusual to see Alexis on campus. But twice in one week?

"There was a typo on the flyers I dropped off yesterday," she explains. "I brought a fresh batch by. Thought I'd bring my lunch, too, so we can catch up on everything that went down last night. Since you haven't returned any of my texts."

Her eyes are sparkling. I'm not going to get out of this.

I gesture to an open chair. "You're welcome to join us, but I can't stay too long."

"So, what's so special?" Alexis asks Noah as she seats herself.

"Noah's taking his mom hiking up in the hills. They're going to be glamping in a rustic Shepherd's Hut," I explain to Alexis.

"It's not *rustic* rustic," Noah defends. "More like 'rustic.'" He makes air quotes with his fingers. "There's a fireplace and Jacuzzi tub. Should be great for her arthritis."

"Oh." Alexis sighs, her disappointment obvious. "You're taking your mom? That's too bad. It sounds very romantic! I thought you were going to say you invited Chelsea."

Noah freezes and looks from Alexis to me. "I mean, I would love that!" he enthuses. "I think Chelsea would really like the place. I was just telling her the other day how lovely it is and how I wish—"

I kick Alexis under the table. Hard.

"Ow!" she says, making a face.

"Stop harassing Noah, Alexis," I say firmly. "You know the school's dating policies are quite strict. He and I are good friends ... and just good friends."

Noah stands abruptly to make himself a cup of coffee. I can't even look at him. That was so awkward. But I should probably thank Alexis. She's given me the opportunity to make it crystal clear where I stand. Politely and firmly.

I already know exactly how it would go. We'd putter along pleasantly enough for a month or two, eating dinners together and seeing a few movies. We'd kiss good night and maybe even fool around a bit. But it would only be a matter of time before the lack of actual sex became an issue—before it became imperative that we take things to the "next level." Three to four months is the longest I've dated anyone before it became a serious issue.

I don't know what's worse ... being called frigid, or making a grown man cry because you don't "want" him like he wants you. I won't put either of us through that. Noah deserves better.

How can I agree to date someone whom I can't see myself taking things to the next level with? I can't see myself having sex with Noah any more than I could see it with any of the other guys I've dated in the last five years. I've tried. I've really tried to make the connection. Maybe if I felt less pressure or was able to give it more time? But thus far, I haven't found anyone I've been tempted to pull the trigger with. *Not counting last night.*

I'm not going to think about Dean. He's unreliable. Bad for me. The sooner I accept that I'll be alone forever, the better.

"Sorry, Noah," Alexis apologizes. "I was just joking around. Sometimes I forget that you are coworkers. That was out of line."

"Sometimes Alexis thinks she's still in high school," I say.

Alexis meets my eye, mouths "sorry," and looks away, cracking open her to-go container and lifting out her wrap sandwich before changing the subject.

"So, that prank was really something last night." Alexis shakes her head and takes a bite.

"Really? I'm sorry I missed it," Noah says, returning to the table with a mug of questionably thick, dirt-colored coffee.

Alexis chews and swallows before continuing. "Jackson was just so floored … his face when he saw Dean making out with you!"

"Dean kissed you?" Noah asks, eyes wide and registering surprise.

"Well," I start to say.

"No, it was totally mutual," Alexis reports. I swiftly kick her again. "Because obviously, they had to *sell it*."

"Of course, of course." Noah nods, taking a big bite of his pasta salad. "I get it. They were acting, selling the story."

113

"Oh, they sold it!" Alexis guffaws. "I had no idea what a great actress you were, Chelsea. Remind me not to play strip poker with you."

"Chelsea is good at everything. She can do anything she sets her mind to." Noah smiles.

"I'd actually like to set my mind to getting those theater sets done, Noah," I say. "Maybe we can get started today?"

"How about I begin by pulling out the pieces from past plays after school today so we can assess what, if anything, we want to use and toss the rest?" Noah volunteers.

"Okay," I say. "Is there anyone else we can get to help? There's some really great stuff, and I think we should use as much as we can. I know it's last minute, but let's see if we can enlist some other faculty and students. Some of those old set pieces are heavy."

"Sounds good." Noah checks his watch. "I gotta get back to my classroom and finish grading some papers before next period, but I will see you"—he jabs a finger in my direction—"after school." Last, he turns to wave at Alexis. "Always a pleasure!"

Alexis waits for the door to shut before speaking again.

"Okay, can we really dish about last night now?" She dunks her chai tea bag emphatically, then squeezes it out. "Because what in the heck was that about?"

"It was nothing," I insist. "I just really wanted to teach Jackson a lesson. I'm sick of him teasing me like I'm still some little kid."

"Mm-hmm." Alexis looks doubtful. "Whose idea was this prank?"

"Actually, it was Dean's. He got the idea after listening to the last Lit Lovers episode." I shrug now. "He stopped by on his way into town and talked me into it. Pulling pranks has always been their thing."

"But when was the last time you saw him? Or even spoke to him?" she asks. "How did you two even get in touch?"

"He messaged me on Facebook." I sip my coffee and blink calmly, as if this is no big deal, as if Dean Riley and I check in with each other regularly. She isn't buying it.

"So, he just messaged you out of the blue yesterday and invited you to pull off this prank? Was this before or after I was here?"

"He messaged me after," I say. "And then he stopped by in person."

"He came to the school?" Alexis looks impressed now. "Damn. So how hard did he have to twist your arm to get you to go along with this plan?"

"Not that hard," I admit. "It felt so good to get back at Jackson."

"Is that the *only* reason it felt so good?" Alexis pokes me. "Because I couldn't help notice that you were practically sitting on that man's lap. Not that I blame you. He's a genuine smokeshow, but—"

I know what she's thinking. He's a genuine smokeshow, *but* you're Chelsea. Buttoned up, ratcheted down, chaste Chelsea. Ever since I mentioned to Alexis that I don't fantasize about movie stars and musicians, she's been grilling me and sending me photos of super-hot guys, as well as a few women, with notes like, "Not even him/her?"

"It was all for show," I reiterate. "I did have a massive crush on him when I was a kid, but guys like Dean Riley aren't the kind of men you date and marry irl."

"Oh, good. So, you wouldn't have a problem with *me* dating him, then?" she asks, a little pointedly. "I'm not looking for a husband. Just a little fun." Chin out, Alexis studies my face.

My apple slice sticks in my throat, and I feel the hot knife of jealousy press into my sternum.

"You probably shouldn't waste your time." I swallow the chunk of fruit and wash it down with a gulp of water. "I just saw a photo of him with Zara Jones."

"Really?" Alexis takes another sip of her tea, watching me through narrowed, catlike, amber eyes. "You verified that relationship?"

"No," I confess. "He said they were just good friends, but they've been so closely linked in the tabloids. And you know he has a rep for breaking hearts." *Mine included.* "I just think it would be prudent not to pursue him at this time. I'd hate to see you get hurt."

"Riiiight," Alexis says, eyebrows raised. "Interesting. But what if I'm just looking for a hookup? I mean, obviously, you think he's hot, right?" She chomps down on her wrap, still eyeing me for a reaction.

"Don't say I didn't warn you." I sigh, trying to swallow my misery with my mudlike coffee.

It's inevitable that Dean's going to date people if he's living here. But why should it have to be one of my best friends? It shouldn't bother me, but it would. I'm not sure I could take it.

———

After seventh block, I take a moment to create a document with the list of all the set pieces we'll be looking for, along with whatever photos I've been able to gather.

Several of the best stage flats date back to Dean's time here at Ephron HS. Nothing has been thrown away. All the old set pieces and props are still here, gathering dust in the backstage storeroom in the high school auditorium. Many of them have been repainted and repurposed over the years. All of them need stabilizing and some amount of reinforcement to be safe to use as backdrops for prom in the high school gym. It's a fair amount of work, but it's certainly easier than building the whole thing from scratch. And it's free.

These kids deserve a decent prom. I am so glad that Noah has finally agreed to pull them out and assess. The printer clacks and squeaks as I print out a copy of the list to share with Noah. I collect it, setting aside and separating it from a copy of the paper that Donovan sent to the printer earlier.

I'm glad that I have my own printer here. It's so much easier than having to run to the print room. I have it here for just this stuff—this and for the occasional student who doesn't have a functional printer at home. They could use the print room, too, but then people would know. I'm happy to print out their papers for them. I remember what that was like. Donovan has used my printer several times.

I slide his paper into a folder for him and tuck it into my bag to give him when I see him later. He's agreed to help go through the sets with us.

Briefly, I consider calling Jackson to come over and help us move some of the heavier set pieces, but I change my mind just as quickly, picturing him going on about last night in front of Noah.

My phone dings with a text. Noah is already getting started. He's sent me a picture of the normally locked-up backstage area, where set pieces from past productions are crammed in tight, floor to ceiling. So tight, it occurs to me we should probably put on hard hats.

Here goes nothing …

Maybe we should get some more help? Those pieces are heavy.

I'll be fine. I'm going to start dragging pieces out onto

the stage for you to look at, and I'll make a trash pile.

See you in a few.

Maybe hold off a minute till I get there?

I hate to think of him pulling out pieces we don't need, only to have to put them back again. Or worse, throwing away perfectly good, reusable pieces.

The hallways are full of students packing it in for the day, and I have to thread my way through the crowd, dodging open locker doors and bulging backpacks. My studio is as far from the office and auditorium as you can get, without leaving the premises.

I run into Donovan outside the auditorium doors and hand him the folder with his paper.

"Mr. Greenberg is pulling out some of the set pieces from past productions right now to see if we can reuse them. Thanks for staying after, Donovan." I smile at my creative student. "Some of the stuff we have dates back to when I was in high school here," I comment.

Donovan tucks a long strand of his blond hair back and out of his eyes.

"That's cool, Ms. Porter. Did you ever work crew with Dean Riley?"

"I did." I nod.

"His aesthetic for the Titanium Man series was so sick." Donovan whistles. "I wish I could meet him!"

"You never know." I smile. It would be so wonderful to arrange a summer job for Donovan working crew at the amphitheater. Maybe I could shoot Dean a text. Just so long as I don't have to discuss it in person.

We push open the door to see Noah dragging out a set piece I immediately recognize. I'd know that paint job anywhere. It's the two-story piece from *Little Shop* that Dean and I were moving on that ill-fated night long ago when I'd broken my leg.

I can practically hear the refrain from "Suddenly Seymour."

"Let me help you, Mr. Greenberg," Donovan calls, bounding toward the stage.

"No, I got it. Stay back. I don't want anyone to get hurt!" Noah insists, walking backward.

"Noah, that's a heavy flat. At least let me help. What made you grab that one?" I call out, dropping my bag on a seat.

"I just started pulling out some of the larger pieces first." Noah looks back over his shoulder, straining noticeably as he drags the piece toward the front edge of the stage.

"Hey Mr. Greenberg, be careful!" Donovan shouts to warn Noah that he's about to back into a footlight, but he's too late. Noah trips, and the huge set piece wobbles ominously close to the edge.

For a moment, it seems like he might be able to save himself. He jumps backward, taking a sizeable step with his long legs in an attempt to regain his footing. And then he takes another … and runs out of stage.

Noah lands on the ground in front of the stage with a sickening thud. Thankfully, the set piece doesn't follow. It teeters precariously but ultimately stays put.

"It's okay! I'm fine! No worries! Just a little spill!" Noah calls out, his voice half-strained, half-laughing. "What a klutz!"

"Just stay there. Don't move!" I shout, already running.

The theater-style seats in the auditorium are blocking our view of him, and Donovan and I dash down the aisle to get to him. Donovan gets there first and freezes.

"Seriously, I'm fine," Noah is still saying.

Donovan looks from Noah to me, eyes wide. "I don't think he's okay, Ms. Porter. His leg is not supposed to look like that, is it?"

No, no it's not. I widen my eyes at Donovan, willing him to shut up.

"What? What is it?" Noah asks, attempting to get up. Which is when he sees the odd angle of his right leg and promptly passes out.

dean

. . .

"SPEAK OF THE DEVIL. I was just chatting with someone about you."

I run into Hudson Holm in the communal work area of the lofts. It's impossible to miss him. He's one of the tallest men I've ever met. He'd be perfectly at home on the set of one of the superhero movies I've styled. Now that I've met my former arch rival for Jackson's friendship, my preteen jealousy seems stupid. Hudson is a great guy with a dry sense of humor. We had a great time sharing embarrassing Jackson stories last night. But Jackson and Ephron are not all we have in common.

He's also my new neighbor. He owns the loft next door to mine.

"This is quite a place you have here." I gesture to the well-appointed co-working space on the ground floor, off the lobby. People are clustered around the juice bar and spread out at the individual workstations.

"Dean! Great to see you again. Everything okay at your loft?"

"Should be, now that the gas and electric are on," I say. "The movers are coming tomorrow with the rest of my stuff, and

I'm looking forward to enjoying this whole work/live experience you have going on here."

"Let me know if you need anything," Hudson smiles. "Not just with your loft. I happen to know a thing or two about coming back to Ephron after an extended leave. Got a minute? I want to hear more about the theater." Hudson gestures toward a booth near the street-facing windows.

"Sure," I say. "There's nowhere I need to be right away. I was just planning to check my email and work on some of the vendor agreements."

Upon closer inspection, I can appreciate the way the booth has been cleverly outfitted with USB ports, wireless charging discs, and outlets.

"So, you moved to Ephron right around the same time I left." Hudson sets his laptop and coffee on the table and takes a seat. "Every time I talked to Jackson, it was all, 'Me and Dean just finished level bazillion on Halo,' and 'Me and Dean built a bike jump in the woods.' Man, I was jealous of you, stepping in and stealing my life."

"You were jealous of me?" I laugh. "That's kind of funny, actually. You were a legend around here. Not only were you some kind of a super brain giant, you were a *Holm*. There was no way I was filling your shoes." I reference the fact that Hudson's family were the founders of this town. The town square is named after them, and they still own many of the commercial properties in and around Ephron, including the converted warehouse building that I'm moving into.

Hudson shakes his head. "Funny how we're both back here now. I never thought I'd end up back in Ephron, but there's something about this place. I bet your dad is happy to have you back here."

"Ha," I laugh and plug in my own laptop to charge. "That's a good one."

"Your dad always speaks so highly of you," Hudson says. "I've talked to him several times about you."

"You talked to my father about me?" I am incredulous at this. It's almost impossible to imagine.

"Sure. When I first came back, I was working with him a lot. You know, your family did most of the work on this building and are doing the renovation on the Feed Co. building in Holm Square. They do such amazing work."

"Yeah, they do." I nod. We may have our personal differences, but when it comes to craftsmanship, I am still proud of my father and the business that he and my brother have built.

"My dad thinks you're a genius for turning this warehouse into lofts and taking the time and care to renovate the historic properties in Holm Square."

"And my dad thinks you're a stud for winning an Oscar and dating Zara Jones." Hudson laughs.

"I hate to break it to him, but Zara and I are just friends and colleagues," I suggest. "Maybe we should swap dads."

"I think I might be getting the better deal if we swap. Walker is a handful. I wouldn't wish my dad on most of my enemies." Hudson shakes his head. "But all things considered, I'm still glad I came back to Ephron. And I don't think you'll regret it, either."

"So, it gets better?" I ask.

"It has for me." Hudson smiles. "I wasn't expecting to stay. Originally, I was just here to see this loft project through. But the town kind of grew on me—again. And it doesn't hurt that I met Georgia. We had a rocky start, but I'm so glad we stuck it out." He picks a bit of cat fur off his sweater and rolls it into a ball as he talks.

"She seems great," I say. Georgia is clearly one of Chelsea's close friends, and I could see the areas where they would bond. Georgia had a punk-rock vibe and arty-looking tattoos that were 100 percent sympatico with Chelsea's teenaged aesthetic. Even though Chelsea's adult incarnation is a lot more conservative schoolteacher, I know that girl's still in there, somewhere. Actually, it's really hot how buttoned up she is. A bit sexy librarian-esque, in fact, with the glasses. It makes me want to kiss her again and unleash that wild streak.

Okay, maybe she's not all that buttoned up. The way she kissed me. Thinking about it still makes me vibrate like an engine revving.

Oh, God. I cannot let myself keep thinking about her.

"I think it's amazing what you're doing with the community center and summer stock theater. It's going to be so good for this town. And for me, too, frankly. Rising tide and all that." Hudson is still speaking. "And bringing in A-list celebrities for the shows?"

"Just a few," I say, "We only have two big names signed for the first run but I'm confident we'll be able to attract even more great talent as we grow."

"Still…" Hudson nods appreciatively. "This town won't know what hit them when this takes off. You're the real genius. This will mean jobs, tourism, and so much more. Ephron needs this."

"I'm so glad you feel that way," I reply, oddly relieved to have his approval. As a member of the most wealthy and influential family in Ephron, his support means a lot. But it's more than that. He definitely gets it, and that is so reassuring. "I think it's going to be great too."

"More importantly, though"—Hudson's lips twitch and twist as he bites back a smile—"the next time you pull a prank on Jackson, you gotta let me know. I want in."

"Careful what you wish for," I warn. "Once you start, it's hard to stop."

"Yeah, but it's a healthy vice, and Jackson is so full of himself sometimes," he argues. "Somebody's got to put him in his place."

Remembering Jackson's shocked reaction to seeing me kiss his little sister makes me smile, too, until I remember the way the night ended. And feel terrible again. What was I thinking? Did I really think I could just show up and start something up with Chelsea? After all those years of getting the cold shoulder from her?

After Hudson leaves, I settle into the workstation by the window and dive into my laptop. I email Rafe Barzilay and Lorelei Dupont the updated versions of their theatrical contracts, and just for fun, I send the photo I snapped with Kenna to Lorelei.

A text from Jackson shows up just as I unwrap the sandwich I've saved for my lunch.

> Chelsea mentioned you spent the night at her place? Still sticking to the story that you two were just pretending?

Absolutely. And it was worth it. Your face!

> I ran the data, and if you ask me, there's actually a really strong convergence in your compatibility matrix.

I am NOT ASKING.

> Seriously. You two sold me. I'm convinced. I can't imagine how else you got my sister to go along with it.

> We didn't think about it much. It was just a spur-of-the- moment plan.

> So crazy it just might work?

> Come on. Chelsea just wanted to get back at you for teasing her. Which btw was a bit much.

> She has no actual interest in me.

I wish I was lying as I type these words. I still wonder what, if anything, Jackson knows about why Chelsea cut me out. She's his sister, after all. But he seems even more clueless than me. He doesn't even know that she kissed me all those years ago. Or that I kissed her back.

> Bullshit. But whatever, dude. Some algorithms resist training. You can lead a horse to water, but a dumbass will die of thirst.

> You're mixing metaphors.

> Don't be a dumbass. I think there might actually be something there.

Since she's been so friendly and responsive to my messages every time I've reached out over the last ten years?

Now he's fucking with me. I feel sure of it.

> Now you're delusional.

Jackson doesn't reply to this, either because he got sucked into something else or because he doesn't have the answer.

Questions pile up in my mind, as well as additional indignation at the way Jackson teased Chelsea so publicly on the podcast.

If she was so into me, then why'd she ghost me for her own senior prom?

After the exchange, I can't stop thinking about Chelsea and how miserably we left things off last night. It's more than a distraction. It suddenly feels like a wrong that needs to be righted. The entire situation. It's just wrong. She might not be interested in me in "that way," but we're still old friends, and I was really looking forward to seeing her again, maybe finding a way to get her involved in the theater. Childhood crush aside, it had been fun working backstage with her. And she is clearly a talented artist, whether she's willing to own that or not.

I wish she would. It would be a dream to work with artists like her on a live production. I never imagined I'd stumble upon talent like hers locally. Let alone that it would be her.

The winking moon in her painting.

For the sake of my sanity, as well as the sake of my theater, it suddenly feels important to try one more time to make things right with Chelsea. I want to show her that I am not someone who walks away. I'm the kind of guy who sees his projects through.

I can't stand the thought of her hating me, and I can't sit still. I'm determined to start over, professional to professional, old friend to old friend, to see if I can salvage this awkward situation.

I pack up my bag and head back to the high school, hoping she hasn't already left for the day.

———

An ambulance is pulling out of the lot as I pull in. A tall, skinny kid in a faded, gray sweatshirt and high-tops is standing outside the school, looking bemused. His shaggy, blond hair is tucked behind his ears, and he is holding a folder. His carpenter-style pants are streaked and splattered with paint. I don't have to go too far out on a limb to guess that he knows Chelsea.

"Hey, what happened?" I ask, pulling up alongside him on my motorcycle. "Can you tell me where to find Ms. Porter?"

The kid points at the ambulance that's just taken off. "Um … she's in there."

I don't wait for an explanation. My heart is in my throat. I just kick my bike into gear and follow the flashing lights.

chelsea

. . .

WHEN DEAN MARCHES into the ER, he's got his helmet under one arm and an endearingly serious expression on his face. He looks around to find whoever's in charge, and when he sees the intake desk, manned by a nurse in the corner, he makes a beeline for her. He's so incredibly hyper-focused that he doesn't notice me sitting by the water cooler. He speeds right past me.

"My friend was just brought here in an ambulance. I need to see her. I need to make sure she's okay!" he demands, a little breathlessly.

"I'm sorry, we can't allow non-family members into the patient rooms, but I can have a message sent back. What's her name?" The nurse looks bored. My ears prick up. He can't be here because of me, can he?

I also wonder if this was how Dean showed up at the ER to see me all those years ago. How had he sweet-talked his way back to see me? Maybe the rules weren't as strict back then. Or maybe he'd ignored the rules. Probably the latter.

"Chelsea Porter," he says, looking absolutely miserable. "Please, I need to know if she's okay."

"I'm fine," I say, speaking loud enough to reach the other side of the room.

Dean spins around to face me, his face flooding with relief. The tension that was holding him rigid seems to evaporate off him. He takes three giant steps toward me, then drops into the seat next to me, clearly reassured. And what else? Is he embarrassed? His pupils are wide, and I notice his cheeks are a bit more flushed than usual. Is he blushing?

"Thank God," Dean says. "Thank God you're okay, Chels. I saw the ambulance and that kid said you were in it, and I thought … I didn't even know what to think."

"Kid?" I ask.

"Shaggy, blond hair, skinny, paint on his pants?"

"Oh yeah, that was Donovan. You'd like him. He's an amazing designer." I nod. "Poor kid was in shock."

"What happened?" Dean asks. "I mean, you seem okay. You're okay, right? You didn't break another leg?" He glances at my legs.

"Funny story," I say.

Dean raises his brows. "Uh-oh."

"Yeah," I say. "The *Little Shop* set strikes again. Noah was dragging out set pieces to see what we could use for prom backdrops, and he tripped and fell off the stage."

"Yikes." Dean winces.

"Yikes is right. He broke his leg pretty badly. I think he might need surgery." I bite my lip. "That freaking flat, Dean. He was carrying the same damn flat as the one we were moving when I broke my leg. I really think it might be cursed."

Dean hums the refrain of "Suddenly Seymour," the epic song that Brittany and her costar were singing the night I threw myself at him.

"Stop!" I shush him, trying not to laugh.

"I mean, that show did end pretty tragically," he says.

"And ominously," I add.

"The set needed fresh blood ..."

When he looks at me, I can't help it. We both start giggling. It's like last night. I don't get it. I'm not a giggler. But I've been in stitches over absolutely nothing with this man twice in twenty-four hours now.

"It's not funny." I struggle to catch my breath. "We shouldn't laugh. Poor Noah."

Dean nods solemnly, and we both struggle to regain composure. He grabs my hand. "Seriously, I'm so glad you're okay."

"Ugh, I'm so screwed," I say, sitting up in the hard, plastic seat, reality dawning on me. My head drops into my hands. "I don't know what I'm going to tell the kids. Noah is going to be laid up for a while. There's no way I'll be able to get all those sets sorted and fixed up in time to use for prom backdrops by myself."

"Prom backdrop?" Dean looks curious.

"Yeah, so the first issue is that we've got to have the prom in the gym this year since the community center was *sold*." It takes him a moment to realize what I'm saying.

"They're planning on holding the prom in the gym?" Dean's nose wrinkles, as if he is offended. *Thank you, Dean.* I wish Noah was here to witness this reaction. I am vindicated.

"I mean, that was their plan." I shrug, hopefully indicating that none of this is my idea. "I am not on the committee, but I offered to help. And they are really counting on me. There's no budget, really."

"Okay. What's the theme?" Dean asks.

"You'll love this. It's 'Theater Lovers.'" I have to struggle not to roll my eyes at how generic and unoriginal that is. Then again, prom themes usually are pretty broad. "The prom committee asked if there were any old sets they could use for the decor. Noah and I were going to repair some pieces over spring break, with a little help from students. But obviously, that isn't happening now."

"No problem." Dean leans back in his seat. "I'll do it."

"Wait. You'll do what?" I ask.

"Help with the sets. Whatever you need me to do. And of course, you can use the community center. I wish I'd known that was a problem. Did anyone try to get in touch? I mean, come on. Who wants to have a prom in a stinky gym? I'll call the school first thing tomorrow."

This is almost too good to be true.

"Are you kidding me?" I study his face, but he's not laughing anymore. "You know there's no money to rent the place."

"It's a community center, not the ballroom at the Ritz. I'm not going to charge the school to host an event that's been held there for decades. It's a tradition." He smiles wistfully, probably remembering going to his own prom there. "One that I'm happy to be able to support."

"That's just ... unbelievable." I'm not sure what else to say. It doesn't excuse him for not showing up for me for my senior prom, but it does feel like an important gesture. It's too late to make up for the past with me, but it's still meaningful to me that he would go out of his way to make things right for my students. I can feel my heart racing and have the urge to call someone, though I'm not sure who. Alexis? Jackson? My mom?

I blush at the thought of calling my mom. There's no such thing as a simple venting session with her. Everything has to become a ritual. This has not improved with age. When Dean broke my heart the first time, she'd taken me to one of those places that let you break shit. If I tell her he's back in town, she's bound to show up with sage, a gong, and some crystals.

"You're sure? You have time for this?" I ask. A part of me worries that he might not follow through.

"First rule of theater," Dean says, smiling and nodding.

"The show must go on." I finish for him. "But it's not a show, Dean. It's a prom."

"Well, prom is still a pretty dramatic event, isn't it?" he asks.

I wouldn't know.

"I suppose."

"How about I come by after school tomorrow? You show me what we're working with for prom backdrops, and afterward, we can swing by the community center. I'll take you on a tour of the amphitheater," Dean suggests. "Honestly, I'd love to get your thoughts."

He runs a hand through his wavy hair, messing it up. When he does this, he looks just like the old Dean I recall from when we were kids—the one who'd get some crazy idea in his head and would have to build it. Usually with me as his willing assistant. So often when Dean was at my house, he'd end up hanging out with me while Jackson was off doing something on a computer. Dean was the king of blanket forts and imaginary space portals. He'd show up with refrigerator boxes from his dad's construction sites, and with just a little bit of paint, and patience, I'd turn them into pirate ships, magic shops, and mobile homes.

He studies me as I wander through these memories and thoughts, and I wonder if he's also remembering our cardboard castles. He seems as if he's about to say something, but doesn't. Instead, he stands, bending to retrieve his helmet from the seat.

"Do you need a ride home?"

"I'm just going to stick around here till Noah is more settled," I say. "And then I'll grab an Uber or something."

"Okay, then." Dean leans across to give me a quick peck on the cheek. It's a kiss your brother or your uncle could give you. But he isn't my relative. And he smells so Deanish. So good. He also doesn't pull away immediately. He lingers there for a few seconds, just long enough for me to watch as my fist closes around the soft, supple leather of his open motorcycle jacket. It's like a weird reflex, something you do without thinking. Like when a jar of pickles jumps out of the fridge and your arm suddenly becomes bionic, catching it before your brain fully registers it fell.

We both look down at my fingers, clutched tightly enough for the metal zipper to leave an imprint. I open my fist and release him.

"I'll see you tomorrow at three," Dean says. Then he pops on his helmet and strides out the door.

dean

. . .

"THAT PIECE HAS GOT TO GO." I rummage through the set pieces with Chelsea the following day. There's plenty worth saving, but only if it can be stored properly, and that means getting rid of all the broken bits. "And this one can go too. It's a menace. Into the scrapper before anyone else gets hurt! In fact, pass me my drill right now."

"How did you bring all those tools on your bike?" Chelsea asks.

"I didn't bring the bike, I brought my truck," I say, quickly disassembling the ramshackle flat. I can't believe this thing is still in one piece. "Why hasn't anyone taken these things apart? It's been over a decade."

"Probably because they wouldn't know how to put it back together again," Chelsea says.

"Would that be so awful?" I ask. I remember how proud I was of the *Little Shop* set, but looking at it now, I see it for the hazard that it is. I eye the backstage area and shake my head, annoyed. It's not safe. I hate the idea of someone getting hurt —again—by something I built. Once was way more than enough.

"This really isn't safe, the way everything is all stuffed in here. It might even be a code violation." God, I sound like such a nerd. But if anyone should know that sets can be dangerous, it's Chelsea. She should be more concerned. Instead, she dives into the closet, hauling out a stack of red-painted plywood pieces that have been hinged together.

"Careful!" I say, hearing the sound of sets shifting and trying to shut down the flashbacks I'm having of the flats falling on her. She looks at me warily. "One of those hinges is loose. Watch you don't get a splinter," I warn her.

"Oh, thanks," she says, repositioning her hands.

"What is that thing?" I ask.

"This one is actually *mine*," she says, a spark of challenge in her eyes. "I can't believe you don't recognize it."

"Yours?" I put down the drill I'm wielding, dropping the last screw into a plastic baggie. I'll stack the pieces in a moment.

"Remember that lemonade stand you built for me and then took back again?" She folds her arms across her chest.

"We needed a kissing booth for the school fair." I think I know where she's going with this. "That can't be it, can it?"

"I was eleven! I was saving up for a new Tamagotchi!"

Chelsea unfolds the wobbly lemonade stand/kissing booth. I can still see the faded remnants of yellow paint beneath the red parts and brown bits that have chipped away.

"Then I did you a favor, didn't I? Those e-pets were a pain in the ass."

"Yeah, but they didn't have any poop to scoop, and my mom wouldn't let me get another pet when we were already struggling with the vet bills for Murphy."

Her eyes cloud over when she mentions their dog, making my heart ache. I almost forgot about Murphy.

"What'll you give me if I rebuild it for you?" I offer.

She eyes me suspiciously. "I'm a little old for a lemonade stand, but I'd actually like to bring it home for a project I'm working on in my studio," she mentions. "If you've got a pickup, I'd love some help getting it there."

"Done!" I exclaim. "Though I was kind of hoping you were going to say you wanted to resurrect the old kissing booth. Who needs lemonade?"

She blushes. "You haven't tasted my lemonade."

"But I have tasted your kisses," I dare to tease her, standing quickly before she has a chance to respond. Why can't I help myself with her? Why do I always need to push it? Probably because I can't get these thoughts out of my head.

I check my watch. "It's after four. How about we pack it up for today and head to the community center before it gets too dark?"

———

The sky is streaked with brilliant colors as we trip down the hill toward the amphitheater. The path has been dug out and graded but still needs to be paved. I hold out a hand to Chelsea to steady her.

"Careful, it's a little slippery," I warn.

"Hang on. I need a photo of that sunset. It's ridiculous!" Chelsea says.

"It's almost as good as the one in the painting that you *didn't* paint," I say, stressing the didn't. We both know that she did paint it. And painted herself into it.

Chelsea rolls her eyes at me. "Tell me, Maestro, what would you call these colors?"

She points at the sky, and it brings back memories of her mixing paint in her backyard. She used to love coming up with silly names for all the colors. We'd put them in old yogurt containers, writing the color names on the lids in a Sharpie pen.

"Flamingo, tangerine, rum raisin, and the little, heart-shaped cloud is"—I stop to think for a moment before I come up with the perfect name for that color—"bruise cruise."

"Bruise cruise?" She snorts.

"You have to admit, it's kind of the color of a black eye." I shrug. Chelsea snaps a few pics and pockets her phone.

"So, how is Noah doing?" I ask.

"He's hanging in there. Probably won't be home for a couple more days because of the surgery."

"He's lucky to have you," I say, "as a friend!" I add on when Chelsea looks askance at me. Noah is lucky, although I wonder if he thinks he is. He's so clearly smitten with her. Who wouldn't be?

I can't help but notice the way Chelsea's skin is glowing in the juicy, gold and fuchsia light of the dying day. I want to pour that color in a jar, stick it on my nightstand, and make it my nightlight.

I pull out my phone and snap a shot of her, then spin it around to show her.

"Ambrosia," I say, tapping the image. "So yummy. Where are the mini marshmallows when you need them?"

"Is this still how you get the girls?" She looks at me skeptically.

"Oh, God no." I smile conspiratorially. "I didn't mean you, I meant the light. I love the magic hour at this time of year. It's practically liquid. A delicious liquid. Peach schnapps. Apricot nectar. But I guess you're okay too."

This isn't how I pick up women. Nobody else in my life speaks like this with me. Color is like a multi-sensory secret language between us, and only us. But I am also lying about the light. It isn't the light that's making my parched soul crawl toward a mirage. It's her. She's what I am so thirsty for. It's almost embarrassing how much I want her. While it's definitely physical, it's not just about sex. It would be easier to ignore it if I was just horny. I know how to take care of that myself.

Seeing her again has stirred up something. I'm viewing her in a different light, both literally and figuratively. Does she know the effect she is having on me? Does she care? Clearly, she doesn't because she rolls her eyes at me again, then looks away, stepping down the slope toward the stage. Poor Noah. I suddenly feel sorry for the guy, having to work alongside her every day, knowing there's no chance.

I text the photo to her via messenger. I don't think she realizes how beautiful she is.

"You really think you'll be ready to open by July?" she asks.

"Dad and Eli will get it done," I assure her. "Most of it is land-scaping. We're keeping the staging and sets relatively simple this summer. The outdoor setting lends itself perfectly to *A Midsummer Night's Dream*."

"*'Love looks not with the eyes, but with the mind, And therefore is wing'd Cupid painted blind.'*" Chelsea sighs. "I love that one. It's such a good choice. And you mentioned it's already been cast?"

"Mostly. I have Rafe Barzilay and Lorelei Dupont confirmed."

"Sounds like a dream come true," she says.

"'*Are you sure/That we are awake? It seems to me/That yet we sleep, we dream.*'" I hit her with another quote from the play.

It all seems so surreal, suddenly. Sitting here on the grass with Chelsea. This dream of mine becoming a reality. Like a sudden zoom of the camera that makes you dizzy, cuing you to some sort of cognitive leap. The sort of moment where you suspect that you might be dreaming. I pinch myself for good measure.

"I guess at heart, I'm still a theater geek," I confess. "It's cool to create worlds on film, and there's so much you can do with CGI. But it almost feels like cheating. I still prefer the challenge of transporting people with a live performance."

"Like putting a kid in a cardboard box, shaking it, and convincing them they're in another world when they emerge?" Chelsea asks.

"Exactly!" I grin.

"You always were my hookup for those coveted refrigerator boxes." She sighs wistfully. "I miss them."

"I loved seeing what you came up with," I say.

"Still some of my finest work!"

"Not by a long shot," I reply, thinking of the images in her apartment. It's getting colder now that the sun is gone, and Chelsea dons her hoodie, pulling it down under her bottom. The ground is cold, but neither of us wants to leave here yet.

"So, what do you imagine doing for the sets this summer, then?" she asks.

"We're installing a giant turntable there." I gesture to the central stage of the amphitheater, which is already a massive, circular-shaped platform. "I like the nod to theater in the round and the ability to spin a scene around, see it from different angles, light it up in different ways," I muse.

"Something behind it for height?"

"Yes, we'll create a raised area, or two. Still working on the final plans for that."

"Color palette?"

"Sticking with the moody forest colors ... greens and purples."

"I like that. I was just thinking about how the colors will change as night falls and how immersive that feels." Chelsea nods. "I'm freezing, but I want to stick around just a little longer so I can see what it's like in the dark."

"Thanks." I nod, scooting a little closer to her to share our body heat. I rub my hands together and use them to warm my cheeks.

"Have you ever been to the Festival of the Arts in Laguna Beach?" I ask, striving for a noncommittal tone. "They do this magical thing where they paint people into their backdrops and bring massive, iconic images to life using trompe l'oeil. I was thinking I would love to implement something like that here."

Something tells me to tread lightly here, and I refrain from mentioning her paintings. Though I'm practically dying to bring it up.

"I love the Festival of the Arts." Chelsea sighs. "I follow their accounts on social media."

"You should go sometime," I say. "I would love to go with you."

"Maybe." She shrugs. "Summers get busy, though."

"Just say the word," I offer. "We could fly down for one night. I always go." And then I change the subject because I don't want to pressure her. "Did you know they use local volunteers for the whole thing? Do you think we can get locals involved here?"

"Oh, I don't know who's going to want to be in a show with Titanium Man, Dean. That's a pretty heavy lift," Chelsea says sarcastically.

"I can't pay them." I shrug. "We're not going to be profitable for at least a couple years."

"Are you kidding me?" She elbows me. "I think people will line up for the opportunity to share a stage with celebrities like Rafe."

"There are so many moving parts." I close my eyes. "It's a lot. And it's all on me. And to be honest, not everyone can picture a theater here. Some people aren't as thrilled about the idea."

My dad, for one. Actually, he's the only one, but he's a big deal around here.

"Sounds stressful." Chelsea's eyes widen. "You mentioned you have an investor?"

"Yes, a silent partner who prefers to remain anonymous," I say. "For now, anyway."

"That's kind of weird," Chelsea says, frowning. "Why wouldn't someone want people to know?"

"That's just showbiz." I shrug. "My investor is taking a risk just helping to fund this, and I'm grateful someone's putting their faith in me."

"Well, I wouldn't keep it a secret. They're lucky to be working with you." Chelsea stands in the dark and brushes herself off.

"Thanks," I say. I don't want to admit how much her faith in me means. I truly wasn't prepared for all the emotions this homecoming was going to stir up.

"For the record, I believe in you too," I say, letting my words hang there. "Your work is so ..." I let my words trail off because I am unsure how to finish the sentence.

I want to tell her the types of pictures she makes are my favorite kind of art because of the layers involved and the way the image tells a story within a story. I want her to know that looking at her pictures is like unwrapping a gift because you have to work a little to get at it, but then when you do, you are richly rewarded. Her art made me feel special and clever because I was able to crack the code and solve the mystery. Presumably, I'm the only one who's done that. If so, not only is it a gift, it's a gift *for me*.

Except, she still hasn't owned up to it being hers. She has remained steadfastly silent, refusing to even argue about it. That makes me the opposite of special. Her denial and subsequent silence make me feel like I've intruded, like some sort of Peeping Tom caught peeking in at something private and intimate. The gift isn't meant for me after all.

I stand up and listen to the wind blowing through the pines. It's almost completely dark now. The clouds part to reveal a sliver of moon and a single, twinkling star.

"I'm glad we're good, Dean. Let's not do anything to screw that up," Chelsea says, holding out a hand to shake.

Her fingers are cold in my hand. I want to blow on them and drag her hands into my pockets to warm them up. But she pulls her hand away.

"Thanks for your help with the sets too," she says. She retrieves her phone and turns on the flashlight, shining it up the path back out to the street. "I should probably get going. I promised Noah I'd stop by with some takeout. He wanted to see photos of what we're doing."

"Sure," I say, flicking on my flashlight as well. "Let's talk more next week. And don't forget, you're coming for that ride with me. Deal's a deal."

"We'll see," she says, bounding up the slippery hill and refusing my arm when I offer it. "If there's time."

chelsea

. . .

Ten Reasons Why I Cannot Tell Dean the Art is Mine: A List by Chelsea Porter

1. If he knows it's me and he says he likes it, I'll never know if he really likes it or if he's just being polite.
2. If I tell Dean, who else will I have to tell? Can I really trust him to keep my secret?
3. What if he mentions it to my mom? My mother would have a field day. She would display my work prominently in her bookstore and hold discussion groups about it. She would probably have a billboard made and mount it to her car, driving around with my art, set to a soundtrack, burning incense.
4. What if it gets out to someone at school? My students? The football players? The principal? Noah? His mom?

5. What if my followers find out I'm just an average, boring high school teacher and not some cutting-edge artist?
6. Everyone will see me naked.
7. Everyone will see me naked.
8. Everyone will see me naked.
9. Everyone will see me naked.
10. Dean will see me naked.*

*TECHNICALLY, I am not naked, I am painted. But still.

I'm trying not to think about this dilemma as I sit in the hospital room with Noah and his mother, Mara. Mara really doesn't want to let me leave this place. It's been like this for the past two days since his surgery. I'm not sure if she's just lonely or if this is some misguided attempt at playing match-maker for her son.

Since spring break started, I've been splitting my time between the hospital, the school, and my studio. But right now, I'd rather be back at the high school theater, painting the sets with Dean and the other volunteers.

"I don't see what the big deal about prom is." Mara looks down her nose as she fluffs Noah's pillow and shoves it behind his back. She uses his napkin to dab at his face. At least she doesn't spit on it.

"Prom is very important to the students," I say. "And to me too. I remember what it was like to be their age. For some of these kids, it's as important as graduation."

"Well, that's just silly," Mara insists. "Proms are just a dance. Graduation is an official ceremony."

"Hey now, Mom," Noah intervenes. "Chelsea cares a lot about prom."

"Obviously," says Mara, disdainfully flicking a piece of lint off her sweater.

"So, who's hungry?" I pull my take-out order from the bag. I stopped by the Ephron Diner on my way here and picked up some of their famous chili and cornbread—enough for all three of us to share.

"What's that smell?" Noah's mom fans her face. "Smells like dog food."

"Um … chili?" I say, sniffing the container. It smells delicious. Hot and spicy and perfect for this cool, spring evening.

"Didn't they have anything a little less heavy? Noah can't eat that kind of food when he's laid up." She looks dubious about the dinner I've provided.

"There's nothing wrong with my stomach, Mom." Noah waves her concerns away.

"Nonsense. If you eat that slop, it's going to give you gas!" She wrinkles her nose. "Or diarrhea. Which is the last thing you need in your current state."

Now Noah does look worried. "Do you know if they use organic beef?" he asks.

I shake my head. "I have no idea." I could probably text Kenna and ask her, but why bother?

There's no way they're eating this chili, and I'm not about to let it go to waste. I put the lid back on the container and pack it back in the cooler bag with the cornbread. My stomach is growling, but perhaps all is not lost. Perhaps this is my exit cue.

"Well, I should probably get going now," I say.

"You're not going to stay and eat something else with us?" Mara looks offended. "Some friend you are," her look says.

"Gosh, I would love to, Mara, but I need to get back to the school to help out."

"Noah tells me you also broke your leg on that stage. I don't know why they don't just pack it in and get rid of the sets. It's dangerous. A lawsuit waiting to happen."

"Nobody says that when football players get hurt." I keep my tone neutral, trying not to sound defensive. But honestly, I'm so sick of football, etc. being glorified as a manly blood sport while anything artistic is regarded as a coddle factory for the most papercut-averse ninnies.

"Well, that's football. Football is different," Mara says confidently.

"Many artists would disagree," I argue. "Glassblowers and ballerinas, for example. Art isn't always safe."

I don't even know why I am being so contrary and arguing with her. Apparently, it's just for the sake of argument. What point am I trying to make? My art isn't particularly dangerous, unless you count catching a chill or being found out. That part does feel risky.

Dean is onto me. I can only hope he'll give up eventually and believe me when I say those pieces aren't mine.

I pat myself down, feeling for my phone, then pretend to read an urgent message that's just buzzed into my pocket.

"Oh, dear. Looks like I gotta get over there stat!" I announce. I cross the room to Noah's bedside, unable to resist the urge to quickly ruffle his hair, returning it back to its naturally floppy state. Mara must have brushed it back earlier, and it looks so unflattering and weird. I can't leave him looking like that. What if a nice, single nurse comes in and is scared off by his giant naked forehead?

Mara twitches as I mess with her handiwork, but I'm at the hangry point where I don't care anymore.

"I feel bad about the Shepherd's Hut. Maybe you want to use the reservation, Chelsea?"

"I'm probably going to be busy working on a painting the rest of this week," I say. "You should cancel it."

"I won't get any money back. They had a strict policy. Maybe you want to go there and go hiking with my mom?" He looks hopeful for a moment.

"Don't be stupid," Mara protests. "I'm not leaving you alone post-op. We'll go hiking next year."

"Think Jackson wants to use the reservation?" Noah asks, halfheartedly.

"He's going to visit my mom." I shake my head.

"Oh, well. I'll put your name on the reservation in case you change your mind. You're a good friend, Chelsea." Noah smiles sadly at me from the bed and pushes himself up on the pillows. "Thanks so much for coming by and keeping me in the loop. I'm sorry I can't help with the stuff for prom."

"No problem. You just focus on getting better," I say, pulling on my coat and heading back out into the corridor.

———

I park next to Dean's truck in the nearly empty school lot. He hasn't brought up the subject of the motorcycle ride I promised him since we went to see the amphitheater last week. And he hasn't brought his motorcycle to the school since then, either. A part of me hopes the motorcycle is in the shop. Permanently.

But another part recklessly wonders what it would be like if we actually went. I can almost feel the wind in my hair and that giddy sensation at a sudden burst of speed. I miss the shot of pure adrenaline that comes with acceleration. My anxiety falls away with the G's. It just can't keep up.

My stomach growls loudly as I pass Madison's car. Thankfully, the windows aren't steamy and there's nobody in it. If I had a nickel for every time I've had to break up a tryst between her and Donovan in the past few days. I've started to question whether they are truly as passionate about the theater as I first suspected, or merely passionate and using this activity as an excuse to hook up.

Who am I to judge? I'm grateful for the help.

I head back into the auditorium, carrying my cooler with its precious chili con carne cargo. It's way too much here for me to eat alone. Surely, someone will want to share it.

"So, this part of the rock is like the crease in your eyelid," Madison is explaining to one of her cheerleader friends who she's rounded up to help, "and the middle is like the highlight area, like when you want your cheekbones to look really high or your nose to look skinnier?" Her friend nods, taking the brush.

"Hi, Ms. Porter." Donovan waves. His hair is piled on top of his head in a messy man bun, and he's wearing painter's overalls, a long-sleeved, thermal shirt, and work boots. Dean has him bracing the corner of the platform they are fixing.

"Darn," Dean says. "I was hoping we'd be finished here before you got back. I was going to ask you to dinner."

"There's going to be nothing left for me to do for the rest of this week at this rate," I complain.

"You deserve some time off," Dean says, screwing in the final screw with a satisfying squeak at the end.

"And you deserve dinner," I say. "Want to split this chili with me?"

"Is that from the diner?" he asks.

"Sure is."

"Then, yes, please!" Dean lays the drill in its case and hands it to Donovan. "Can you finish packing it in for the day?"

"You got it!" Donovan grins. It's been so wonderful to watch him working with Dean. I'm not sure if it's the attention he's been getting from Dean, or if this sudden infusion of confidence has more to do with the head cheerleader, a senior, going public about her "relationship" with a junior theater nerd, but Donovan is practically glowing.

"What a cool kid," Dean comments as he joins me in the theater seats.

I pass him the chili. "I think Donovan's really excited to be working with you."

"Yeah, he asked me to write a rec for his college ap!" Dean laughs.

"You'd better do it," I say.

"Don't worry, I will. And I've offered him a summer job at the Turning Table Theater."

My heart swells, hearing this.

"Oh, wow. I bet he was thrilled. You know, he reminds me a little of you," I offer. "Minus the jock status."

"Really? In what way?" Dean observes Donovan and Madison sucking face—again. He whistles loudly, like he's hailing a taxicab. "Break it up, you two. Express your affection on your own time. I want to get home before midnight!"

"In the way that you dated the hot cheerleaders and worked backstage on crew?"

"Hey now, I did not make out on the job!" Dean argues quietly, for my ears only. "I was nothing if not professional.

151

But I'm not sure *you* could say the same, Ms. Porter." His eyes sparkle as he points his chili-laden spoon at me. And the accusatory way he says my name? Like I'm some buttoned-up, old biddy he knows has a secret sex dungeon. He raises his eyebrows in challenge, as if to say, *What do you have to say about that? Are you going to let me get away with it?*

It should be getting old, but every time he challenges or teases me this way, it makes me want to climb him like a human ladder. I want to kiss the smug grin right off him. Which of course isn't an actual option.

What is going on with me? I find myself staying late and getting here early, making excuses to do extra work on the pieces. As much as I'd like to get to work on my own art, I don't really want this project to be done. Because when it is, these verbal volleys will end, and I can't pretend … what? That there's a possibility? It's even more ridiculous than when I was fourteen.

This is a moment. A moment to savor, perhaps. But not too much. Because it's going to end. He's going to end up dating someone eventually. They might even get serious and get married, have kids. I consider the possibility of junior Dean Rileys coming through my classroom someday. Or maybe he'll change his mind about the summer stock theater and leave again. Go back to LA. That might actually be easier for me.

"So, what are you doing on Friday?" Dean asks suddenly.

"I hadn't really made plans," I say. "Jackson is heading to my mom's for Easter, and Emily and Alexis are also out of town for the holiday weekend. The only thing I was planning on doing for sure was some painting in my studio."

"I'd love to watch you work sometime," Dean says gently. "I'm so curious about your process."

"No!" I snap, reflexively, before remembering to dial it down. "No offense. I just can't work with an audience. And my paintings are really bad. Nothing I'd ever want to share."

"Hmm ... if you say so. But anyway, that's not what I was going to ask you to do." Dean smiles and lets it go. "I had another suggestion. Something I wanted to go see with you."

"What is it?" I ask warily.

"The wildflowers are starting to bloom up in the Blue Mountains. With all the rain we had this winter they are saying it's going to be a superbloom. Think of all the colors we can name. And you still owe me that motorcycle ride."

"You're sure you don't want to ask someone else?" My heart is pounding wildly as I consider this. Why is he so fixated on taking me for a ride? Does he think he has to? Do I have to go?

I'm dying to go. But I'm also terrified.

"Well, I asked Jackson, but he said he's headed to the coast, and he also claims that motorcycles make his balls go numb."

"Really?" I grimace. "Gross. I'm not sure I needed to know that."

"No, Silly, I didn't really ask Jackson to come see the wildflowers with me. You're the only one I've asked to come with me."

I open my mouth to answer, but instead of words, butterflies come pouring out. Not actually. But I can feel them fluttering there. I'm imagining myself on the back of his bike, arms wrapped around his waist. There's a low heat fluttering in my belly. My lady parts are the opposite of numb.

I feel like a flopping fish. I close my mouth.

"You okay, Ms. Porter?" Brittany blows a bubble and sucks it back in with a pop. "You look a little weird."

"Just the chili." I fan myself for cover. "Super spicy!"

"Come on, Chels. Come with me? I'll get you your own helmet. I promise you're gonna love it." Dean's pale eyes are so imploring that I can't say no.

dean

. . .

I MEET Jackson in Holm Square on Thursday. When we arrive, he surprises me.

"I almost forgot, we're recording a podcast episode this afternoon," he says. "Everyone is already over at Chelsea's house. They're waiting for me."

It's a short walk, and Jackson is walking briskly, forcing me to match his stride. I'm guessing Chelsea doesn't know I'm tagging along. It feels like an ambush, and I'm wary.

"Okay, here's the deal," Jackson says to me as we ride up in the elevator. "You have to be super quiet. No eye contact. Especially with my sister."

"Why no eye contact?"

"Because no good comes of it." Jackson shakes his head.

"No good comes of looking at Chelsea?"

"Not while we're recording. If we look at each other, we end up cracking up. It's a natural thing, a way to release some of the tension. But it breaks the flow and fucks up the session. I saw you and Chelsea the other night, and you two are wound far too tight. I need to get this episode in the bag. I don't have time for twenty retakes."

"You know I make my living on movie sets, right?"

"Whatever." Jackson rolls his eyes. "Not with my sister, you don't."

"Pardon?"

"Look, I know you don't want to hear it, but I reran the process one more time with updated data points for the two of you, and for whatever reason, it's *obvious* you two are meant to be together, so go with God. I could do worse for a brother-in-law."

"Ha, ha, ha. Nice try. You are not getting me back like that. I'm onto you."

"Fate is fickle, my friend, but logic isn't. You can't argue with logic. The algorithm is smarter than both of us." Jackson shakes his head sadly. "I mean, it's a little gross to imagine the two of you together, but trust me, I've run multiple models now, and I'm afraid it is what it is."

———

Chelsea's compact apartment feels crowded with most of the Lit Lovers crew assembled there. As I suspected, Jackson didn't bother telling anyone he was bringing me along. They all looked surprised to see me.

Alexis arranges herself in a yoga pose on a pillow beside the coffee table.

"Namaste," she says, concentrating as she bends her legs like pretzels and balances on her wrists.

"You too." I smile and nod.

We head the three steps over to the kitchen counter where Chelsea is huddled over a laptop screen. There's a woman facing the camera on the other side of the conference call. The image is static, awkwardly frozen.

"Emily keeps freezing," Chelsea says to Jackson.

"It's my Wi-Fi," I hear the woman on the other end apologizing. "I'm so sorry. Tuscany is amazing in every way, except for the Wi-Fi."

"They don't need you on camera, do they, Em?" I hear a male voice in the background.

"Hey, Blaze." Jackson waves. "Good point. Why don't you try shutting off your video feed, Emily? We'll do the same."

"Yes, that's so much better," Chelsea says, a moment later. "I think we're all good now."

"Let's do this." Jackson dons a headset and moves the laptop to the coffee table. He takes a seat on one end of the sofa, and Chelsea settles on the opposite end.

Tentatively, I sit in the chair beside the sofa. I smile at Alexis, who is still looking curiously at me. Her eyes dart to Chelsea before she smiles back at me. And then Jackson frowns at me and removes his headset.

"What did I say to you? No eye contact with the talent. None. If you are going to make faces at Alexis, you're getting banished to the kitchen."

He's being ridiculous. "I am not making faces!" I defend myself.

"Cut it out, Jackson," Chelsea protests. "He's a grown man and allowed to look wherever he wants. Stop being so controlling."

Thank you, Chelsea.

"He can look at whatever he wants. Except at Alexis. Or you," Jackson growls.

I make eye contact for the briefest moment with Chelsea, and that's all it takes. We're cracking up again.

"See! What did I say? Get in the kitchen—NOW!" Jackson commands. "You're on time out."

"For how long?" I whine.

"I think it's one minute for every year of your age," Alexis volunteers. "So that's like half an hour?"

Give or take.

"Fine." I cave. "But I would like to register a complaint that this is extremely unfair."

I resettle myself at the kitchen counter as they attempt to go on. I'm tempted to study Chelsea's art in the hallway again, but that would probably be rude. How is it that none of her friends or family have figured out that she made these images?

"Shit, we lost Emily again," Chelsea says. "No, wait. She's back. Can you hear me, Em?"

"I can, but you're cutting in and out. Blaze had an idea for you guys. Can you still hear me?"

"We hear you," Jackson says.

"Did I hear correctly? You have *the* Dean Riley there with you all today?" Blaze's voice comes out of the computer, clear one moment and sounding like he is underwater the next. Emily's boyfriend is a celebrity in his own right—a relationship guru who's pretty famous in LA. I'm looking forward to meeting him in person when they get back from their trip. We can commiserate about tabloid drama.

"Is that *the* Blaze Smith?" I ask. "Looking forward to meeting you!"

"Likewise. I can't wait to meet you, Dean," Blaze says. "Meanwhile, why don't you fill in for Emily today? We can barely hear ..."

"Shit," Jackson curses, as the connection is abruptly severed.

"Just mic him up," Alexis says. "What's the big deal? We've had guests on before. What do you say, Dean, you want to play?" She is using that husky, sexy voice on me now, flirting with me a little. She's attractive. Normally, I'd be all over that. But there's something about the mic and recording equipment that ruins it. It feels forced.

Nevertheless, I roll with it, accepting the role that I've been cast in today.

"Sure, I'd love to play," I answer.

Moments later, they mic me up and I'm back in the chair, and we get going. Jackson does the podcast intro and shares the sponsor info, plugging The Grumpy Stump before plunging into the segment.

"Well, folks, we have a special treat for you today. You'll love this. Remember last week's episode of Lit Lovers when we discussed the 'brother's best friend' trope?"

"Who could forget that guy," Alexis plays along.

"Well, my sister for starters. She obviously couldn't forget him," Jackson deadpans. "And as luck would have it, guess who we have in the studio today? Wait for it. No, you don't have to wait because he's right here, sitting in the room with me. None other than my high school bff, Dean Riley, the dreamboat."

"Girl, I get it now," Alexis says, almost too appreciatively. "This man is dreeeeamy."

"Ugh, not you too," Jackson says. "What's so sexy about a guy who can burp the alphabet?"

"Let's start with his eyes, shall we?" Alexis enthuses. "Then we can work our way down to his beautiful butt." She is really laying it on. It's flattering but also off-putting.

I can feel my face growing hotter, but now that I am mic'd up and we are recording, I try and maintain my cool. Zara would love this. She's constantly telling me that I don't know what it's like for her when she does press junkets. She wants to talk about her work, but all people care about is how hot she is, what color lipstick she's wearing, and who she's dating. That's really why she insisted on a silent partnership. Considering how many times the tabloids have shipped us, she didn't want to run the risk of changing the Turning Table Theater's initial press into another vapid series of stories about her sex appeal. I got it. I understood why she wanted it that way. But I'm feeling it on a more personal level at the moment.

"I'm feeling rather objectified by this banter," I complain. "I'm a real person here. What is the point of this show, exactly?"

"Usually? We discuss modern romance. But if you caught our last episode, it was mostly about my brother picking on the fourteen-year-old version of me," Chelsea says. "Now it appears as though he's moving on to you. I'm sorry, Dean. I'd like to say you weren't warned, but you've been friends with Jackson for what, twenty-something years?"

"Yes, I have," I admit. "And I do know what he's like. He's always pulling pranks. Someone had to stick up for you."

"Exactly. You were always my hero," Chelsea agrees. "Thank you for your chivalry."

"Someone, get this guy a suit of armor," Alexis suggests. "I am only half-joking here. I would really love to see Dean

Riley in a suit of armor. You do all that cool movie CGI stuff, right, Dean? Can you make that happen?"

"Nope," I say.

"Well, it actually seems like the joke's on me now"—Jackson sighs—"since everyone is ganging up on me, and more importantly, since I've determined that the two of you were actually always meant to be together."

"It was just a joke, and you know it," Chelsea protests.

Alexis fills in the listeners, "For the record, Dean and Chelsea played the most spectacular joke on Jackson the other night. They tried to convince him that they're madly in love. Pretty damn convincing, actually," she mumbles.

"Exactly!" Jackson says. "I don't know why I didn't see it sooner. Once I ran their profiles through my system, it was *so obvious*."

"My profile? You made a profile for me?" Chelsea looks indignant.

"I mean, yeah, I make profiles for a lot of people," Jackson says, "in the name of science. And it's not like you're winning at dating. How many guys have you dated and dumped over the last five years?"

"Over a dozen." Alexis furnishes the number. "She's a heart-breaker."

"Well, to be fair, none of them were *Dean*, right?" Jackson supplies.

"Is this your idea of getting back at us for pranking you?" I ask. "Dude, you need to let it go. Stop torturing your sister. So what if she had a crush on me when we were kids? Maybe I was into her too? What if I was just dying to get it on with your sister? Let's lean in and discuss it from that angle. We're all adults here."

I break the rules and look directly at Jackson. Game on. Predictably, he's squirming.

"Ugh, I don't know. It's like incest. You were practically a member of our family. Blech." Jackson pretends to gag.

"No, I wasn't." I laugh.

"Chelsea is like three years younger than you!" Jackson looks horrified.

"Oh yeah, that's gross," I say ironically. "What's the metric again? Half your age plus seven?"

"Enough, you two." Chelsea shuts it down. "I'm not in the market for a boyfriend. Dean is awesome, but he's not my type."

"Can he be my type then?" Alexis purrs. It's clear she's only saying this for dramatic effect, but I notice she glances over at Chelsea.

"Help yourself," Chelsea says. "He's all yours."

I can't help it. I look over at Chelsea. She's sitting with her knees pulled up, and her hands are balled into fists. Does she really want to invite Alexis to "help herself" to me? Is that what she really wants? She's not going to fight for me, even a little? Even if it's just for the show? I can't help but feel offended. But I shouldn't be surprised. That is her MO. Chelsea has always blown hot and cold with me.

"So, refresh my memory about how this show works?" I feign ignorance. "You talk about different films and movies every week?"

"Yes, but we usually theme it with a trope," Chelsea answers.

"Like the big brother's sexy verboten bff," Alexis volunteers.

"Can you give it a rest already, Alexis?" Jackson asks. "Keep your clothes on."

"You're not the boss of her, Jackson." I chastise him while still watching Chelsea. "Alexis, you should go ahead and make yourself comfortable."

"Why, thank you, Dean." Alexis peels off her hoodie and throws it at Jackson.

"Okay, so while Alexis is stripping, how about we move on to a new trope!" Jackson says. "Some of our listeners might not know this, but we've adopted a new system for choosing tropes to discuss. We've set up an electronic spinner on our website, using your suggestions. Chels, you have the wheel of tropes open on your browser. Do the honors, would you? Give it a spin. Here we go. It's spinning … spinning …"

"Oh, fuck me!" Chelsea exclaims.

"Excuse me?" Jackson says, eyes wide.

Alexis snorts. "Did my ears deceive me, or did our dear, sweet, proper Chelsea just drop an f-bomb?"

"I heard it," I say. "Put a dollar in the swear jar, Chelsea."

"Just read the trope." Jackson sighs.

"It's the 'Losing It' trope," Chelsea says.

"The 'Losing It' trope?" I ask.

"You know," Alexis says, "the one where someone gets deflowered."

"Who can think of some examples?" Jackson asks.

"*Blue Lagoon*!" Alexis is first to comment.

"*American Pie*?" I offer.

"*The Forty-Year-Old Virgin*," Chelsea says through clenched teeth.

"Oh, I loved that movie," Alexis says. "Steve Carell was so cute. It ended up really sweet."

"Ugh, I hate this trope," Chelsea says. "It's the worst."

"How so?" I ask.

"Well, in so many of them, it involves a sexually experienced man and some poor, innocent girl who freezes like a deer in the headlights, utterly mesmerized and confused by his throbbing member or some such bullshit."

"For the love of all that is holy, *never* use the words 'throbbing' and 'member' together on my podcast again, Chelsea," Jackson groans.

"How about me? Can I say 'throbbing member?'" Alexis asks.

"Yeah, whatever. You're not my sister."

"It's just so misogynistic. It's all some male fantasy about deflowering a woman. Even the term deflower is offensive. It literally means you are depriving her of something precious and beautiful. Stripping away her beauty."

"With your throbbing member," Alexis agrees. "But it sounds much sexier than calling his thang a weed whacker, amirite?"

"Weed whacker has definite manscaping overtones," Jackson offers.

"Stop. I'm being serious here. Why does every fictional virgin have to be some kind of idiot? Maybe some of them just haven't met anyone they actually *wanted* to do it with."

"They could just be asexual," Jackson suggests. "That's more common than you think."

"Who says they have to be asexual? It's entirely possible for a grown woman to have sexual feelings and sexual pleasure without having sexual intercourse," Chelsea fires back.

"Absolutely. Sexuality is a spectrum," Alexis says soothingly. "It's okay wherever you're at. The important thing is that you do what feels good for you and your partners and stay true to yourself. Nobody else gets to dictate that to anyone. We're all LGBTQ *plus* friendly here."

"What's so terrible with people waiting to have sex, anyway?" Chelsea goes on, "I mean, everyone wants to lose it in high school, but once you've waited past a certain age... I mean if you haven't done it with anyone by the time you're a proper adult, you're not going to squander it on just anyone," Chelsea says, amending with, "I imagine."

"I was just reading how some people need a strong emotional attachment *before* they can feel anything physical," Alexis mentions. "And that's totally normal. Isn't that interesting? For me, it's always physical first and emotional second. But ever since Chelsea told me she doesn't fantasize about Henry Cavill making her breakfast in bed, I wonder if she might fall into that first category."

"For all you know, Henry is a total asshole," Chelsea defends, voice cracking a little bit. "I'm just saying. You don't need to make this about *me*! My fantasy life is alive and well, thank you very much!"

"Seriously," Jackson says, "I do not want to know anything more about this, so moving on ..."

"You know, not all guys fantasize about deflowering women," I volunteer, weighing in. "It's actually a lot of pressure, I imagine. Particularly, if you care about someone. You don't want to hurt them, and you don't want them to have a bad time. What if you ruin sex for them?"

"Seriously?" Alexis asks doubtfully. "There are men who think that?"

"Seriously," I say. "I would think that."

"Oh, my. It's getting hotter in here," Alexis asserts. "I think I may need to take off another article of clothing now."

"Suit yourself," I say, risking another glance at Chelsea. I don't know what I'm looking for. Gratitude that I'm taking her side in the argument? A nod of solidarity? That's not what I see, though.

If I didn't know better, I'd swear she was wiping away a tear.

chelsea

. . .

FINALLY, it's over, and I have a moment to collect myself. I thought the last episode was bad, but it had nothing on this one. I was blindsided by Dean's sudden appearance in my apartment. And then to have the trope of the week be *that one*?

I go into the bathroom and splash some cold water on my face, forcing myself to get a grip on my out-of-control feelings. It's been all of a week, and Dean is still here. Really here. Integrating into my social life, helping me out at work, and showing up for podcast episode tapings.

If anyone had asked me how I felt about Dean Riley two weeks ago, I probably would have stonewalled. Ever since he broke my heart all those years ago, I shut those feelings down. I thought I was safe, that my wall was solid. But his bulldozers have been working on me as much as they have been working on the theater grounds. I need to accept that the landscape is changing.

I have a good life. I make good choices. I duck into my bedroom for my notebook and write up a quick list.

Ten Ways to Deal with Dean Being Back in Ephron: A List by Chelsea Porter

1. *Spend more time on my art.*
2. *Volunteer at the pet shelter. Get a dog?*
3. *Get serious about training for a half marathon.*
4. *Join a book club.*
5. *Start a new Social Media account dedicated to teaching painting techniques.*
6. *Learn to crochet.*
7. *Plan a trip.*
8. *Do yoga.*
9. *Grow some plants, preferably succulents.*
10. *Try dating again?*

I cross #10 off the list. What's the point? There's not a huge pool of candidates here in Ephron, and hookup culture is not my thing. Alexis is right. It takes time for me to bond with people and feel something physical. Possibly too much time. It took years for me to bond with Dean. It could happen again, in theory. But I'm not even sure I want it to, considering how I feel right now. I can't imagine feeling that way about someone else when I still feel so attracted to him.

Having no feelings at all would be much easier than having the right feelings for the wrong guy.

When I come back out to the kitchen, Alexis is flipping through a magazine while Jackson and Dean argue over takeout menus, trying to decide what to get for dinner. At least Dean isn't looking at my art in the hallway again. Hopefully, he will drop it and forgot about it.

"I can't stick around. I gotta get home and pack for my trip to Florida," Alexis apologizes. "Walk me to my car?"

"Why?" I ask warily.

"I just want to show you something."

"Fine," I say. It's ridiculous, but I'm still having a hard time meeting her eye. Did she have to flirt so shamelessly with Dean? I need to develop a thicker skin.

"It was fake, you know! You *know* that, right?" Alexis blurts the minute we are out the door.

"Okay, sure. Whatever," I say.

"Chelsea, you know I'm not really like that. Thirsty Alexis is a persona. It's just an act I do for the show. I'm not really like that. I mean, I enjoy sex—a lot—but I would never prioritize a hookup over a friendship, okay?"

We take the stairs, spiraling our way down. The fluorescent lights flicker overhead, and I hear everything twice, thanks to the echo.

"Well, you said he was your type," I point out. "And he seemed sort of interested."

"I'm pretty sure he was only flirting to make YOU jealous."

"Don't be ridiculous," I say.

"You are the one who is being ridiculous, Chelsea. And possibly, he is too. There's no way he's interested in me. Every time that man spoke to me, he was looking at *you*, looking to see how you would react."

"We're not supposed to look at each other when we are recording," I say, primly.

"Yeah, well, he wasn't following the rules. He was looking at you. He only has eyes for you."

169

My hand is dragging down the metal handrail and is gripped so tightly, I feel my palm burning. I let go before it gives me blisters.

"I don't believe you."

"Look, I just want you to be happy," Alexis insists. "You deserve that. Maybe there's a reason you had such a crush on that guy in high school. Maybe you actually had your shit more together than you were giving yourself credit for. Sometimes I think I knew what I wanted when I was younger much better than I know now, you know? Life fucks you up. Makes you overthink."

I sigh and sit on the bottom step of the stairwell.

"Can I just hide here for the rest of the night?" I fold my arms across my lap and bury my face.

Alexis sits down beside me and gives me a hug. "Oh, honey, I'm sorry. I pushed it too far in there, didn't I?"

"No, you were just doing your schtick. I don't know what's wrong with me," I say.

"Tell me this," Alexis says. She pauses for a moment, like she is trying to choose her words carefully. "What do you really want from Dean? I don't mean on paper or one of your lists. I mean, in your heart. And not just you're pushing thirty and worried about your 401(k) and biological clock, heart. I mean in your sixteen-year-old, hopelessly romantic heart."

"That's not fair. I am not that sixteen-year-old girl anymore. This isn't a sweet romance," I argue.

"We are all that sixteen-year-old girl, Honey. She's still in there. She's just getting silenced by her bitchy, jaded big sister. You gotta let her have her say, too, though. Her voice counts."

The tears start rolling.

"I can't, Alexis. High school things never work out. My parents' relationship nearly killed them both. I'm not going there."

"Yeah, I know. You've got your heart locked up in a cage for its own safety, and your brother, meanwhile, has dedicated his life to trying to crack the code so he can achieve some kind of perfect pain free union.. Meanwhile, neither of you are really letting yourself live. It's seriously fucked up. Love is messy and sometimes it hurts, but it's worth it."

"Big talker." My lips twitch, but I wipe my eyes.

"Let me tell you, if I had a guy like that looking at me the way that your man, Dean, was looking at you?" She shakes her head. "Damn, Girl."

"I can't," I repeat, shaking my head again. "It would never work."

"You never know till you try. And I think you gotta try," she says. "If you want to, of course." She looks at me seriously. "And I think you want to, don't you?"

"I do," I admit, "I really do. But I can't." I groan, flashing back to how bad it felt the last time I laid my heart on the line. "I really can't."

Alexis stands and raises her eyebrows at me. "I think you have to explore this," she says, "or you won't ever be able to move on. It's move on or move out of town."

"Urgggghhhh," I groan into my hands. "Why did he have to come back here?"

"Because maybe the two of you were meant to be?" Alexis smiles. "Even your brother sees it, although I hate to say Jackson is right about anything."

We sit for a moment in silence before she stands up. "That's all I got, Chels. What do you think you're going to do?"

"Target run!" I announce, grateful that I brought my phone, wallet, and keys with me. "I don't really need anything, but it never hurts to stock up on toilet paper and conditioner." Quickly, I text Jackson to let him know not to pick up dinner for me and to lock the door on his way out.

"I get it," Alexis nods approvingly "Sometimes you just need to push a red cart around to clear your head. Make sure you get yourself something nice and frivolous off the clearance rack."

dean

. . .

TWELVE YEARS AGO ...

I've packed way too much into one weekend. The wedding shower. Packing up my childhood bedroom so my mom can use it as a design studio. Getting fitted for a tux for Eli's wedding, plus a job interview and finishing a paper. I can't concentrate in my parents' house. My dad hasn't spoken to me since I broke it to him that I won't be spending this summer here, either.

"Three summers in a row, you've stayed away. The writing's on the wall, then. You never planned on coming back to Ephron. You're not interested in building a life here. You're not interested in us," was the last thing he'd said.

I take my old motorbike out for a ride to blow off steam. I'm going in circles. Literally. I'm riding in circles around Holm Square.

What did I think? That things would never change? That I could go off and do my thing and everyone else would stay the same here, perfectly preserved in a little time capsule? That my dad would get over it, and everything would go back to normal? That I'd have all the time in the world to make up my mind about the future? Why does it need to be so black and white?

I rev my engine, taking the empty block with way too much speed and loving it. The community center where Jackson and I used to go for Scout meetings flies by in a blur. I slow down for the next block, passing the diner where we always went after games, doubling up on our French fry orders.

I'll be back here again, albeit briefly, in a couple of months. Eli's wedding is just a few days after my term ends. Nothing's radically changing overnight, but it won't ever be the same again. I don't know why that surprises me. Sometimes it takes me a while to catch up and see the writing on the wall. My brother is marrying Brittany, the girl I took to senior prom. Awkward.

The word vomit came out, along with a lot of actual vomit, on the night of our prom. She'd had a crush on *him* since her freshman year. I was a consolation prize.

It isn't the wedding that's bugging me. I never had strong feelings for Brittany. And it's not the pressure from my dad. It's something else. Something else feels wrong. Something's missing here. *I'm* missing. I can't help but feel like I've misstepped somewhere, somehow. Like my family members, and everyone else in this entire town, are performing a musical number, and it's going great, until I step to the right at the exact moment when they all step to the left. I want to rewind and pick it up from the beat where I fumbled, but I can't. There's no going back. They've finished the number without me, and there's a giant round of applause. No thanks to me. I'm not even a member of the crew anymore.

As I cruise up Main Street for the third time, I notice a familiar figure in the gazebo at the center of the square. Chelsea Porter. She's got her nose in a book. Just seeing her sends such a surge of happiness through me, and all my melancholy thoughts instantly evaporate.

I turn the bike up the paved path into the park.

"Team Edward or Team Jacob?" I ask in a teasing voice. Chelsea looks more delighted to see me than anyone in my family was.

"Dean! What are you doing here?" She grins. "Jackson is not coming home for a few more weeks. That's so weird … I was just thinking about you."

"Wedding shower," I say. "And I had to come home to pack up some things. My folks are losing their minds getting everything ready for Eli's wedding."

"I heard about Eli and Brittany." Chelsea screws up her face. "Didn't *you* take her to your senior prom?"

"Yep." I nod.

"Isn't that awkward?" she asks, raising her brows.

"Honestly? Not too bad. It's not like we were madly in love or anything." I shrug. "It was just prom. And we were both too drunk afterward for anything to actually happen in that hotel room."

I don't know why I bother telling her that. Why do I want her to know? Chelsea blushes her signature shade of red, and I change the topic.

"Speaking of prom," I say. "Who's the lucky guy taking you? It's just a few weeks away, right?"

"You, you idiot. You're still taking me. Don't joke." Chelsea bats her lashes at me and grins. She's gotten taller and lankier. Prettier and cooler than I remember. So different from the plastic Barbie types back at school. She's not into a lot of makeup or labels. But she's so well composed. Everything about her style feels intentional, from her oversize, fuzzy, gray sweater to her patent combat boots, laced with lavender, velvet ribbon.

"For real? You seriously still want me to take you to your senior prom?" She's not blinking, just staring at me like that, with her lips slightly parted. I can see the remnants of a sparkly lip gloss on her lower lip, and instantly, I'm wondering if it's flavored.

"Of course I'm serious. Why are you looking at me like that, Dean? You promised. I don't have a date. I'm not letting you off the hook."

I can't tell if she's messing with me, but it's doing something to me. Rearranging things in my mind. And my pants. Of course, I haven't forgotten about that kiss, or my promise. But somehow, I had assumed she had moved on. She's only mentioned it the one time, over break. I thought she was just kidding around.

"You can't tell me nobody has asked you to prom," I challenge.

"Nobody I actually wanted to go with." She licks her lips and closes the book. "What if I said I've been saving myself for you?" She raises her eyebrows and studies me, intensely, leveling me with those stormy, gray eyes of hers.

I'm pretty sure she's just winding me up. But it doesn't matter. I reach out and wipe the rest of the gloss off her lower lip, tasting the sweet tartness on my thumb. *Lemon meringue pie.*

"Sorry. You had something there." I smile.

I'm not thinking about our families now. I'm not even thinking about the kiss that happened three years ago. I'm thinking about all the other things I'd like to do to her now, right now, if I could. And now, I'm thinking that I'm actually looking forward to coming home again in two months.

"Come for a ride with me?" I ask her, holding out my hand.

"Where to?"

"I dunno. Just around the block. I gotta go home in a bit, but I was trying to clear my head. I'll drop you at your house."

"Only if you confirm you're definitely still taking me to prom." Chelsea tosses her book in her backpack and hesitates.

"Wouldn't miss it for the world," I say. I take my helmet off and place it on her head.

"I miss you so much, Dean," she says before jumping on the back of the bike and wrapping her arms around me. "It's not the same here without you."

"Love you, Chels," I say. I feel her arms wrap tighter and her head pressed into my back as we take off, and suddenly, everything feels okay again. Sure things are changing, but it's not like my entire past is vanishing. There are still people here who care about me. My family isn't going anywhere. And I still have Jackson and Chelsea to come home to.

chelsea

. . .

I CHECK the weather report as soon as I wake up on Friday morning. Cloudy and temperate with blue breaks and very little chance of rain.

No excuses there. The weather's cooperating perfectly with Dean's plan to take me out on his motorcycle. I set the succulents I got at Target on my windowsill. I should probably make sure I can keep these alive before considering adopting a pet.

"I'll just give you guys a little water before I go, in case I don't make it home alive today," I say to the plants. I'm only half-joking.

I lock the door to my studio before I leave the apartment. If anything happens, I don't want it to be too easy for someone to wander in there. My work in progress is coming along nicely. I've settled on a split screen composition using the old kissing booth/lemonade stand as the centerpiece. Half of the painting will be bathed in light, with cool tones of ice, white flowers, and lemon slices. The other will be fiery reds and oranges, flames, and roses. I'll paint myself into the scene as the server on both sides, impossibly facing two directions at once, lips puckered.

"Hey, I recognize those shoes," Dean says, looking up from the phone he's punching directions into. "Aubergine and orchid, right?" He smiles and points at my purple, patent combat boots, laced with lavender, ribbon laces. "Oh yeah. I've had these forever." I stick out my foot, surprised he remembers them.

"I thought they seemed like sensible footwear for a motorcycle ride. I also can't picture myself dying in purple boots," I admit. It's oddly reassuring.

"You ready for our ride?"

"Ready as I'll ever be." I gulp. "It's fine if you'd prefer that I drive to see the flowers, though. I mean, I have the heated seats ... and what if it rains?"

"The forecast is fine, and we'll be fine. You're not going to die. I promise. Come on." Dean gestures to his motorcycle, parked casually on the street.

He stretches as he walks toward the bike. I try not to stare at the sliver of skin exposed as he raises his arms overhead. He rolls his neck from side to side and reaches for a helmet.

"Here," he says, handing me the shiny, black one. "Take my helmet." I notice that the letter Z has been scraped off the purple one as he pulls it on. I slip his helmet onto my head, smelling his shampoo. It's weirdly intimate. Like I'm slipping into his head, not just his helmet.

"Let me check the fit." He steps closer, placing one hand on my shoulder and maneuvering the helmet with the other.

I hold my breath as he tugs and jerks a few more times, finally slapping the side lightly when he's satisfied with the fit.

"There we go," he says. "Hop on. You remember how?"

"Like riding a bike," I assure him. But it isn't. Everything feels different. Had it really been teenaged me who so confidently jumped onto a motorcycle with this man? I can still picture him in his T-shirt and jeans, handing me his helmet.

Now I'm not sure where to put my feet. Dean takes his place between my thighs and reaches back to adjust my legs, pulling me closer. "Scoot forward a little."

"The seat's a lot cushier than your old bike," I comment, bouncing a little. Dean reaches back again and grabs one of my hands.

"It's a smooth ride, but you still better hang on, okay?" He pulls my hand to his belly. I hope he doesn't notice how much it's shaking. It's not just my hand. My whole body is shaking. I reach my other hand around and clasp my fingers together as he revs the engine.

"You good?" he asks.

"Mm-hmm," I say, squeezing my eyes shut, laying my head against his back and holding on tight.

Just go already. Please.

And then we do.

———

I don't open my eyes until we're out of Ephron, heading up into the hills.

"You okay back there?" Dean asks, shifting slightly in his seat. His voice is all around me.

"How is your voice in my head?" I ask.

"Bluetooth helmets," he says. "You want to listen to anything? Coldplay maybe?"

"I'm good," I say. "I like the sound of the wind."

"Me too," Dean says. "I do some of my best thinking on my bike."

It beats a red cart.

"I should have brought some gloves for you. Are your hands cold?" Dean asks. "Put them in my pockets, if you want."

I adjust my grip, feeling my way with one hand, then the other across his hard torso, sheathed in soft leather, until I find the pockets. I gratefully snake my hands inside where I can feel the warmth radiating from his skin. I have to resist the urge to stroke his hard muscles, and I scoot closer still, enjoying the constant vibration of the machine and road beneath us.

"I think I see some flowers already," Dean says. "Look at the ridge on the right."

"Poppies." I nod. I like the sound of his voice in my helmet and the feel of his warm skin under my hands. I like it a lot. In fact, I realize it's kind of turning me on. Suddenly, I'm intensely aware of the heat pooling at my core. The vibration of the road is a constant buzz that's become impossible to ignore. All of it together is turning me on, and I don't know how to turn it off.

Uh-oh.

I shift my position, tensing my thighs to raise my body slightly and lean harder against Dean, in a vain attempt to mitigate the sensations that are threatening to overwhelm. It doesn't help. I feel the fabric of my sports bra rubbing against my nipples, and it's an exquisite torture.

I need a distraction.

"Hey Dean," I say, hopefully not too breathily. "Want to play the color game?"

"Sure," he says. "But I'm a professional production designer now, you know. I might have an unfair advantage. I eat paint chips for breakfast."

"And I'm an art teacher," I comment, attempting to do a Kegel squeeze, then thinking better of it. That's only increasing the blood flow to the affected area. "And I'm also a girl. I buy a lot of nail polish."

"Okay, what should we start with?"

"How about the poppies?" I suggest, picturing the red flower in my head. The term "deflower" pops in out of nowhere, and I banish it. "How many words can you come up with to describe the color red?"

I close my eyes and do everything in my power not to see red, but it's difficult. What is wrong with me? Everything feels so … sexual. Everything I picture is bringing me closer and closer to …

"Carmine," Dean says. His voice is low and deep in my ears.

"Mm-hmm. Keep going," I say, feeling fluttery.

"That's not how this game works, Chels. It's your turn. You say a color now."

"Uh … poppy." I breathe.

"No, you can't use poppy. We started with that." Dean speeds up to pass a slow-moving RV, and the adrenaline surge of the sudden burst of speed blessedly holds back what was starting to feel like an inevitable climax.

Thank God. I murmur a quick prayer of gratitude, wondering if I'm the only woman who has ever been grateful for not coming.

"Scarlet," I say, catching my breath and squirming in my seat.

"Crimson," Dean replies. It's like he's whispering in my ear. I have goose bumps.

"Ruby." I can't help myself. I rake my nails gently against his belly and feel his muscles tense.

"Vermilion." Dean takes one hand off the handlebars and rests it over my hand in his pocket, pushing it closer in.

"Chili." I breathe out, starting to feel a light sheen of sweat on my forehead as the feelings resume their slow climb.

Ironically, the motorcycle is also climbing. We are gaining altitude as we reach the peak of the hill. More and more fields of flowers are revealed as we take each curve.

"Carnelian," Dean says. Is it just me, or did that sound like 'carnal'ian?

"Lipstick." I lean in closer, deliberately smashing my breasts harder against him now and working my fingers lower against the taut ridges of his six pack. The fabric on his pocket lining doesn't allow me to dig deeper than the top edge of his jeans.

He grips the handlebars tighter. I can feel his entire body flex.

"You okay? What are you doing back there, Chelsea?"

His voice has a low, growly tone to it. It bites into my ear and nibbles at the lobe. Of course, that's just my imagination.

"I'm fine. It's your turn." I rotate my hips against his tailbone to distract myself, but there is no relief from this relentless buzzing between my legs and between us. It's tickling nerves I didn't know I had.

"Oxblood," Dean states.

"Ew." I laugh.

"What, you don't like that one? Oxblood is a very virile color," he insists.

"Sangria," I answer quickly, noting the sign we've just passed for the pullout. We're almost at the overlook.

"Rose petal." Dean's thumb is stroking the underside of the handlebar grip, slowly and gently. Oh, Lord. I wish I hadn't noticed that.

"Lollipop." I moan slightly, gripping him tighter, if that's possible. I hear his sharp intake of breath, and the bike slows down. "Don't slow down, Dean," I whisper. "We're almost there."

"Cherry," Dean says, speeding toward the peak and setting me off like a bomb. All around me are fields of bursting colors, but I don't need to open my eyes to see them. Sensation after sensation washes over me as I come. Colors, textures, tastes. I gasp, and I could swear I smell black cherries mixed in with the leather of Dean's jacket.

"You sure you're okay?"

"Oh, yeah. I'm fine," I manage to mumble as he pulls off to the side so we can take in the view. Thank goodness it's so awe-inspiring and breathtaking because it takes a few moments before I can speak or process anything. I'm still sitting there, clinging to him, limp, spent, and shaking off sparks, even after he cuts the engine.

Finally, Dean pulls off his helmet and hangs it on the handlebars. Then he unzips his jacket. His hair is damp and clinging to his neck. He twists and looks over his shoulder at me. I'm grateful for the helmet. Hopefully, it's hiding how beet-colored my face is at the moment. I'm not sure how I will wipe away the tears rolling down my cheeks.

I have never had an orgasm that powerful before. The force of it has me questioning everything. Sex. Mortality. The meaning of life. If someone offered me a cigarette right now, I would probably smoke it.

"Chels, what's up?" he asks. "Did I do something wrong? Was I going too fast? I mean, I know you were a little scared to come out today, but you used to love it. I'm sorry if I pushed you to do something you weren't into."

"No, it's not that." I shake my head. Dean deftly swings a leg over the center of the bike and hops off.

"Then what is it?" He reaches for my helmet, but I hang on to it, protectively.

"Um … I think you should take this off," he says, tentatively. "We've stopped. You don't need it anymore."

"But you got it perfectly adjusted," I insist. "And you can't be too safe, right?"

Dean quirks an eyebrow at me. "We can readjust it again when we are ready to go." He lifts the helmet up and off my head. My hands fly to my face.

"Are you crying?" he asks incredulously.

"It's just from, you know, the wind," I say, scrubbing away the tears with my fists.

"In a windproof helmet?"

Dean wipes away a tear with his thumb. My eyes close reflexively as he moves his hand to my jaw.

"Fine, they were tears. But not the sad kind. They're happy tears." It's so unfair this effect he has on me.

"Happy how?" he asks.

"Happy as in …" I try to think of a way to finish the sentence without the word "ending." Nothing comes to me, so I just continue to sit there at the overlook, blushing. After a few more moments of awkward silence, I sweep my hand across the stunning vista. "Pretty flowers," I say.

Dean isn't looking at the flowers. He's looking at me. His thumb has started making slow circles against my neck. His eyes are practically the same light cyan shade as the sky at its

185

brightest edges. And his lips … Dean Riley red. I take a deep breath, leaning toward him like he's the sun and I'm a helpless bloom, about to get stripped.

"Screw the flowers," Dean murmurs, and then he leans in and kisses me, simultaneously pulling me off the bike and crushing me with those irresistible lips.

I can feel the gravel under my feet, but at the same time, I feel weightless. Dean's hands course over my body, roaming from my shoulder to my ass. He pulls me roughly against him, our jagged angles colliding and softer parts cushioning the blow. I can feel his hip bones and the hard thrust of his need. A truck zooms by on the road, blaring its horn in passing and startling us apart.

It takes a moment for the dust to settle and the birds and bees to resume their background hum. I smell grass and flowers on the wind. But I choose to look at Dean, drinking in the sight of him and wanting more.

Wordlessly, Dean takes a step back and holds his palms in front of me, almost like someone who is warming their hands in front of a fire, not daring to get too close.

"Tell me." He speculates. "Was that what I thought it was back there on the bike?"

"What did you think it was?" I ask, no longer bothering to blush. I wonder if he can feel the heat and the humidity that is still radiating out of me.

"You told me not to slow down. I thought you weren't happy with my driving."

"Actually, I was extremely satisfied with your driving. I don't think I've ever been that satisfied with anyone's driving ever before," I confess. My fist closes around the open edge of his jacket again, and I bite my lip.

Who even am I?

"Jesus, Chelsea." He moans. "I don't know what I'm going to do. I can't ravish you by the side of the road, and I don't think I'm going to make it all the way back to Ephron."

"Me, neither," I say. I don't want to lose my nerve. I don't want this moment to end. Alexis is right. I have to give this a chance. I have to give us a chance. And I know exactly what I want. I've waited so long for this. I don't want to wait a moment longer.

I can hardly believe the next words that come from my lips.

"The Shepherds Hut."

dean

. . .

CHELSEA PROGRAMS the address into my GPS, and we get back on the road. It's a good thing the Airbnb is only about twenty-five miles away, farther up in the hills. Not too much time to second-guess things. Are we really doing this? Granted, I'm already in my head about her. Maybe Jackson is right. Maybe there's a reason why I haven't been able to commit to anyone all these years. Maybe …

I've never been able to forget the way she kisses.

Neither of us speak on the way up into the mountains. I feel every shift of her body against mine. Her arms are wrapped so tightly around my waist. Her hands are in my pockets, pressed to my flesh. I want to turn around and lift her shirt, feel her skin against mine. But then, who would drive? If this were a movie, my bike would magically take us there on its own.

Finally, we reach the gates marking the entrance to the private road.

"There should be a red mailbox on the right side of the road," Chelsea says, squeezing me. "The driveway is just past there."

"What color mailbox, did you say?" I ask. I feel her nails digging into me.

The host is waiting for us when we arrive. We park near the hut, which I'm pleasantly surprised to see is actually a yurt. The building is circular, with canvas-covered lattice walls. The host is rocking in one of the two rocking chairs on the covered front porch. He jumps up and waves excitedly at us. Chelsea is off the bike first, walking rapidly toward him.

"Hi, guys! Welcome to The Shepherds Hut!" He bends and picks up a basket. "You must be Noah and Chelsea. I have some goodies for you two to enjoy—champagne, chocolate-covered strawberries, and some artisanal, lavender massage oil made right here on the farm. I wasn't sure what the occasion was, but I can see now I was right to make it romantic." He squeals delightedly as he passes the basket our way.

I steal a confused look at Chelsea. She takes the basket, flushing a little. "What a nice surprise!" she says.

"Thanks for letting us in," I say to the host. "We should be good from here."

"Well, let me just do the walk-through," insists the bearded man. He's short and wearing a green, flannel shirt. He has a bushy beard and twinkling, blue eyes. He looks around confused, suddenly.

"Where are your bags? Don't you two have bags?"

"We're traveling light," Chelsea says.

"Oh, dear. I can bring some extra blankets and toiletries by later. What can I get for you?"

"Nothing, we're fine," I insist. "Long day on the road. We'll probably head to bed early. Motorcycles really drain you. It's all the vibration." I wink at Chelsea, enjoying her blush.

"Okay. Well, I'm Ben, if I didn't already say." He continues his spiel. "And The Shepherds Hut is a very special property, very near and dear to my heart. There's a wood stove over here and a basket of logs on the porch. Would you like me to show you how to build a fire?"

"No, I've got it," I reassure him. "I was a Boy Scout."

"Okay, Noah. I thought there was something about wanting a fire-building lesson in the original reservation email. I must be remembering wrong." Ben looks confused for a moment but shakes it off and continues his tour.

"Here's the bathroom, and there are towels on the bed. Make sure to turn the water heater on at least half an hour before you want to take a shower."

While Ben continues on his tour, I step closer to Chelsea, wrapping my arms around her and sliding a hand up under her sweater to stroke her ribs. I take a deep breath, smelling the scent of her shampoo before quickly kissing her neck and releasing her. I do all this before Ben turns around or looks back. I've completely missed whatever he was saying about the thread count on the sheets.

"Which brings us to the kitchen. Feel free to use any of the items in the pantry and fridge. It's a ways to the nearest grocery store, so we keep the hut stocked with the basics. Pasta, sauce, oatmeal, bread, jam, some canned stuff. You won't starve. Oh, and coffee. This is a Nespresso coffeemaker. There are two kinds of pods. The red ones are decaf and the brown ones are regular. Do you want me to write that down for you? Have you ever used a pod-style coffeemaker before? I'd be happy to show you how it works. Of course, I'd have to use one of the pods, but I can bring back some more in a bit."

"We're fine. We don't drink coffee," Chelsea says. She sets the basket of goodies on the kitchen counter before returning to my side and putting an arm around me. "We've just really been looking forward to spending time *alone*, Ben."

Ben looks from her to me and back to her. "Oh, dear. I get it. I'm so sorry. I'll leave you two lovebirds alone. I hope you enjoy your stay here, and if you do, please don't forget to give us a five-star review! And if you need anything, I'm just up the road. You have my email. Do you want my cell phone too? I can write it down for you."

"That's okay, Ben. Thanks for the tour." I look pointedly at the door.

Finally, thankfully, Ben leaves, and it's just the two of us.

"I'm so sorry about that," Chelsea says. "Noah was going to cancel, but there wasn't enough time to get a refund, so he put my name on the reservation, too, in case I could use it. I had almost forgotten about it until we were just looking at the flowers and I realized it was so close, and—"

"It's fine. I don't want to talk about Noah," I interrupt, running a finger along her jaw and down to her jacket. "In fact, I'm not so sure I want to talk at all."

She still seems flustered. "Okay, but I just want you to know, I had no idea ..."

"It's really okay," I reassure her.

Chelsea nods and takes off her jacket. "I have to admit, this place is nicer than I thought it would be when he offered it up," she observes.

"It's not so bad," I agree. I peek inside the basket. "This is decent champagne too. Want some?"

"Okay," Chelsea acquiesces. She seems so shy, suddenly, and a little nervous.

"Are you okay, Chels? We don't have to do anything. Maybe we just sit on the porch and watch the sunset. We can play the color game some more. I still have a few good reds in me."

She blushes again. "You will never ever let me live that down, will you?"

"That depends on whether you let me put together a dedicated palette of all my Chelsea shades. It's going to take a little while. I'll have to do a thorough investigation, looking into the subtle variations of tone and texture here"—I lift her hair to kiss behind her ear—"and here." I nudge at her sweater sleeve to kiss her wrist. She closes her eyes. "And I might have to use my tongue." I push the sleeve up farther and press my lips to the crease in her elbow, pausing to flick my tongue in the hollow there. She moans and steadies herself against the counter.

I release her arm and turn my attention back to the basket of goodies. I set the two flutes on the counter and take out the plate with the strawberries. They look juicy and delicious.

"Don't go anywhere," Chelsea says. "I'm just going to use the restroom. I think I'll turn on the water heater. I wouldn't mind a shower later."

Or a bath. That Jacuzzi tub looks pretty incredible and is definitely big enough for the two of us.

I untwist the metal cage and pop the cork on the champagne, pouring it into the flutes, watching the bubbles rise to the surface. This is really happening. Maybe Jackson is right. Maybe it's the only logical thing. A part of me has always been waiting for her. I'd just given up hope that she was also waiting for me.

God, I've missed her. I've missed the easy camaraderie. Bouncing creative ideas off each other. Her sense of humor. Even all of her silly checklists. Jackson may have been my best friend, but Chelsea was something more. She might be my soul mate.

Why have I waited so long to come home?

chelsea

· · ·

> We're at The Shepherds Hut. I think
> something might actually happen. Help!

I TEXT Alexis from the bathroom. I'm trying not to freak out.
This is exactly what I wanted. It's what I have always wanted.
And even if it's not exactly what I pictured all those years
ago, it does feel like a second chance.

I'm not an idiot. I know that Dean is probably going back to
Hollywood and dating celebrities. I don't think he's interested
in anything long term. Whatever this between us is, or was,
we both have to get it out of our systems. Once and for all.

> Wait, what? You're at The Shepherds Hut
> with Noah? Didn't he just get out of the
> hospital? Where's his mom?

> No!!! Not Noah. I'm here with Dean.

> How did that happen?

We were already in the mountains, checking out the superbloom. It wasn't too far. Noah put my name on the reservation just in case. One thing led to another.

OMG. Do you even have protection?

No.

I smack my forehead. What am I even thinking? I'm an idiot.

That's ok. You can do other stuff, right? This doesn't have to happen right now.

Alexis punctuates her text with the devil emoji, three chili peppers, an eggplant, and the Easter Island guy. Easter Island guy?

No! I don't want to do other things. I want to do THE thing. The thing we were supposed to do on prom night all those years ago.

Oh, honey, you've waited this long. You sure you want to rush it like this?

This is not a rush! I'm 29. I want to do it. I want to get on with my life already. I want to be able to have normal relationships. I'm ready to surrender my V Card.

My plane is about to leave. Are you sure you want to do this? Seriously, Chelsea, you've waited this long.

Yes.

What does Dean think? Does he even know?

Dean hands me a glass of champagne when I come out. He's put on some music. I recognize the '80s' song "Don't Dream it's Over," and it brings me right back to a moment in my living room all those years ago, shortly after I broke my leg. I remember exactly how I felt sitting there, leg propped up, listening to my parents' music and pining so impossibly for him.

It's starting to rain outside, and I hear the patter of raindrops on the canvas.

"To us," he toasts. "Maybe Jackson wasn't yanking our chain."

"Jackson never jokes about his AI." I smile and clink glasses before taking a sip. "I just don't know that I put as much faith in it as he does."

Dean raises an eyebrow. "What do you put your faith in these days, Chelsea?"

Good question, Dean.

"I'm not sure," I finally admit.

"Well, it's nice to have your brother's blessing, but it's not his permission I need." Dean takes a long drink of his champagne before setting it on the counter. He grabs my flute and sets it beside his. Then he pulls me close. Our bodies fit together so perfectly, it's crazy. Like we were originally one unit, before being separated by a cosmic jigsaw.

His lips are hovering just above mine, close enough to feel the electric spark of the atoms fuzzing and reacting between us, pulling us back together.

He steps me back toward the bed, stopping a few inches away.

"I can't believe this is happening," he says, expressing my thoughts perfectly.

"Me, neither." I hum.

"Have you ever thought about it before?" he asks, brushing his lips softly against mine.

"Are you kidding me?" I shake my head.

"I don't mean then. Not when we were kids. I mean since." Dean slides my cardigan sweater off my shoulders.

"No," I say. It's the honest answer. I haven't allowed myself to even think about this possibility.

"How about you?" I ask as he reaches behind my back, under my tee, to deftly unhook my bra.

"Honestly?" Dean asks, lifting the shirt over my head and taking his time to admire my uncovered breasts.

"Yes, please," I murmur, although I'm not sure whether I am asking for his honesty or something else.

"No," he says with his mouth. But his head is nodding, and then it's bending, and his lips are featherlight against me. I tangle my hands in his hair and laugh.

"What does that mean, Dean?"

"God help me, Chels. I tried not to. You were too young, and I hated myself for thinking of you like that. And so, I just … I don't know, shut it down. You were just a kid, and I knew you'd forget about me. And I was right. You did.

"Now this is truly rose-petal pink, by the way." He nips gently at my breast, kissing the areola and making me moan. Then he pulls back to look into my eyes.

"Is it terribly selfish that I'm dying to make you remember me now?" he pleads. "I don't want you to forget about me. Nobody knows me like you do."

"Take off your shirt," I direct him, adding my bra to the pile of clothes on the floor. I run my hands over his torso, realizing that the grown-up, flesh-and-blood version of him standing in front of me right now is a thousand times better than the teenager version that was trapped in my juvenile dreams.

"What is it you'd like me to remember?" I quiz him, kissing my way across his chest, amazed at my newfound ability to make him tremble.

"Everything." He wraps his arms around me, and we tumble back onto the bed, limbs tangled, lips kissing, tongues seeking.

There's no moment where I question myself. No need to calm myself with one of my lists. No awkward moment where I need to make excuses. I set my phone on the nightstand when I wriggle out of my jeans. And who knows where my underwear went. I shiver, half in delight at what Dean is doing to me with his fingers, and half at the rapidly falling temperature in the yurt.

"I should build a fire," he says, breaking free from a trail of kisses along my hipbone.

"You already have," I say, warming myself with a blush. I don't want him to stop now.

"No, really. We're going to freeze if we put it off too long. And I don't want to freeze. I want to take my time with you."

Now would probably be a good time to tell him, it occurs to me. If I were going to tell him. But it's probably better if I don't. It might make it weird if I do. And it's been so perfect so far that I don't want to spoil it.

"What are you looking at?" I ask, realizing that he's stopped stroking me and is just hovering above me now, gazing down at me.

"I was just thinking that I really want to see you by the firelight. And that I like the idea of laying you down in front of that fireplace."

"There's even a sheepskin rug," I note.

Which could be a bad thing if I bleed. Would I bleed? Would it hurt? Would he figure it out? Oh, God.

Stop it, Chelsea. Get out of your head. Think about Dean in the fire-light. Naked Dean.

"Okay, fine," I say. "Do what you gotta do." I sit up and wrap the down comforter around myself.

Dean reaches for the throw blanket off the chair next to the bed and wraps it around himself like an oversize poncho. Then he pulls on his boots. "I'll bring in some firewood from outside. I should probably grab some protection, too, unless you have something on you?"

"I don't," I admit, trying not to panic. I really want this to happen, but not so much that I'm willing to be completely reckless. How is it that I was so much better prepared to have sex at seventeen?

"I have something in my first aid kit," Dean says.

"Wow, you really are a Boy Scout," I comment. It shouldn't bug me that he has an emergency condom. It's responsible. And fortuitous.

"You'd be surprised how many alternative uses condoms have." He smiles wryly. "But I'm happy to use it as the manufacturer intended."

He looks at my phone on the nightstand. "Can I use your phone's flashlight? It's pretty dark out there."

"Sure," I say, unlocking it and handing it to him. He promptly uses it to take a photo of me, which he then texts to himself.

"Hey," I protest. "That wasn't fair! I'm a mess."

"Just making a memory, Chels. You're gorgeous, and I don't want to forget this."

And then he heads out the door.

dean

. . .

I HEAD BACK to my bike, holding the phone up to illuminate my path. The rain has slowed to a steady mist, the likes of which we never had back in LA. I inhale deeply. I've missed this lushness in my life. My teeth are chattering, but I'm grinning, nonetheless.

I can't wait to get back inside and get the fire going. I can't believe my luck.

Quickly, I locate the first aid kit in the compartment under my seat. I pull out the condom and chuckle. I keep it in there for emergencies, but not the sexual kind. Condoms make great ice packs in a pinch. You can use them to keep your phone dry, to cover a bandage, plus a dozen other "off brand" uses. Good thing I just repacked this kit before my drive up to Washington because I wouldn't trust a condom that sat too long.

Next stop—wood. Fortunately, Ben left a basketful of supplies on the covered porch. It shouldn't be too difficult to get a fire going with a couple of those good, dry logs and kindling.

Chelsea's phone dings as I am coming up the stairs to the porch, and I see that the message I sent to myself failed. Probably because the signal isn't terrific here. I pause on the deck and tap into her messages to resend it. It's not a great picture in terms of lighting or framing or anything like that, but none of that matters. Wrapped up in the blanket like that, hair a mess, lipstick kissed off her, Chelsea is recognizable as the kid I knew and loved. But she also looks like the woman I can't wait to get closer to. The incredibly smart, sexy, and creative woman whom I haven't even dared to dream might be out there waiting for me. Or not waiting ... Chelsea hasn't been waiting for me. She's moved on with her life. But not so far along that I can't play catch-up.

I don't want to forget anything about tonight. I hit the button to resend. This time, it seems to work, but it's taking really long to get through. I listen for my phone's chirp in response to the sent message, somewhere inside the yurt. I think I left it in my jacket.

While I'm waiting for the message to be sent, I set the phone on the stool by one of the rocking chairs, light shining on the wood in the basket. There are a couple of good-size logs that should last a few hours. I tuck them under my arm, being careful to keep the blanket between my bare skin and the wood. The last thing I need right now is a splinter. I don't want anything getting in the way of the activities I have planned for the rest of the evening. Shades of pink, coral, and peach-colored activities.

Chelsea's phone screen lights and dings again. Frustrated, I reach for it, determined to try one last time to send the message again before giving up.

But the ding isn't that at all. It's a new message that I clearly wasn't meant to see.

> Flight was delayed. I hope that finally losing your virginity to Dean Riley means you can move on with your life already.

Losing your virginity to Dean Riley? What. The. Actual. Fuck? The night suddenly feels colder, wetter, and altogether foreign to me. The sky actually seems larger and darker, clouded over the way it is, with no moon or stars in sight.

I hate myself for doing it, but I scroll back and read through the entire conversation. This has to be a joke. I'm just missing context, right? The messages are from Alexis, I see.

> Do you even have protection?

No.

> That's ok. You can do other stuff, right? This doesn't have to happen right now.

No. I don't want to do other things. I want to do THE thing. The thing we were supposed to do on prom night all those years *ago*.

> Oh, honey, you've waited this long. You sure you want to rush it like this?

This is not a rush! I'm 29. I want to do it. I want to get on with my life already. I want to be able to have normal relationships. I'm ready to surrender my V Card.

> My plane is about to leave. Are you sure you want to do this? Seriously, Chelsea, you've waited this long.

Yes.

> What does Dean think? Does he even know?

No! Dean doesn't know, dammit. He most certainly doesn't know! And what the hell does she mean about "supposed to do …" With me? She didn't end up going to prom with me. It all goes back to that night, doesn't it? What game is she playing now?

My head feels like it's going to explode.

I storm back into the yurt, dropping the logs by the wood-stove. Chelsea is still wrapped in the comforter. All rosy-cheeked and expectant-eyed. I feel like I've been catfished.

"Everything okay?" Chelsea asks. "Did you find your emergency condom?"

And then she sees my face.

"Oh no," she says. "What happened?"

"This." I toss the phone on the bed. "When were you going to tell me you're a thirty-year-old virgin, Chelsea?"

"Twenty-nine," she argues, looking horrified from the phone to me. "Not that it matters. Or that it's any of your business."

"Bullshit!" I snarl, pointing at the phone. "I thought I knew exactly what was going on here, but it turns out the joke's on me. This whole situation with you and me is some kind of a setup?"

"A setup?" Chelsea fires back. "What's so false about wanting to have sex with someone you're attracted to and actually getting to do it? Most people would call that living the dream."

"No!" I fume. "It isn't. It's certainly not my dream. Not like this. Not when you're not being straight with me. Is it because of what I said the other day, about not fantasizing about virgins, that you didn't tell me? Or is it simply because you're only sleeping with me so you can "get it out of the way" and move on with your life? I was willing to overlook how weird you were being about your art, but this is too much. Too fucked up. Too many secrets."

"Fuck you, Dean!"

"It's 100 percent not happening." I hurl the condom in the trash. "Maybe you should quick send a text to Alexis and let her know before she buys you a congratulatory floral arrangement for losing your ' V Card.'"

"How dare you read my messages!"

"How dare you treat me like your personal fuckboy gigolo? You couldn't have found some other piece of meat who hasn't known and loved you since you were eleven years old to service you?"

I'm angry now and pulling on my clothes. Jeans, boots, tee, jacket. Screw my socks and underwear. I don't want to be here a minute longer.

"Where are you going?" Chelsea asks.

"I'm leaving," I announce.

"It's raining and dark out there," Chelsea says. "Is that even safe?"

She has a point, but not one I'm willing to concede at the moment.

"Thanks for your concern, Chelsea. So thoughtful of you." The sarcasm drips from me like acid.

"So that's it? You're just going to leave me here?"

"I don't want to spend another minute in this fucking hut with you, let alone take your V Card."

Chelsea is pulling her clothes on angrily now too. And as anxious as I was to see her naked before, I can't even look at her now. I don't want to see her. I snatch my keys off the counter and grab my helmet.

"Later," I rant. "I'm out."

I hear her voice through the canvas walls of the yurt as I'm walking away in the rain. And I know she's crying. But I'm too mad to turn back.

"Fan fucking-tastic, Dean," Chelsea yells. "Go! Just go! Leave! Fool me twice! Shame on me! Story of my life!"

dean

. . .

TWELVE YEARS AGO ...

Jackson and I are cooling our heels, waiting my turn at the tailor's shop in Ephron. I'm here to pick up the tux I'm wearing to my brother's wedding tomorrow and to take Chelsea to prom after. I'll probably have to get it dry cleaned in between, but it's easier than renting twice. There's a line because of prom next week. Pretty much every teenage guy in Ephron is getting fitted for their tux today or tomorrow. The tailor is looking harried.

"My tux had better fit. I've got a million things I need to do between today and tomorrow," I complain. As the best man, I've got to see that everything's set for Eli's bachelor party tonight, making sure he doesn't get too drunk to show up fresh tomorrow. Plus, I still need to finish up writing the toast. I decide to leave out the fact that my future sister-in-law was my former prom date.

"So how do you feel about Eli marrying Brittany?" Jackson asks me.

"I mean, it's a little weird, but as you know, nothing happened after the prom," I say. "She was pretty wasted. And frankly, so was I."

"Yeah, I remember," Jackson says. "I lost my deposit on the limo because of the cleaning fees. I hope Eli knows he's marrying a puker."

"We weren't that annoying, were we?" I point out the three jockish guys checking themselves out in the triple mirror. They're shooting selfies and making stupid, inane peace signs. One of them can't seem to keep his tongue in his mouth. He's got a lot of product in his hair.

"I definitely wasn't," Jackson says. "I was the nerdy sidekick. You were the football player."

Football player/theater geek. I don't bother making the distinction. High school feels like it was another lifetime ago, not a mere three years.

The teenagers are giving each other high fives now, and we can't help but overhear their conversation.

"Oh, yeah. We are *so* getting hotel sex on prom night. Who else has hotel rooms?" asks the meaty guy with the overly coiffed hair.

"What kind of room did you get, Bryce?" asks the shorter one.

"Presidential Suite," he says, puffing himself up and flexing in the mirror.

"Best part about my room is I'm off the hook. I don't even have to pay for it. My date reserved it," says the third dude, who is preening like a peacock, despite a scorchingly bad case of acne. "She got some kind of group deal with a bunch of her friends."

"Oh really? Which girls?" Bryce looks interested.

"Danielle, Lacey, and Chelsea ... not sure who else."

"Lucky you. Maybe they're into group sex too." Bryce snorts. "But Chelsea Porter? Seriously? I thought she was a frigid little bitch! Then again, maybe it's all a front. Have you seen her mom? Talk about a MILF!"

Jackson goes rigid beside me. My hand is already clenched in a fist. I elbow him, looking at the guys and then back at him, raising my eyebrows significantly. I hope I'm communicating what I'm thinking. *We can take them. We can teach those little shits a lesson.*

I don't care if I show up at Eli's wedding with a black eye. How dare they talk about Chelsea and her mom like that?

But Jackson shakes his head at me. "Not worth it," he asserts. "That's my friend Hudson's younger stepbrother. He's a little piece of shit, and I'd like to kick his ass too. But we'd just end up getting thrown in jail. You don't want to miss Eli's wedding, do you?"

"Did you hear what he just said about Chelsea?" My fist is aching to connect with Bryce's flappy jaw. "And what the fuck is he even talking about with the hotel room? That's a load of shit. I mean, I ..."

Jackson is looking at me with the strangest look, and I don't like it. He knows I'm supposed to take Chelsea to the prom. But he doesn't know how I feel about her. As far as he's concerned, I'm taking her out of pity. I've left it off too long. I just don't know how to tell him I have feelings for his little sister.

"You what?" he asks, eyes narrowing. "You said that you'd be her backup if she didn't have a date, right? Am I missing something here?"

"Hey, Babe." A teenaged girl with orange hair pops her head into the shop, and her cotton candy perfume hitchhikes in on the breeze. It's cloying in the tight space. "Hurry up. We got a booth at the Ephron Diner."

"Calm down. You can keep my seat warm for a few more minutes, Danielle," the acne-scarred guy says. "I was just telling the guys about the hotel room deal you got. Bryce didn't believe me when I said Chelsea was in on it." He doesn't turn to look at his girlfriend while he speaks. He's too busy smugly checking himself out in the mirror.

"LOL! Chelsea is the one who got the deal," Danielle trills. "You should thank her for scoring such a cheap rate because you're still paying. You didn't think I was footing the bill, did you?"

"Who is Chelsea going to prom with?" Bryce asks, eyebrows raised.

"Dunno. Some guy from out of town, I think." Danielle blows a bubble and sucks it back in. "Quit admiring yourselves and get your fine asses over to the diner." She ducks back out, and the boys go back to the dressing rooms to change back into their clothes. But they don't stop talking.

"Lucky bastard," we hear from the back. "I'd tap that ass. Wonder who the ice queen is planning to screw?"

"I dunno. I'd still rather do her slutty mom."

Jackson is even paler now. His fist is clenched. I can't believe he won't let me beat the shit out of that obnoxious kid. Who cares if he's a Holm? But Jackson appears to be glaring at me now.

"Jackson, you know this has nothing to do with me, right?" I ask. Hopefully, my guilt isn't showing. What if it was true about the hotel room? The thought gives me a thrill. I'd been on the verge of booking a room myself. But I didn't want to presume.

210

"Of course I know it's not about you." Jackson snorts, releasing some of the tension. "Didn't she tell you? She doesn't need you to take her anymore. She's going with some other guy. Someone she met online. I'm going to have to have a talk with her now. The last thing she needs is a rep like our mom."

I feel like I've been punched in the gut. She's planning on going with someone else? And she didn't even bother telling me? When was she going to let me know? When I showed up with a corsage and a limo like some sad fuck? Is this her idea of revenge for rejecting her all those years ago? Some kind of twisted prank? I have to hand it to her … she plays a long con.

Outrage over the teenagers' slurs twists together with the fresh offense of discovering I've been played. I was to be served a cold shit sundae. The horror must show on my face because Jackson elbows me in the ribs.

"Come on, Dude. You didn't really think she was going to make you take her to prom? You're like *twenty*. She was just playing a joke on you, yanking your chain."

I'm still trying to process his words. I'm such an idiot. Why didn't I say something sooner, to either of them? Of course Chelsea has a real date for prom. Hell hath no fury, right? But honestly, this is a little over the top, even for her. Was it really necessary for her to go to such lengths to get back at me?

Then again, she has no idea how I actually feel, does she? I've been leading her on for years.

The three guys drape their pants back on the rack and call out to the tailor, who tells them to come back tomorrow to pick their suits up.

"Dude, Chels will probably kill me, but it's not fair of her to do this to you, so I'm just gonna do you a solid and tell you now. You're off the hook," Jackson reveals. "This should make you happy. Weren't you in a hurry to get down to Ashland for your internship, anyway? Now you can head down there sooner. I know you didn't really want to stick around for a whole extra week at your parents' house."

"Okay, Dean Riley, you're up. You need your tux through next week, no?" The tailor checks his list before looking our way.

"Actually," I say, "I guess I'll only need it through Sunday."

"Okay, but I still gotta charge you for the whole week," the tailor says. "I'll be right back."

"Well, that sucks," Jackson says, "but at least you're free to leave, right?"

I should be relieved. He's looking at me like he's just done me a huge favor. So, I nod, trying not to let the shit sundae leak out onto my best friend. None of this is his fault. I'm the stupid, fucking idiot. I look down and realize my fist is still clenched.

"Hey, don't worry." Jackson speaks in a low tone, "We're still going to teach those little shits a lesson."

Before the tailor returns from the back with my tux, Jackson swipes a seam ripper from behind the counter and grabs the chalk-marked pants the boys left on the rack. He ducks into a fitting room with them. It doesn't take him very long to unpick every third stitch in the butt seams of those assholes' pants. He's finished with the job and has discreetly placed the pants back on the rack before I'm even done trying on my suit.

chelsea

. . .

I STAND ON THE PORCH, watching Dean's taillights disappear down the dark, lonely road. I can still hear his motorcycle, even when I can't see it anymore, and I stay there for a little while longer, until it's just me and the cold, wet, foggy night.

He actually left. I can't fucking believe it.

And even though I'm furious, I'm also scared because I don't think it's safe out there on those roads, and he was so mad at me. It hardly seems fair, given our history. He was the one who stood me up. He was the one who broke my heart. Not the other way around. What does he think this is, anyway? Surely, he is planning to go back to LA and his real life eventually. If not sooner, then later. As soon as the summer stock season wraps.

My throat feels like I've swallowed a blade. I want to scream. And who cares if I do? If a perfectly composed and uptight small town art teacher screams in the woods, does anyone actually give a shit? I throw back my head and wail, a proper, horror movie, banshee howl. And then I do it again. And again, for good measure. By the third scream, the fight has gone out of me and the tears come. Thick, fat, hot tears, the likes of which I have not cried since I was seventeen. But there's nobody here to comfort me. I kind of miss my mom this time. As misguided as her offers to build and burn an effigy may be, it's still nice to have someone there who cares. And in the end, are we really so different? We both got screwed by our high school crush. Although not literally, in my case.

I go back inside and grab the strawberries, the open bottle of champagne, my phone, and the throw blanket Dean discarded and drag them all back out onto the covered porch. Then I park myself on one of the rocking chairs. I just can't stand the thought of being alone inside there. I don't want to look at that sheepskin rug or sleep in that bed where I thought all my foolish adolescent dreams were about to come true. Nope. I'm not going back there, I vow. I will sit here all night. But what am I sitting vigil and waiting for? Dean *left*.

Stupid. Stupid. Stupid Chelsea. And now I'm stranded here with nothing. Not even a clean pair of underwear. Why did I get on his bike this morning? Will I ever learn? I should be home in my studio right now, finishing the piece I started.

But The Shepherds Hut was my idea.

I should probably call somebody, but who? I've barely got any signal. I pop a chocolate-covered strawberry in my mouth and wash it down with the champagne that's already started to go flat. Alexis is in the air. Jackson is over on the coast with our mom. They couldn't get here till morning even if they left tonight. Emily is still in Italy with her family and Blaze. And Noah? I picture Mara answering the phone. Nope. There's no way in hell I'm calling him. I bite into another strawberry, spitting the stem over the side of the railing.

It was actually quite thoughtful of Ben to bring the basket. I think about how the night might have gone differently if I'd agreed to come here with Noah. But I can't picture being here with anyone else or doing those things with anyone besides

Dean. No other man has ever given me an orgasm. Even if it had been a complete accident.

He literally took me for a ride. And then he left me here, alone—again. I take another gulp of champagne and scream again. Dammit!

I've been waiting for ages to find my person. I think Alexis is right. I can't even imagine having sex with someone first and falling in love afterward. I don't want to have sex with just anyone. It has to be the right guy for me. And I've just never been able to picture it being anyone but Dean. Even if it's not destined to last.

I may as well just give up now. I'm going to die a virgin. *Alone.*

I can't help it. The tears won't stop. My nose is running too. I wipe it with the back of my hand and realize I've smeared chocolate all over my face, and I don't even care. They'll find me here at some future date, hair matted and eyes wild, and assume I've gone feral. That's the effect that Dean Riley has always had on me. He turns me into a wild and unhinged version of myself.

I shove the last strawberry into my mouth and slide a sticky finger over my phone screen. The last message from Alexis taunts me.

What does Dean think? Does he even know?

Well, he sure as shit does now!

I exit out of the text and see the stuck-in-progress message that Dean was sending himself. The photo of me in the bed, looking ridiculously fucking happy. Before I can delete it, it dings to alert me the message has gone through.

Splendid.

I hold up the phone and see there are two bars. I wonder where Dean is now and if he got the message? What if the sound startled him and he was taking a turn too fast in the rain and he rode off a cliff? I want to text him to ask him to let me know he's still alive, but I also don't want to risk being his cause of death. And I'm so mad at him. So incredibly mad at him. And myself. Why hadn't I just been honest with him? Maybe he would have run for the hills, like he literally has now. But maybe he wouldn't have.

God, I miss Murphy. I wish I had a dog to sit on my foot right this moment. Maybe I should get a dog.

I settle back into the rocking chair and swaddle myself more tightly, hitting play on an old playlist. Songs that remind me of high school—and Dean. I don't listen to it that often anymore. Just when I really feel sorry for myself and need a good soundtrack for a wallow. I drain the last of the champagne and rock to the music, soothing myself with tears and motion until I start to fall asleep.

I don't hear the motorcycle till it's pulling up into the driveway. The headlight washes over me, startling me awake, and I squint and squirm like a mole rat in the beam.

Dean cuts the engine and stomps onto the porch, holding his phone up like a torch to light the way.

"You came back," I marvel, not entirely sure if I'm awake or dreaming. Then I burp, tasting champagne and acidic berries. Definitely awake.

"I have a question for you," Dean says. "And I'd like you to tell me the truth."

"Okay," I answer warily.

Dean shines the flashlight on me and startles. "Jesus Christ, Chels! What the hell happened to you? Is that blood?" He reaches out to touch my face, and I shy away. I don't have to look in a mirror to guess what I look like. I swipe a finger across my cheek and lick it.

"Strawberries," I say. "Delicious. You missed out." I hope he knows that I'm not just talking about the berries.

"I'll have to take your word for it," he says, dropping down into the other rocking chair. He lifts the bottle of champagne, shaking it gently to verify that it's empty.

"You snooze you lose," I note, unable to hold back the snark in my voice. Still not just talking about the berries.

"It's freezing out here. Why don't we go inside," Dean suggests, "and I'll build a fire. And then maybe you can tell me what the hell you were talking about in those texts when you mentioned prom?"

dean

. . .

I START a fire and put the kettle on while Chelsea washes her face in the bathroom. The yurt begins to warm immediately. She's taking forever, and I really need answers. When I hear the shower come on, I feel like punching something. It was such a simple question.

What did she mean by "the thing that was supposed to happen at prom," and what did that have to do with me? *Maybe there was more to the prank she'd planned?* It doesn't add up. It doesn't make sense.

I hadn't taken her to prom. And I have no idea who she even went with, let alone what happened that night. That part couldn't have been about me.

I recall the painful episode at the tux shop where I found out she didn't actually need or want me to take her. I'd happily shelled out an extra hundred bucks for a weeklong tux rental, thinking I'd wear it twice. But then I found out the truth, thanks to those stupid kids Jackson and I had run into. I'd hated the way they trash-talked about Chelsea and her mom. Possibly even more than Jackson.

Those little assholes had gotten theirs, though. Bryce Holm's pants splitting at prom was one of those epic Ephron stories. At least his pals had been wearing boxers. But Bryce had gone to prom commando. It was even worse than when he puked all over himself at homecoming. His junk was on full display. The memes probably still exist, thanks to Jackson's programmatic sharing of them on every site and subreddit list his bots could hit.

But I still feel like I don't know the whole truth about what went down. Something, some essential part of the story, is missing. Why had she secured a hotel room? And then, why hadn't she even ended up going after she went to all that trouble? Chelsea has rejected every attempt I've made to contact her over the years. I've always assumed she was angry at me for having foiled her prank. Suddenly, I'm not quite as sure.

What exactly happened that week?

I dig around for more memories while I walk around the yurt, straightening things. I make the bed and put the dishes in the small sink, wishing I could just hit rewind on this whole day.

Eli's wedding was such a "big day" for my family. My dad had been so proud of his son, the high school football hero, marrying the prom queen cheerleader and stepping up to help run the family construction company. His dreams were finally coming true. Everyone had conveniently forgotten that she'd gone to prom with me. Even me. Brittany had only dated me in a bid to get Eli's attention. And it had worked.

I so desperately wanted my father's approval that summer. I wanted him to see my awards and achievements and the plum internship I'd scored with the production company down in Ashland. I was already starting to field job offers with production companies for after graduation. But if my dad had asked me again that week, I would have gladly come

219

home and worked for him. Especially if he'd asked before I went to pick up my tux.

Too little, too late. He was content passing the torch to Eli, the "good" son. The only son, from the sounds of the new "Riley and Son" signs he ordered for the home office and the trucks.

So, I'd made up my mind after the wedding. Why the hell would I want to ever come home again? I had bigger fish to fry. Hotter cheerleaders to date. Better cars to drive. I'd been mad. So mad. I couldn't get to Ashland quick enough. That summer, we'd staged *The Tempest*, and I'd slept my way through the cast. I'd been a real asshole. It was easy.

I shake out the down pillows, giving them a karate chop. I don't like the blue color scheme of the cushions. If I was styling this shepherd's hut yurt, I would have stuck to warmer colors. Neutrals, tans, and reds. Earth elements like that sheepskin rug. My eyes travel to the flickering firelight, casting a glow there, and I'm reminded, in a slow motion, multi-sensory, carnal flashback of everything I'd imagined this night might hold. The amber light on her skin. The golden strands of her hair tangled in my hands. Her scent— earthy paint and vanilla with a hint of roses. I can't. I can't let my mind keep going there.

She was just *using me* to get on with her life. Kind of like Brittany, in a funny way.

"Okay, I'm ready to talk," Chelsea says. She's scrubbed clean and wrapped in a waffle-weave robe. The steam coming from the bathroom smells of lavender. I close my eyes and inhale it like a palate cleanser. Mixed in with the wood smoke, it's an incredibly calming smell.

We eye each other warily. Chelsea curls up on a chair near the fireplace.

"Tea?" I ask, pouring the hot water into two mugs.

"Thanks," she says.

"There's only chamomile," I say, dunking the bag for her. "I hope it's okay." I hand her the tea and wait for her to speak. She blows on it, takes a sip, and sets it down on a side table. Then she stares at me, unblinkingly, in that way of hers. Like she has nothing to hide and is willing to be an open book to me. But I know that's not true. Chelsea has always been a book of secrets.

"So … prom?" I say tentatively, prompting her in case she forgot the topic.

"Prom," she repeats, nodding. I can't help but notice a slight tic. Her left eyelid is twitching. Both of her eyes still look puffy and red, something I really don't want to claim responsibility for.

But it's Chelsea. I have to resist the automatic urge to comfort her.

"You want to just tell me about what happened that night?" I ask, trying my best to be diplomatic. I remember my own fucked-up prom night, Brittany puking in the limo before falling asleep on the tile floor in the bathroom. The best laid plans. Except nobody got laid that night.

"Dean, are you fucking kidding me?" Chelsea looks incredulous now. And angry.

"Look," I say, holding up my hands. "I know it's none of my business, but it seems to be some kind of sticking point with you, and while I appreciate that you're taking steps to work out whatever it is, I don't see what it has to do with *me*."

Chelsea stands and strides to the bed, where she picks up one of the freshly fluffed throw pillows. She hugs it tightly to her chest as she paces in a semicircle.

"You don't see what it has to do with you?" she repeats. "How can you even say that?"

"Because I *wasn't there*, Chels. I didn't take you to prom."

"Exactly!" She flings the pillow at my face. I duck in the nick of time, but a small, ceramic owl figurine isn't so lucky. It smashes on the floor.

"What the ...?"

"You fucking asshole! It's bad enough that you stood me up. But the fact that you can't even be bothered to remember? That makes it so much worse. I hate you, Dean Riley. I can't believe that I ever thought you were anything special."

Suddenly, I wish I had something stronger than tea to drink. I sit myself down on the edge of the bed, attempting to process what she is saying.

"What the fuck are you even talking about, Chelsea? Have you lost your mind? Jackson said—"

"Jackson! Jackson? Jackson said what? I'll tell you what Jackson said. He told me that you'd decided to head down to Ashland early because you met a girl at Eli's wedding and the two of you really hit it off. And then he laughed at me for getting a hotel room. Said he just saved me from making an ass of myself. Because 'It's just prom, Chelsea. It doesn't matter. You've got your whole life ahead of you. You're not like those stupid girls who lose their virginity at their prom and end up pregnant. You're not like mom,'" she says, mimicking her brother's words.

She can't be telling the truth now, can she? I cradle my own head as I shake it side to side. No. *No, no, no!*

"He didn't." I reel in horror.

"That was the frosting, actually. Shitting on our mom like that. She's not perfect, but she hasn't had it easy, and she never once said she regretted keeping Jackson."

"So, the hotel room you got. You were thinking … you thought that after prom, you'd be having sex … with *me*?" I can barely say the words.

"I know it's stupid, right? But I was seventeen, and for what it's worth, I had a *plan*, Dean. I had protection and everything. And I don't know, maybe you would have laughed at me, maybe you would have let me down easy. I was ready to accept it if you did. But just leaving me hanging without a date for prom after I had gone to such great lengths to plan this incredibly important, life-changing night? That was cold. That was more than cold. It was cruel."

Chelsea dabs at her eyes, but there are no more tears. Perhaps she's run out. She seems to have run out of words.

"Your fucking brother," I say. Chelsea doesn't move a muscle.

"Yeah, he's a lot," she finally agrees. "But his heart was in the right place. Over time, I've come to realize he was probably right. I didn't want to be one of those girls. And I certainly didn't need to waste my time pining over someone like you."

"Someone *like* me? What the hell does that mean?"

"How should I characterize a guy who coldheartedly stands up his best friend's dopey little sister on what she has built up to be the biggest night of her life?"

"How about hoodwinked," I say. And I look up to meet her eyes. "Tricked. And dumbass. I was a total dumbass for not checking out your brother's story."

"What are you talking about now?" Chelsea stops pacing and looks at me through narrowed eyes. The tic is gone, though.

"There wasn't any girl at the wedding. I went down to Ashland because they'd said they needed me there ASAP, and I didn't want to spend any more time with my family that week. And most of all, I didn't think you wanted or needed me. Whatever. I thought you'd made other plans for prom."

"Why would you have thought that?" Chelsea asks.

"Because of the whole incident with Bryce Holm." I shake my head again.

"Who? What?" Chelsea takes a seat in the chair again, tucking a leg under herself. Her hair towel comes loose and she takes it off, shaking out her mane and hanging the towel on a hook by the fire. It acts like a diffuser, spreading the smell of her. I'm reaching my limit. My mind wanders back to the text messages with Alexis, and I have to remind myself that even though my assumptions about the past are obviously wrong, she's still just trying to "get me out of her system so she can get on with her life."

I go on, anxious to finish clearing the air.

"Jackson was with me when I picked up my tux for the wedding—and prom—or so I thought at the time. We ran into Bryce and some other guys, and they were talking about who was going with who and who had hotel rooms. Your name came up. There was a girl there, too, who said you helped her get a cheap room."

"Fucking Danielle," Chelsea says. "She had such a big mouth. And you know what's funny? She *did* get knocked up that night. She's divorced now. Works at the supermarket pharmacy. She'll tell the whole town you have herpes if you buy wart remover."

I bite my lip at the random non sequitur. "I'll have to remember to buy my wart meds elsewhere."

"But I still don't get what any of this has to do with you standing me up," she challenges.

"When we heard Bryce talking, and he said you had reserved a room and a bunch of other bullshit, I wanted to kick the shit out of him. Jackson stopped me. And then he said you were planning on going with some other guy and hadn't gotten around to telling me." I think harder. That wasn't quite right. "Actually, I think what he said was that you were just winding me up. That it was all a joke you were playing on me."

"And you believed him?" Chelsea is the one shaking her head now.

"I don't know … it made sense at the time. I was a little surprised that you were even asking me to take you, why you thought you still needed me. I couldn't imagine why you'd still be hung up on me. You were gorgeous, Chels. And so cool. Any guy would have been lucky," I tell her. And since we're finally telling the truth, I don't stop there. After a moment, I continue, speaking more slowly and quietly. "*I* would have been lucky. I was really looking forward to taking you. I'd picked out the flowers and everything. I was really disappointed. More than that, I was hurt."

"I'm going to fucking kill him." Chelsea polishes off her cup of tea and slams down the cup.

"Get in line," I respond.

The log crackles, and we both sit there for a few minutes, staring at the flames and processing.

"Thank you for coming back," she finally says.

"The roads really weren't safe," I concede. "And I was going back over the texts in my head. It didn't make sense." *And then that photo came through. That damn photo. I'm not deleting it.*

"Why didn't you say something sooner?" I sigh, still staring into the fire. I'm not sure if I'm talking to her or to myself.

"I'll sleep on the couch. It's way too short for you." Chelsea collects a pillow and takes the throw blanket from the bed. "I can call for a ride in the morning if you don't want to take me back."

"No, I'll take you back," I say. "And I'd like to repay Noah for this place. It was presumptuous of me to come here with you on his dime."

"It was presumptuous of me to use the reservation like that," Chelsea objects. "You were just being a guy."

"Come on, Chelsea, that's bullshit, and you know it," I protest.

"Look, Dean, we both know you're not here to stay. When the summer's over, you'll be back in Cali. It really sucks what Jackson did. But all things considered, maybe it was for the best. Maybe he saved us both from making a terrible mistake."

"Is that really what you think?" I ask.

"I don't know. But yeah, maybe it is," she asserts, punching the pillow and snuggling on the sofa in front of the fireplace.

"Maybe," I say. I'm not sure she's right, but suddenly, I'm too tired to argue. I just want to stretch out on the bed and fall into a deep, dreamless sleep.

"This clears up one thing for me, at least," Chelsea speaks up again before we both drift off.

"What's that?"

"It explains how those photos of Bryce Holm's ass went viral," she says.

chelsea

. . .

TWELVE YEARS AGO ...

*Items to Pack for Prom Night: A List by
Chelsea Porter*

Hairspray
Bobby pins—for updo
Breath mints
Clear nail polish
Tylenol
Converse sneakers
Jeans/tee
Safety pins—just in case
Blotting paper
Candles and lighter
Bubble bath
Nightshirt
Condoms (!!!)

"Has anyone seen my overnight bag?" Jackson barges into my room just as I'm shoving a box of condoms into the canvas duffel bag I got down from the shelf in the garage. I scramble to shove it down farther where he can't see it.

"Oh, good. There it is. Give it here. I need it."

"No can do. Get another bag," I say.

"You get another bag. That one's mine," Jackson demands imperiously.

"No, it's not yours. I don't see your name on it. It was Dad's. He left it here for whoever wanted to use it," I argue.

"Yeah, and I'm the only one who uses it." Jackson swipes at the bag.

"Wrong, obviously, because I am using it right now!" I say, batting his hand away.

"Not anymore." Jackson swoops toward my bed and snags the bag, spilling out the contents on my bed. "What are you packing for, anyway? You're not going anywhere, are you?"

"Stop! Cut it out!" I yell. All of my stuff tumbles out.

"Condoms, Chelsea? Seriously?" Jackson says, picking up the box. "Are you running away from home to a brothel?"

"Shut up," I say. "They're for prom. For a *friend*. A bunch of us girls got rooms at a hotel." I am not about to tell Jackson about my plans to spend the night with Dean. It's none of his business.

"I'm not judging." Jackson shrugs. "But I'd be careful if I were you. I'd hate for you to get a reputation. People already talk enough shit about Mom around here."

"You think I don't know that?" I roll my eyes at my brother. "And so does she."

"Well, maybe she should be a better example for you," Jackson says. "You don't want to end up pregnant in high school like she did, do you?"

"Are you kidding me, Jackson?" My mouth falls open. "I can't believe you're even saying this."

"I just think it might have been better all the way around if Mom and Dad had never hooked up in high school."

"Then neither of us would be here."

"Maybe." Jackson shrugs. "But I bet they both would have had much happier lives, and we wouldn't have had to deal with all their dysfunctional bullshit, and maybe Murphy would still be around."

Seriously? He's bringing up Murphy now?

"I think you're being dysfunctional now. Mom can date whomever she wants. She's happy for the first time in years. I can't believe that you, of all people, would judge her for dating and having some fun."

"I heard some guys talking, Chels. It wasn't okay. And one of them mentioned you."

"What guys?" I ask.

"Bryce Holm," he says.

"That tool is just mad because I turned him down for prom," I say. "Why are you even listening to him? Everyone knows Bryce is a loser."

"Bryce Holm asked you to prom?" Jackson looks vaguely amused. "And you shut that asswipe down?"

"Yep." I lunge for the bag, narrowly missing it. He holds it just out of my reach.

"Good for you. I thought Dean was taking you because nobody else even asked you," Jackson says.

"No, he's taking me because nobody else I *wanted to go with* asked me," I say. "Now, give me back my bag. I'm really busy. I've got a lot to do to get ready between now and then, and I would appreciate it if you'd just give it back."

"And you wanted to go with Dean? Seriously? I thought you got over your crush.

"Shut up," I say. I'm not even going to honor his comment. I've occasionally wondered if he's a bit jealous of my relationship with Dean. But I don't think it's that. Jackson just doesn't understand. He doesn't see me as a peer. I'm still twelve in his eyes. There's nothing I can do about that right now. I change the subject. "Where are you going now, anyway? You just got home."

"About that …" Jackson is looking at me warily. He sets the bag down and doesn't try and fight me when I snatch it back this time. His eyes are a bit sad, and his look gives me the chills. It's an about-to-deliver-bad-news kind of look.

"What is it?" I ask. "Is it Dad?" A thousand scenarios go through my head. He could be in the hospital again. Or jail. Or he could be dead. "Is he …" I can't finish the sentence.

"Oh, God no. It's not Dad. It's just … prom is tomorrow, right?"

"Yes." I stick out my chin defiantly. "Obviously. That's why I was packing my overnight bag and prepping."

"Well." Jackson sighs and looks skyward. "This is awkward, and I hate to be the one to tell you, but I think Dean forgot about it. He met some girl at his brother's wedding, and they decided to head down to Ashland early. He invited me to come down for the weekend."

"Sure," I say, rolling my eyes. "Very funny, Jackson. Nice try. I'm not falling for your prank." I commence shoving my stuff back into the bag.

"Chels, I am not kidding. You can call him yourself. See? Here's the text he sent me earlier with the address of the place." Jackson holds up his phone. "Shit. He's going to feel terrible when I remind him. I'm really sorry. I hope it's not a big deal."

A text comes through on Jackson's phone while he's talking. It's from Dean. It's a picture of an outdoor theater and a keg.

> What time are you getting here? Crew party tomorrow night.

Jackson is not kidding.

My face is hot, and my skin feels too tight. Everything is itchy, irritating. My clothing, the carpet, the walls. I'm having an allergic reaction to my life.

This isn't real. This isn't happening. Dean would never do this to me.

I glance over at the dress hanging on my closet door. I might have been able to return it, if only I hadn't handsewn all the beads onto it. Three hundred dollars. Plus, the prom tickets. That motherfucker. How could he?

"Chels, are you okay?" Jackson asks tentatively.

"Yeah, whatever," I say, dumping out the bag of stuff on the bed. "Who cares. Prom is stupid. I didn't really want to go anyway."

I will not let him see me cry. I will not let him see me cry. I will not.

"You sure? I mean, you can still go, right? It's not like Dean was your real date. He's just a friend. I'm sure you can find someone else to go with."

231

"Nah." I shrug, pretending to be fine. "My friends were just pressuring me. I'm glad to have an easy out. Now I can stay home and paint. I've been meaning to repaint this room."

My mom had mentioned we'd need to cover up the mural before she listed the house, and I'd resisted because I didn't want to cover all the work Dean and I had done together.

"Okay, if you're sure. Can I get you a smoothie or anything before I go?" Jackson offers. "I'm catching a bus in an hour."

"No, Mom will be home soon. I was planning to eat dinner with her." I hand him the bag. "You'd best get a move on if you're leaving in an hour."

I have to get him out of my room. I'm not sure how much longer I can hold back the tears.

"Honestly, Chels, I know you don't feel this way right now, but you're probably better off skipping it. My prom sucked. I ended up paying a fortune in cleaning charges when Dean's date puked all over our limo. And my date ended up making out with her best friend and coming out that night. I wished I never went," Jackson says. "But I'll be sure to give Dean hell about this. I can't believe he didn't even call you."

"Don't bother," I say. And I mean it. There's really no point. I'm never speaking to Dean Riley ever again.

dean

. . .

WHEN I WAKE UP, I notice there's a note from Chelsea in the kitchen, telling me she's gone for a walk. The yurt is still warm from the fire I built last night.

I make myself some coffee and take it out on the porch while I wait for her to come back. The weather is warmer today, but foggier. The overnight rain has left a mist. It's not long before I hear her footsteps crunching up the gravel drive.

"Good morning," I say.

"Morning." She nods shyly back at me. She's holding a small sketchbook and some wildflowers.

"You woke early," I comment.

"Teacher's life. I'm used to waking at the crack of dawn. I went for a walk to see if I could get some signal, and I ran into Ben. He's going to give me a lift down into town, and I'll get an uber from there."

"You don't have to do that," I say. "I'm perfectly happy to take you home."

"I think it's for the best." Chelsea shakes her head sadly. "This was a mistake."

"Was it?" I ask. I have so many other questions I want to ask her. So much I want to discuss as a follow-up to last night's revelation.

"I think it was," she says.

"We have unfinished business, Chelsea."

"I don't know. I think we dodged a bullet." She presses the wildflowers carefully into her book and tucks it under her arm.

It doesn't feel like I dodged a bullet. It feels like I got hit. Square in the chest. Last night was awkward and awful in so many ways. But it was also amazing, and frankly, a long time in the making. I have feelings for Chelsea—I always have—and I don't want to pretend I don't or that I didn't.

"I just really, really want to punch your brother in the face right now," I say.

Chelsea just stands there, tracing circles in the gravel with the toe of her boot.

"Yeah, I'm not sure what I'm going to say to him," she admits, "if I ever speak to him again. I suspect his heart may have been in the right place, but he really fucked things up."

"For both of us." I take a sip of my coffee, but it has already gone cold.

"Yeah, well," she says, "I should probably get my shit together. Ben will be here any minute." She comes up the stairs and I stand up, too, catching her arm as she passes.

"Don't you want to talk about anything else?" I ask. "You were ready to sleep with me last night. I didn't realize how big of a deal that was for you. But I think you're ignoring the fact that it was also a big deal for me."

"Oh, come on!" She shakes me off. "You can't convince me that it was *that* big of a deal. It's just sex, right? I'm sure

234

you've had one-night stands and plenty of insignificant sex before."

"Not with you," I say. "There's no way sex could be insignificant with you. And I'm not interested in a one-night stand."

Chelsea ignores me, rushing into the yurt and looking around for her things. She's yanking her phone charger out from the outlet as I come in.

"Didn't you hear me?" I ask, getting frustrated by her lack of a response.

"I did," she says.

"And you don't have anything else to say? Were you really just planning to use me to 'get on with your life,' Chelsea? What does that even look like? What does your post V Card life look like?"

"I don't know!" She rolls her eyes and shoves her charger in her small backpack, along with the notebook. "I guess it doesn't involve me wringing my hands over every guy I date, trying to decide whether he's worthy of being 'the one' to the point that I drive myself crazy and don't end up sleeping with any of them."

"Has that really been a problem up until now?" I ask. I'm curious and a bit confused. The Chelsea I know is a passionate person. She's always been passionate.

"Yes, it has. It kind of gets in the way, if you want to know. I was hoping to lose my virginity to you before I started college because I knew I wouldn't regret doing it with you. I didn't have any expectations that it would lead to anything, back then. I just thought it would set me free, like it wouldn't be this 'thing' I had to worry about anymore." She pauses. "That actually sounds kind of stupid now, but there it is, since you asked."

"So, you were planning to use me back then too?" The words taste bitter in my mouth. "Thanks, Chels. I wish I'd gotten the brief. Maybe Jackson did do us a favor after all."

"Oh, come on, Dean. What do you think would have happened if he hadn't intervened? Would you actually have slept with me? Would we have gotten married and lived happily ever after? You know how that worked out for my mom."

"I don't know," I say. "Maybe? What's so terrible about that? It worked out okay for my parents."

"Yeah, but your dad never had big dreams about making it somewhere else. He never left."

"So that's your problem with me? I'm too much like your dad?" Anger flares in my chest, along with hurt. "That's kind of a low blow, Chels."

"I don't mean it that way. I know you're nothing like him. But your dreams have never been thwarted, Dean. You don't have a wife and kids anchoring you to a town you couldn't wait to get the hell away from. I'm happy here in Ephron. I have a good life. A quiet life. I'm just an ordinary art teacher."

"No, Chelsea, you are not ordinary. You're extraordinarily gifted and talented, and I'm not sure why you want to blend into the background. You should be center stage. You should at least take credit for your work."

"Stop it," she says. "Just stop it, Dean. Like I said, we dodged a bullet. It's a good thing it didn't happen then and probably an even better thing it didn't happen now. I'm sorry I was being so selfish. I guess I just got carried away by the memories."

A car horn honks outside. "Ben's here," Chelsea says. There's a single tear streaming down her face, and I want to wipe it away. I want to kiss her. I want to tell her that we have the rest of our lives to make new memories.

I feel my own eyes starting to prickle. "So, I left, so I did some other stuff. Why does everyone I love feel like they have to punish me for that?"

She freezes in the doorway when I say the word love.

"I guess," she says without turning around, "it's because we can't stand the thought of losing you again."

Then, without another word, she leaves.

chelsea

· · ·

I CAN'T GET into my studio quickly enough. I change into my painter's overalls and crank my playlist of show tunes and punk classics. Then I turn off the phone. The world can piss off for the next forty-eight hours.

This piece. I'm not coming out till I get it done.

I unlock the door to my studio and survey where I left off. The high-ceilinged room where I paint is essentially a blank box. White walls and theatrical lighting. The windows are draped with sheer, white fabric that lets the light in and keeps prying eyes out. Centered at the far end of the room is a mini stage composed of three set walls and a platform that I drape and paint and repaint to create the backgrounds for my work. My camera is set up on a tripod facing the stage. Everything is reflected in the mirror on the back of the door. There's also a monitor mounted to the back wall behind the camera that allows me to see what the camera sees.

I've made some progress on this concept, but I'm not ready to paint myself in. I've still got some work to do on the background part, and there's a headpiece I have to make that will help me create the illusion that I'm looking in two directions at once. I'm planning to photograph my painted face first. I'll go back and Photoshop it into the larger image after I've got the rest worked out.

I'm happy with it so far. It's ready for the personal touches. I sketch Murphy into the puffy, cloud-filled sky behind the lemonade stand. He's an angel dog, holding a bow like Cupid. His arrow is drawn and pointed at me. Another arrow is sticking out of a bag of sugar on the counter. The sugar is spilling onto the ground.

On the kissing booth side, my dad's old guitar is leaning against the wall, two strings snapped. The sky is stormy and filled with lightning. In the foreground, I've staged a bunch of roses in an overturned vase. I'm planning on holding a big knife with a curved blade in one hand and a lemon in the other. If I position myself the way I'm thinking, the lemon will be my shield and the knife a lightning rod.

Who needs therapy, right?

Time passes in a blur as I get into the flow of my work. Everything drops away, and it's just me, the colors, the music, and a kaleidoscopic barrage of emotions. The music is a catalyst, helping me release the feelings and express them. Sometimes it feels like I'm forcing out the toxins. And sometimes it feels like I'm applying armor, painting on a thicker second skin.

I can live without Dean Riley. I've done it before and I'll do it again. It's better this way. I repeat this like a mantra.

I don't know what I was thinking, taking him to The Shepherds Hut. That I could turn back time? That sleeping with him would somehow make me more whole?

I smear together two shades of red, feeling my face grow hot as I remember the conversation on the motorcycle. I'm so frustrated with myself. Confused, frustrated, and embarrassed. How will I ever look Dean in the eye again?

239

And I have no idea what I'm going to say to Jackson. I can't have a conversation with him till I've calmed down. Maybe next week. After I finish this piece.

I mix in a smidge of black to darken the colors, matching the blood tones of the crushed, silk roses. Then I rip off a few petals from my props to scatter on the floor. Tearing the flowers apart feels pretty damn good right now.

Of all the excuses and explanations I've imagined Dean might have served up for what happened on the night of my prom, none of them even remotely resembled the truth. How could Jackson have lied to both of us like that? And why?

I kick the guitar, and it goes clattering across the room. One of the pegs pops off. Good. I'm fine with the damage. It's a wonder that this old thing is merely scarred and not entirely smashed to smithereens. I've certainly come close on a couple of occasions, but electric guitars, it turns out, are really hard to smash. This fucking guitar has given me two cuts and a black eye. I don't even know why I've kept it around so long. Enough already. After this piece is done, I'm putting it in the trash. I'm moving on.

I have a pretty good idea why Jackson lied. He was trying to save me from the humiliation of rejection. And he was trying to save Dean from the mortification of being propositioned by his best friend's kid sister. He thought he was doing both of us a favor. He was so wrong. Or maybe he was right. Either way, he had no idea. None at all. Because we've never discussed it.

I got so good at pretending I didn't give a shit that it practically became second nature. For the last ten years, I've been pretending to be this carefree, simple, happy-go-lucky high school art teacher with quirky taste in music and fiction. I've convinced everyone that this is all there is to me. I don't know myself anymore.

But Dean knew me. He knew me in the parking lot of the school, and he recognized me in the images in my hallway. All my friends and family members have walked past those pieces dozens of times. A few have commented that they thought my artwork was "cool," but none of them ever considered the possibility that I'd made them myself. That it was literally me in the pictures. Not once had it occurred to them. Dean knew the minute he saw it. Somehow, after all these years, Dean saw me.

I turn up the volume on a Kings of Leon song, remembering, letting the feelings stream over me. "Sex on Fire." It's everything I pictured when I envisioned myself with Dean. Struck by lightning, burning up the sky.

What if we *had* gone to my prom? What if Jackson had never intervened? Dean asked me that question this morning, and I've been doing my damnedest not to think about it ever since because it's the most taboo fantasy for me. The most painful and embarrassing dream, considering the fact that he'd left town and stood me up without even bothering to call me. I locked the door to this particular fantasy long ago. But now the door is cracked, and I can't stop myself from peeking in.

I have new information now. Vital information. Dean had wanted it too. He'd wanted me. Possibly as much as I'd wanted him. The feeling of his lips on mine. His skin on my skin. Just the memory of it makes me feel drunk. The way the world fell away, and it was only the two of us.

It's not hard to let my imagination run wild as I strip naked and begin to paint myself into the scene. It won't be the final version. I will probably need to attempt this several times before I get it right.

I can't stop myself from wishing Dean was here, imagining his hands applying the paint all over my body.

dean

. . .

IN THE PAST TWENTY-FOUR HOURS, I've barely slept. I've been too busy, going in circles in my mind and on my motorcycle. My first instinct was to jump on the bike and ride until I got to the Oregon Coast, so I could smash my feelings into my old friend's face with my fist. But after a quick reckoning with my better self, I turned back. I didn't need to go off like that. What good would it do? What I did need was the time to cool down and process all the new information revealed by our trip into the mountains.

It's been a lot to process. It changes the way I look at everything. When I asked Chelsea the "what if" question, I wasn't just asking her. I was filtering my memories through the same sieve. What if we had gone to prom that night? What if we had admitted our feelings to Jackson and everyone? What if we'd admitted our feelings to *ourselves*?

We'd been as much in denial about our feelings as everyone else, hadn't we? I can't put all the blame on Jackson, much as I want to.

I'm certainly not blameless. Why hadn't I said something to Jackson? Why hadn't I said something to *her*? I can't even picture her sitting alone in her room on the night of her prom.

How much had she hated me? No wonder she hadn't responded the times I'd reached out. As shitty as I felt, with my wounded ego, I suspect she felt worse. So much worse. My absence that night was a betrayal. It's a miracle that she'd spoken to me at all, let alone gone along with my silly prank when I got home.

I park the motorcycle on the street near the park where Chelsea and I chatted when I first got back to town. There's nobody there this morning, which is perfect. I need a quiet place to sit while I make this call. And I can't be indoors. I need more space. I kick one of the stupid, bouncing mushrooms as I pass by on the way to "our" bench.

God, I'd been excited when I saw that Facebook like from her, after all this time. The slightest scrap of acknowledgment from her, and I'd been ready to come running. Even if I hadn't already been on my way home, I'd have wanted to come. And seeing her again, that day … it was like everything clicked. Like no time had passed. We were different. But the essentials, all the feelings I was feeling, were all the same.

> You coming soon? Mom and Dad are already here getting the egg hunt set up.

Eli texts that my parents are already at his house. He's hidden a rabbit costume in the back of his truck, which he parked down the street from his place.

> Hope you're close. Braden's only got two hours before naptime, and he's going to be useless after that. Some of the neighbors are bringing their kids over too.
> Hippety-hop, bro!

How appropriate that I've got to wear a costume to my family's celebration. It only serves to highlight how much I feel like an outsider. When was the last time I'd felt like I belonged? It had to be before my brother got married. That was the last time I'd seriously considered coming back to Ephron.

The week of Eli and Brittany's wedding I'd finally been ready to consider coming home and working for my dad. That was when I'd first started to speculate about the community center and the amphitheater. I had decided I could still be involved with the theater in my spare time, while taking my rightful place beside my dad and my brother in the family business.

Is that what would have happened if I'd taken Chelsea to her prom? Would we be living next door to Eli now, decorating Easter baskets for our own kids? Who'd be the bunny then?

The alternative time lines plague me. Infinite possibilities. I could drive myself crazy considering all of them. It has to stop. I pick up the phone and make the call. I've got to get it over with before I head to my brother's house.

"Hey, Dean." Jackson picks up on the second ring. "How's it going? Are you spending Easter with your family?"

"It's going," I say, attempting to keep my tone even when all I want to do is shout WHAT THE FUUUUCK loud enough to instantly render him deaf. Instead, I say, "I'm on my way to Eli's now. How's your mom?"

"She's really good," Jackson says. I can hear a smile in his voice. "She finally caught a keeper. Ed's a great guy. She didn't want me to run their profiles with my AI, but I did it anyway and didn't tell her. Perfect match. Gives me hope."

"Why do you have to do that?" I ask. I wasn't sure how to broach the topic of his big lie, but it seems he's given me the perfect in with his admission about his "benevolent" meddling in his mother's love life. I take a deep breath. "Why do you have to insert yourself into other people's lives like that?"

"Uh-oh. What's wrong?" Jackson asks.

"Have you heard from Chelsea?"

"What is it? Is Chelsea okay?" I hear Jackson's mom in the background. I hadn't realized I was on speaker.

"Chelsea's just fine, Mrs. Porter," I reassure her. "I just saw her yesterday. Not to worry."

"Oh good. And Happy Easter, Dean. I'm glad to hear you and Chelsea are speaking."

"Thanks, Mrs. Porter," I say.

"So, what's up now?" Jackson asks distractedly. I can tell I've already lost his attention. He's already dismissed whatever seemingly small drama his sister might be involved in. He's probably back to thinking about his AI and using me and his sister as guinea pigs, playing us like pawns. A part of me still wishes that I'd driven down there to punch him.

"Maybe you want to take me off speaker?"

"Yeah, uh … okay." Jackson does something, and the background noise dissipates. "Better now?"

"Chelsea and I had a long talk about prom," I say.

"Ugh. Our prom or hers?" Jackson asks, a little too flippantly for my taste.

"What do you think, Asshole?" I jab.

Jackson makes a sound that is halfway between a groan and a sigh. "Aw, shit. Okay. I guess you guys did finally figure it out, then. This has been a long time coming. But honestly, Dean, you have to admit, I did you both a tremendous favor. I mean, even without the wisdom of hindsight, it was a kindness."

"You think you did us a *favor*?" I ask. "How do you figure? You lied to us."

"Yeah, but do you remember what those guys at the tux place were saying about her getting a hotel room? I knew she had a crush on you. She was a really intense kid. And you were always such a good sport about it. But I was afraid she was going to try and proposition you or something. It was kind of weird that she even wanted to go to prom, honestly. It wasn't really her scene. I think her friends talked her into it, and the hotel room too. How awkward would that have been? For both of you. I don't know what she was thinking. She would have been embarrassed about it to this day. It was bad enough that you had to be her pity date."

"Pity date?" I snap. "You think I was her pity date?"

"Weren't you?" Jackson lowers his voice now before going on. "You heard the way those guys were talking about my mom too. I didn't want Chelsea's rep getting trashed. As adults, I think we can agree that the whole episode was rife with cringe. It had the potential to be the sort of thing people take years to get over. Trust me, I've seen it time and again in my research for the dating app."

"You Massive. Fucking. Idiot," I growl, rubbing my temples. "Has it ever occurred to you that people also take years to get over getting stood up for prom? And what about me? You lied to me too. You made me the bad guy. And for what?"

"Come on, Dean. I mean, she was a little tweaked about not being able to return the dress, but she said she didn't care. She was only going to prom because of the peer pressure. We talked about it."

"You're wrong," I say. "Wrong about her and wrong about me. How dare you do that to us?" I can't sit still. I have to pace and kick another mushroom. It bounces back without any sympathy.

"I knew this day would come, but I didn't think you'd be so bent out of shape about it. Honestly, I thought the whole reason the two of you pulled that prank on me at The Grumpy Stump was because you'd figured the whole prom thing out. I thought that was your way of getting me back," Jackson says.

"Figured what out? Getting you back for what?" I hear Jackson's mom in the background.

"Nothing, Mom," Jackson shushes her. "Just a prank."

"Holy shit, Jackson. Give me the phone." Her voice is getting closer.

"No!" Jackson argues. "This is just guy talk."

"The hell it is."

I hear a scuffle as, I can only assume, Mrs. Porter wrestles her son for the phone. It clatters to the ground, and I hear him yelp in pain. "Ow! Mom! That was my shin!" Jackson says.

"Serves you right," Mrs. Porter says. And then she puts the phone to her ear.

"Hi, Dean," she says in a perfectly pleasant tone of voice. "Sorry about that. Jackson wasn't being cooperative. I assume you two were just chatting about why you stood my daughter up for prom?"

"We were," I say. I can't help but smile. Mrs. Porter has always had a certain unbreakable quality about her. She's not like other moms. Perhaps that comes from having to hold her head high through the many challenges of being married to Jackson and Chelsea's unreliable rocker dad. Whatever. I can see where Chelsea gets her spirit.

"Mom, this is between me and Dean." Jackson is protesting. "Give me back the phone."

"It's between you and Dean and Chelsea," his mom says. Her voice is muffled, as if she is holding the phone away or speaking over her shoulder as she chastises her son. "And me. You are in my house. What did you expect? This is a small cottage. I couldn't help overhearing. For God's sake, Jackson, how did you turn out to be such an idiot? I love you, but any fool could see that Dean and Chelsea were crazy about each other. Sometimes I think your dad must have dropped you on your head when you were a baby."

There are further sounds of a scuffle, and I can hear another voice, possibly Ed, telling Jackson to back off and let his mom say her piece.

"So first off," Mrs. Porter resumes talking to me and pauses to mess with the phone, pressing several buttons that have me holding the phone away from my ear. "Wait … how does your phone work, Jackson? Just a sec. I'm putting you back on speaker." She fiddles some more with the phone, finally succeeding. "I think I owe you an apology, Dean. I've spent the better part of the past ten years hating you for standing my daughter up. Such a shame because I always liked you. I just couldn't figure out what went wrong. I always thought you'd be her first."

"Ugh, MOM! Why?" Jackson is groaning in the background.

"I like you too," I say, biting my lip and rubbing my forehead. This phone call is not going as expected. I don't know whether to laugh or cry about my day so far. And I have yet to don a bunny suit.

"Were you cursed by some sort of stupid fairy, Jackson?" Mrs. Porter addresses her son. "Just because I got knocked up with you at *my* prom is no reason to ruin everyone else's. Shame on you. Whatever your sister and Dean had planned that night, it was none of your business. Get your butt back in here."

"I'm just getting an ice pack," he says, from a distance.

"Okay. Actually, that's all I wanted to say. I'm sure Jackson will find a way to make this up to both of you. Right Jackson?" she concludes.

"Got it, Mom." I hear Jackson coming closer. "Give me back the phone now?"

"You mind my words, Jackson. And you take care, Dean."

Jackson snatches the phone back, shutting down the speaker function, and places it to his ear. "I can't believe my own mother just kicked me in the shin."

"Yeah, well," I say, "I would have punched you in the face if I was there. I almost came there to do just that, but I had some other plans for today that I couldn't get out of."

"So, you were really into her." Jackson sighs. "And she was really into you. Fucking hell. I didn't know. Why didn't either of you say something to me?"

"I'm sure that would have gone great," I say, voice dripping with sarcasm. "Tell me, didn't you think it was strange that she hasn't spoken to me for the last ten years?" I ask.

"I didn't really think it was a big deal. I mean, she hasn't stayed in touch with a lot of people who have left town, and you were *my* friend, not hers. I guess I thought maybe she was embarrassed because she'd had a crush on you, and that's maybe why she didn't want to talk about it. I mean, we joke about it all the time."

"No. You tease her. Relentlessly. And, as it turns out, cruelly."

"Oh, my God. Holy shit. I really am a massive, fucking idiot," Jackson groans. "Although, on the plus side"—his voice perks up—"this confirms everything that my AI was saying about you two."

Does he really sound smug about this? Too soon.

"I don't give a shit about your AI, Dude," I say.

"That's fair," Jackson attempts to assuage me. "I'm so sorry, Dean. I don't know what else to say. I never meant to hurt either of you. The opposite, if anything."

"But you did hurt us. Both of us," I say. There's an awkward pause as we both sit with this information. It's a bit of a lightning strike. It's going to take time to assess the damage. I go on. "I honestly don't know how you're going to make it right, but I have faith you'll try. Starting with Chelsea. You better kiss her ass. She's home, and I don't think she has any plans for Easter. Maybe you should give her a call."

––––––––

I don't exactly feel better when I get to Eli's, but I do feel okay enough to put on a bunny suit for my nephew and pose for photos with all the toddlers on the block. It's bittersweet, watching their shining faces as they shyly approach me. I may be the most jaded Easter Bunny of all time.

"Turn back now! It's all a trap! Your friends will betray you, and true love will evade you," I want to yell.

"Is it true that your Easter Bunny won an Oscar?" one of the assembled moms whispers to Brittany. She's speaking in low tones, so as not to tip off the kids, but of course, that only makes them pay closer attention.

"Is Oscar Grouch here? Where? I want Trashcan Man! I wuv Trashcan Man!" wails a tiny, little girl. When I try to placate her with a chocolate egg, she knees me in the groin. "Go home, you big, dumb bunny!"

Out of the mouths of babes.

Once the neighbors leave, and Braden is down for his nap, we finally sit down for the family meal. By some miracle, we make it through the main course without arguing. Eli regales us with tales about toddler hip-hop, and my mom and Brittany discuss plans for building an addition on my brother's house.

My dad weighs in on materials for the kitchen reno, and I alternate between pretending I'm a fly on the wall and thinking about the conversation with Jackson.

We're still sitting around the dining table when I suddenly get a text from Zara. I wait till my dad goes to the kitchen to grab a few more beers to slip my phone under the table and read it.

> How's the family stuff going?

I'm doing Easter with my parents and my brother and my nephew rn.

I also type my response under the table. My father doesn't like seeing cell phones at the table, and the last thing I need today is more drama.

> I'll add you to my Club 33 membership if you send me a pic of yourself in the bunny suit.

Not happening.

> Aw, come on, Dean. How am I going to convince my future kids that you're the fun uncle if I can't show them a picture of you in a bunny costume?

My dad returns with the bottles, and the displeasure shows on his face as soon as he catches me texting under the table. He sets my drink down by my plate, but not before I read the next message. It's not one I can ignore.

> We're going to lose our director. He's waffling. He doesn't want to work for such a new company. You have to talk to him. I can't be you. You gotta get your ass down here, stat.

Where did you hear this?

> We just had lunch.

On Easter? I thought you weren't supposed to work this week, Z. You're supposed to be taking it easy for the rest of this trimester.

> I am taking it easy. I gotta eat, though, and I love the salads at The Ivy. Can you get down here by tomorrow?

"Is that really necessary, Son? We're having a family meal here." My dad looks pointedly at my phone.

"It's no big deal, Dad." Brittany stands to clear plates. "We're pretty much done here, unless anyone wants seconds?"

"Thanks, Britt, you've outdone yourself. I'll take seconds!" Eli smiles proudly at his tradwife.

Zara's text is cause for concern. Without the director's commitment, I'm worried all the other contracts for the summer stock theater are at risk. Everything could still easily fall apart. She's right. The only way it's all getting sorted is if I fly back to LA for a week or two and meet with everyone face-to-face. I'm kicking myself for leaving before the ink dried.

> How soon can you be down here? Can you come tomorrow morning? I can arrange a private flight if you need.

My dad raises his eyebrows at me, challenging me not to look back down at the phone.

"I'm sorry," I say, "but it's work. It's kind of an emergency. I have to take it."

If anyone should understand this, it's my dad. How many holiday meals did he miss because of work emergencies? Someone always had a burst pipe or a roof leak. I can't recall a single Christmas dinner that wasn't interrupted by something. So, he should really be giving me some space right now instead of scowling at me when I glance back down to reply.

"What kind of theater emergency is more important than your family? I thought we were going to have a nice meal together," he says.

"Kevin, please. It's Easter, and we were all getting along so well," my mom attempts to intervene.

"No really, I want to know," my dad demands. "Is Titanium Man demanding a last-minute color change for the costume on his next movie?"

"This is about the theater here, actually," I say, standing to go outside to call Zara and finish the conversation on the phone. I am not even going to point out that the Titanium Man franchise has already wrapped its final episode. Everyone knows that. Except for my dad. "I'm going to have to go back to LA tomorrow. I have to make a few calls and book a flight."

"If you leave this table now, you better not come back," my dad says.

"Seriously, Dad? What is your problem?" I explode. "What do you want from me? I get it, you're never going to take anything I do seriously, but surely, even you can see that the theater I'm opening is going to benefit this town immensely, and I'd think you would give a shit about that, even if you don't give a shit about me."

"I don't give a shit about you?" My father's face becomes florid. "I've done everything for you boys my whole adult life. Everything I do is for my family and my community."

"Well, the only members of my family who have shown up for my last three premieres have been Mom and Eli," I point out.

"You know it's hard for me to get away. I haven't taken a day off in ten years. And I didn't see you there to celebrate at the ribbon-cutting ceremony when we completed the Holm Warehouse Lofts!" My father turns the accusation around.

"I was in freaking Croatia, wrapping a film!" I shout.

"Of course you were. Ephron's never been good enough for you, has it?" he barks back at me.

"Would you have preferred for me to let the community center rot and fall down? Maybe I should have allowed the amphitheater to become a festering swamp? That would be great for everyone, wouldn't it? Give it a rest, Dad. I'm back home now, and I'm making a difference in this community. You don't have to take a day off to support me when the Turning Table Theater opens. What's your excuse going to be this time?"

"Who wants more …" Brittany freezes in the doorway with the platter of meat. She looks from my dad to me. "Ham?"

"Thanks, Britt. I've had enough." I push my chair back in and throw my napkin on the table. "I'm really sorry, but I have to run."

Swiftly, I'm back on my motorcycle and driving. I pass by the community center and tear past Holm Square several times in circles, like I did as a teenager. I need to burn off some steam before I call Zara and finish making arrangements for my trip. The gazebo is empty today, but it seems like Chelsea should be sitting in there with her book and a half-eaten apple.

As soon as I'm done with the calls, I jump back on the bike. But I don't head home. Instead, I pull around the corner and park in front of Chelsea's apartment. When I get to the door, I'm surprised to see a familiar face. Donovan is also there, ringing her buzzer.

chelsea

. . .

"JUST A MINUTE!" I grab my black, cotton, knit robe from the chair in the studio. I can't believe it's already this late in the afternoon. I've almost got the composition ready to shoot, though I'm not exactly sure how I'll trigger the camera. I'll be sitting on a counter with both arms above my head. I can't use my fingers or my toes. I'm going to have to figure something else out.

But first, I need to eat something. I've forgotten to feed myself, yet again. This frequently happens when I get lost in a project. I don't want to stop, I don't want to pull away, and I don't even notice that I'm starving until I've let it go too long. Which is exactly the situation I find myself in now. I'm absolutely ravenous. And since I haven't gone grocery shopping in days, there isn't anything in the fridge to take the edge off. I polished off the last of the dry cereal yesterday. Thank goodness The Onion Bar and Grill is delivering, even though it's Easter.

I buzz the delivery guy into the building. I can practically smell the chili fries. My mouth is watering. I wait with my ear against the door, listening for footsteps.

256

"Just leave it by the door!" I call out through the door. My bathrobe is covering most of the paint, but I still don't want to take any chances of being seen. It's a small town. I don't want to have to explain why the high school art teacher is spending Easter alone, covered in body paint.

Much to my surprise, the delivery person knocks.

"You can just leave it!" I repeat. "Thanks! I'll send a tip through the app!"

"I'm sorry, ma'am. I'm going to need you to sign for it." The voice is muffled.

"Really? You guys always do doorstep delivery. Is that really necessary?"

"Sorry, ma'am. New policy. We've been having issues with the chili fries attracting porch pirates."

"What the?" That's ridiculous. I crack the door open and peer out through the gap. Dean Riley is in my hallway. He's leaning against the wall across from my door with his arms crossed. And he's holding my bag of food.

"These smell so delicious. I'm seriously tempted to sail off into the sunset with them." He grins.

"What are you doing here? How did you get in?" I ask.

"I bumped into your delivery guy." He smiles. "Your student? Donovan?"

"Oh, wow. I didn't know he was doing deliveries."

"Yeah, just for a couple of months till the theater opens. Then he's going to work for me as a PA and an usher. It was fortu-itous, though. I was just on my way over here to see you. You busy?"

"Actually," I say, narrowing the crack in the door so that only my eyeball is visible, "I was kind of in the middle of something. Shouldn't you be at your brother's place?"

"My dad kicked me out for texting at the table." Dean looks weary. He's still holding the bag, and my stomach is growling. "Can I come in for a minute?" I can see the shadows under his eyes. Those beautiful eyes. They look so uncharacteristically sad. I can't take it.

"Please, Chelsea? I've just had such a shitty day. And that doesn't even include the part where Eli's neighbor's kid kicked me in the balls because I was dressed as the Easter Bunny and she wanted me to be Oscar the Grouch.

"That does sound tough." I stifle a smile. "But I'm a little indisposed at the moment."

"Really?" Dean raises his eyebrows and steps forward, trying to see in the crack. "Indisposed how?"

"Oh, fuck it," I say, sticking my head out into the hallway and looking both ways to make sure nobody else is there. This whole charade is getting tedious, and *he knows*. He already knows. I throw the door open, grab his jacket, and yank him toward me. "Get in here quick before my fries get cold."

Dean is so shocked, he almost falls through the door, but he recovers quickly, laughing it off. "Jeez, Chels. You're a beast when you're hungry."

"You have no idea." I snatch the bag from him, kick the door closed behind me, and tear it open. I take it to the counter and commence eating out of the container while he watches me, amused.

"When was the last time you ate?"

"Honestly? I can't remember," I admit.

"Were you working on something?" he asks.

"Mmmph, yes." I grunt and nod, still shoveling food in.

"Slow down, you'll get a cramp." Dean rummages in the kitchen for a plate and a fork and pours me a glass of water. "I get it, though. I forget to eat, too, when I get into that creative flow state."

He sets the glass of water down next to me and runs a finger along my collarbone, revealing the streaks of dried red and black paint there. His touch is like fire, but instead of burning me, I feel like I'm melting. I hold my breath, trying not to puddle when he pulls his hand away and steps back to study me.

"So, what are you working on?"

"Can you keep a secret?" I'm studying him now too. His pale eyes. The perfect arch of his brows. His sturdy shoulders. The way his dark hair always seems to be lit with undertones of burning embers. What had Alexis called him? A smoke show.

"You can trust me with your art, Chelsea." He's staring directly into my eyes, and I know he's telling the truth.

"Okay." I nod my head and stand without breaking eye contact. What I'm about to share with him is probably my biggest secret. But suddenly, I'm burning with the need to share it with someone. Not just someone. Him. I want him to know. I want him to see. I want him to help.

I know how I'm going to get the shot now. I've never done this before, but I know what this piece is missing now. I need him. I need him to help me.

"Come with me," I say, beckoning him to follow. "I want to show you something."

The music is still on in my studio, which is lit up like a surgery. Light is spilling into the hallway through the half-open door.

"Once I let you in, there's no turning back," I say dramatically, trying not to smile. It's a reference to our childhood creations. The spaceships, the portals to other worlds. But this time, I'm only half-joking. I can't believe I'm sharing this with him. Nobody has ever been allowed inside my studio, allowed to see me work. It's my private place. For my eyes only. Until now.

"Are you sure this is what you want?" he asks.

"Yes," I whisper, and I mean it. I can feel every nerve in my body as I back through the door, pulling him into the light with me.

It's warmer in the studio, thanks to the lights, and more humid, thanks to the paint. Dean takes a deep breath as he steps inside, looking around with wonder.

"It smells like you in here … paint, and what is that, vanilla?"

"I mix essential oils into the body paints." I nod. "I make them myself."

"Oh my God, that's the kissing booth!" Dean laughs, checking out the tableau I have created at the far end of the room.

"Lemonade stand," I correct.

"Yes, that too." He nods, looking over the way I have painted the structure to reflect both uses. Lemonade to the left, kissing booth to the right.

"It's both," I say.

Dean is looking up at the rest of the scene, the cloudy sky. He steps carefully, so as not to disturb anything. He's checking everything out now and spins around, taking in the camera setup on the tripod that is connected to the large-screened monitor on the wall.

"How do you paint yourself in?"

I kick the door shut, revealing the mirrored back. Dean turns back toward the tableau, still shaking his head.

"This is amazing, Chelsea, just amazing. You're amazing."

His back is still turned when I undo the sash on the robe, letting it hang open. I take a deep breath and pick up a pot of paint and a brush from my rolling art cart.

"Do you think you could help me with something, Dean?" I ask. When he turns to face me, I let the robe drop. I don't need to see myself in the mirror. His eyes are all I need. Presently, they are dark pools, pupils wide. The music thrums, and I take a step forward.

"Whatever you need," he says as he advances toward me. "I'm here for you."

"I can't think of anyone else I would trust to help me with this." I hand him the brush and pass the pot of paint.

"My art is usually all about illusion," I explain. "In most of the pieces, I'm painted somewhere in the background. Everything about me is a part of the background. I disappear into the woodwork. I'm still there, but you don't see me."

"I saw you," Dean says. "You can't hide from me." He smiles slightly. His eyes are still devouring me, covered in a mask of paint, but still essentially naked, standing in front of him. He holds out a hand and then drops it. "My God, I'm dying to touch you, but I don't want to fuck anything up."

I smile a little wickedly. "The paint is actually pretty smear resistant once it's dried, but it's best if you don't touch it with your hands. I'm going to ask you to do some strokes once I get myself set up on the counter of that booth." I gesture to the structure.

"What's different about this piece is that I'm not going to disappear entirely into this one." I explain, "In this one, you'll see me. Not exactly *me*, since I'm painted, but you'll know I'm

261

there. Normally, I'd do all of this alone, but I think it's going to be so much easier to get this right with your help."

I position myself on the counter, one leg tucked under me, and drape some silk fabric across my lap. It's pure white on one side, but the other side is permanently streaked with smears of the same red paint I've used on the flaming half of my body. It occurs to me I ought to warn Dean about stains.

"You might want to take off your jacket and anything else you don't want to get ruined. The paint will definitely leave a mark if it gets on your clothes. That's why I have a black robe."

"Are you telling me to strip?" he asks, arching a brow. His accompanying smile is positively smoldering, adding extra heat to the already warm room.

"No. Just suggesting you make yourself comfortable," I say. I don't look away as he peels off his clothing. He doesn't stop till he gets down to a pair of black boxer briefs. Too late, I realize he's aware I'm staring at them.

"These should be fine, right?" He winks. "They're black. They won't stain."

"Get over here and paint me already." I snort.

"You'll have to tell me what you want me to do." Dean steps close. He's standing between my legs, running the dry brush along my ribs. "I don't want to do anything you don't like."

I shiver, feeling myself contract at his touch. I close my eyes, just a little concerned that what happened to me on the motorcycle might happen again if he continues to stroke me gently like that with his brush. I want to finish the piece. But I don't want him to stop.

"How much time do you have?" I ask, peeking at the mirror. Big mistake. The reflection of him standing between my legs is only making it hotter and more humid in here.

"I have all night. There's nowhere else I need to be right now." Dean runs the brush from my neck to my navel. I can feel his breath against me.

"So, just checking. You're okay with my using you for this?" I ask. "Even if it's a one-time thing?"

"Are you asking me to suffer for your art?" he asks.

"I guess I am," I admit. "And maybe that's selfish, but I don't want to suffer alone tonight." I point at the red paint and gesture at my inner thigh. "Brush some of that one here, maybe mix it with some of the pinker-toned one. I'm going for an organic look."

Dean nods, and I have no doubt that he gets it. He's always been great at sharing my visions, plucking the seeds of an idea from my mind and coaxing it into bloom.

"Just to be clear," Dean says as he strokes the exact spot where he ran his thumb against me the night I got my cast, "we're just talking about art here? Not another kind of one-night stand?"

I can see he's also not just thinking about art. There's no mistaking the bulge in his shorts. I am dying to reach out and touch him. I want to see him naked as well. I'm dying to grab a brush and paint him. I'd like to run my brushes all over his body, while he does the same to me, then sink to the floor of the studio, rolling on the canvas, mixing new colors with our bodies and …

My breath catches as he circles my left nipple with the pink paint, tracing petals.

"Rose-petal pink," he says. When he lifts the brush, my back arches and I lean forward, without meaning to. My body is reaching out to him like he's the sun. My breasts have their own agenda.

"Thank you for helping me out." I swallow my desire and try to refocus on the art. "I needed to finish this piece, and it wasn't happening. I think I really required some help with it. Not just the paint part, by the way. I'm going to need you to press the button. I can't use my hands or my feet in this position. I can't do it alone."

"Okay, Chelsea, I'll press your button," Dean says, leaning to switch to another pot of paint before continuing his journey to my other breast. "You can use me tonight for the sake of your art, but I'm not sleeping with you. That's not something I'm willing to do casually with you. If and when that happens, it's going to be special."

"If and when." I nod as I repeat his words mindlessly, aching for him to touch me some more.

"What were you thinking for your face?" Dean hesitates before placing his hand on my cheek and studying my mouth. Looking at his lips is making me feel buzzy again.

"I already shot myself with the face paint," I explain. "I'll Photoshop that in later. You can just leave my face alone."

"No, I really can't," he corrects, leaning forward to kiss me. He's incredibly careful not to touch any other part of me as he does this. The kiss is electric, and it goes on for an impossibly long time. It starts out tender and builds in intensity, moving from subtle seeking to thirsty passion. As I rock and suck on his thrusting tongue, I'm alternating between a world of color and sensation, losing myself between the physical and the sensual sensations flowing between us. It's unreal. How can a single kiss contain a whole universe like this?

I'm on the brink of abandoning my entire project to the throbbing demands of my body when he suddenly pulls away, taking a step back and spilling some paint.

"Jesus, maybe we need to play the color game with shades of blue next." Dean looks down, his face revealing his discomfort. "I'm sorry, Chelsea. This is harder for me than I thought it would be."

"That's okay," I say. My heart is pounding, and I feel my soul sinking like I've something significant. This is why I shouldn't be with Dean. I can't even stand it when he stops kissing me. How am I supposed to survive if he leaves again?

"I should probably figure out a way to get it done by myself," I mumble.

"No. Just give me a minute. I'm not leaving you hanging." Dean steps back farther and surveys the whole scene again, looking past me at the parts I've spent the entire weekend painting.

As soon as Dean steps aside, I catch a glimpse of myself in the mirror and gasp. Dean's done an incredible job with the paint he's applied to my body. His brushstrokes have called out the highlights on the lighter half of my body and deepened the shadows on the other. My body is a burning canvas of all the light and dark parts of womanhood, from bud to blossom to fruit. It's like he's seen me from the inside out and discovered a way to light me up. It's everything I could have wanted— and more.

"My God, Dean, I can't believe what you've done to me," I marvel.

"It's pretty mutual." He groans, glancing down again.

"I think I'm ready," I say. "Let's shoot this." I reach for my props. I don't want to waste another moment. I just want to capture this while I still can.

"Okay, tell me what to do." Dean crosses to the camera and flips it on.

"Can you turn on the TV monitor too? I need it to see what the camera sees."

"Sure thing." Dean moves to the side, standing behind the camera as I arrange myself, arms up, blade touching the lightning in the sky. I've got to hold up the knife at the perfect angle and form a claw with my hand, so it's evident the lemon is being squeezed. I'll digitally add the drops of juice in later.

"Now," I say.

Dean presses the button … once, twice, three times, and a few times more, capturing me in all my painted glory.

"That's it," I say, feeling more certain than I ever have about a piece. "We did it!"

I jump down and proceed to hug him, but much to my surprise, he moves away, picking up my robe and holding it out for me.

"When do you think you'll finish editing it?"

"A couple of days probably," I say. "You could come over to see it next weekend."

"Actually, I can't." Dean shakes his head sadly. "I'll be in LA."

"You're going back to LA?" I ask. "When?" My heart starts to race.

"Tomorrow morning." Dean pulls on his jeans.

"I see," I say, folding my arms across my chest. "When were you going to tell me?" Here we go. It's exactly what I feared would happen. I just didn't think it would happen this fast.

"I was coming over to tell you tonight. Something came up. I've got to go down and sort out some contracts."

"What does that even mean? How long are you going for?" I refuse to let the lump in my throat solidify. I swallow it down.

"I don't know. A week? Maybe two? Don't worry. I'll be in touch with the prom committee, and they can reach out to my brother while I'm gone if they have any questions or need to get into the building."

"Great," I say, tying my robe shut. "Sounds like a plan."

"This was …" Dean searches for an adjective to describe what we just did together.

"Super fun! Just like when we were kids, not counting the friends with benefits part, right?" Stupid words come out of me. I'm talking too fast. My tone is overly bright. This isn't me. I'm delivering someone else's lines.

"Chelsea, you are not my friend with benefits." Dean tilts his head down to look at me. "Have you had a chance to talk to Jackson yet?"

"No." I shake my head. "I was busy with this stuff, and I figured it could wait till after the break when he got home. It's not really such a big deal, is it?"

"I think it is," Dean says. "I called him earlier."

"Did you?" I pick up his jacket and head toward the living room, gesturing for him to follow.

"I did. We had a long talk," Dean says.

"Good." I thrust his jacket at him. "I hope you guys worked it out."

"I was hoping he called you. He owes you a huge apology," Dean says. "Did he call?"

"I don't know. My ringer has been turned off all weekend," I admit. I glance pointedly at my phone. "Oh, God. Look at the time. I've got to clean up, shower, and get to bed. I've got to be up early for work tomorrow."

"Chelsea," Dean says, "are we okay? You seem like you're done with me suddenly, and I didn't get that feeling earlier."

"I appreciate the help, but I'm tired now," I say, walking him toward the door. "You must be tired, too, and I'm sure you have to pack, right?"

"Will you call me tomorrow?" he asks.

"Sure," I lie, holding the door open.

"If you're worried that I'm going to tell anyone about the art, don't. I'm not about to betray you, Chelsea. We're not done here."

I want to believe him, I really do. But it's hard to get past the leaving part. Just when things start to get good, he's gotta go.

dean

. . .

I SCROLL Chelsea's social feeds while I wait for Zara at The Ivy. Nothing. She hasn't posted anything on Facebook or either one of her Instagram accounts since I left, almost three weeks ago. I'm dying to see the final version of her piece. But she has barely responded to my messages. It's like pulling teeth. I'm lucky if I get a two-word response to my texts, two days later.

If only she'd speak to me on the phone. When I spoke to Jackson last week, he told me she wouldn't speak to him, either. I even called Noah. I wanted to settle the bill for The Shepherds Hut, but more than that, I'd wanted to make sure Chelsea was okay.

Short of calling her mom and Alexis, I don't know what to do. She's freezing me out. It's like we've gone all the way back to the non-relationship we had before I came home. I'm miserable, and I still haven't wrapped everything up here.

"You look like dog shit," Zara says, settling into her seat and taking me in. "What are you even still doing here in LA?"

"Apparently, I like paying forty bucks for Eggs Benedict." I grimace at my friend and business partner.

"Highway robbery," she agrees. "Last week, I paid fifteen dollars for a side of grits. I'm surprised they didn't want an extra five for the organic butter."

"So, I'm still working out a few of the final details," I admit to her. "We've got the director and the talent. But there are still issues with the costume designer. I thought we had him, but the jerk just signed with a cruise company instead. Apparently, a summer in Ephron can't compete with the Western Med and free food. There's also the matter of craft services."

"I dunno. Seems like we should be hiring local talent for anything else we need." Zara looks over her menu at me. "You should go home already. Why are you dragging your feet? Anything else you need to talk about? Construction issues?"

"No!" I reassure her. "If anything, things are going better than planned. We're slightly ahead of schedule."

"So?"

"So, nothing." I shrug. "I don't know. I just feel like I'm not needed as much up there. LA's still home." Even as I say this, I know it isn't true. LA doesn't feel like home at all anymore. My favorite taco place shut down, and I'm annoyed by the incessant sunshine. I miss the Ephron Diner's chili con carne, and I miss playing with my nephew. I even kind of miss arguing with my dad. He's called me twice since I got down here to update me on the progress at the amphitheater. And the last time, he actually apologized for being so gruff at Easter. He asked me when I was getting back.

I miss Chelsea.

"Where's your motorcycle parked?" she asks.

"Ephron," I admit. "But that's just because I rode it up there in April."

"Let me see your phone. What's the last thing you looked at on social media?" Zara holds out her hand for my phone.

"Don't be silly." I shake my head.

"I'll bet you an order of Eggs Benedict that the last thing you looked at was Chelsea Porter's profile."

"Excuse me?" I feel my face coloring as I slip my phone back into my pocket. "Where did you even pull that name from?"

"Come on, Dean. I listen to that podcast, the one your friend does—Lit Lovers. And I heard the episode you were on with her. I was waiting for you to talk about it with me, and the fact that you haven't mentioned it at all yet?" Zara shakes her head. "Well, that tells me everything I need to know. In fact, it clears up a lot of questions."

"What kind of questions?" I ask. "I've always been an open book to you, Zara."

"Well then, this is a bonus chapter," she says, "and I can't wait to read it. Just as soon as you get your ass back to that cute, little town of yours and deal with whatever bullshit you're currently avoiding."

"You know, it's not that simple," I argue.

"Yeah, it never is, right?" She rolls her famously huge, amber eyes at me before holding up a finger and waiting for a waiter to rush over so she can order her own Eggs Benedict and some fresh-pressed juice.

"Let me guess." She continues her assault as soon as her order has been placed. "You've both always secretly had a thing for each other, but it could never work out because you're her big brother's best friend, and now you're all grown up and the sparks are flying, and oh gosh, you just don't know what to do about it."

"Not exactly," I say defensively, feeling my brows furrowing.

"Honey, I know this story. I've read the book, and I've acted it, and now, I'm going to give you a little stage direction, if you don't mind."

"Fine." I capitulate. There's no arguing with Zara when she puts on the director's hat.

"It's so simple, you idiot," she says. "You gotta haul your ass back there and not only tell her, but *show* her how you feel."

"It's not that simple. There's more to the story," I insist.

"Let me guess, a tragic misunderstanding?"

"No, not exactly. I mean, I was supposed to take her to prom, but her brother fucked it all up."

"This would be Jackson? I can't wait to meet that boy and smack him upside his head. He sort of reminds me of my brother. So, what happened?"

I fill her in on the story, minus a few sensitive details, as we eat. She listens with rapt attention, only retrieving her phone a couple of times to field messages and pull up the old memes of Bryce Holm.

She laughs at the video of Bryce trying to cover his ass. "Your pal Jackson is not messing around. This shit never goes away. Remind me never to cross him."

"He meant well," I concede. "But I can't help but think about what might have happened if he never interfered. I mean, maybe it wouldn't have led to anything. We were so young. But now, we'll never know."

"Wait. Hold up. Rewind!" Zara holds out a finger and rotates her hand counterclockwise.

"What? Which part?"

"The part where you said you wish he never interfered, and you'll never know."

"I'm not sure I get what you're talking about."

Zara is typing furiously on her phone now. "I'm booking you tickets to Washington for tomorrow. Now all you have to do is figure out how we're going to do it."

"Do what?" I'm getting frustrated now.

"The do-over. The rewind. Just … fix it!" she says.

"I don't have a magic wand." I shake my head. "She isn't even returning my calls."

"I can't believe I even have to explain this to you." Zara rolls her eyes. "Obviously, you can't actually turn back time, but you know what you have to do. Lock it down. Commit to the vision. We're talking *grand gesture*. If anyone can pull it off, it's you. You're the king of movie magic, Dean Riley. I have faith in your ability to spin it." She emphasizes her words with her hands again, spiraling her pointed finger clockwise this time.

Maybe it's the word spin. Maybe it's the motion of her fingers. But I get an idea. I know what I'm going to do.

I lean across to kiss her on the cheek.

"What's that for?" she asks.

"For helping me to look at things from a different angle," I answer. "You've given me a lot to think about. And here's some cash for breakfast. I gotta go pack."

chelsea

. . .

JACKSON SLIDES into the booth at the Ephron Diner. I've finally agreed to meet with him, if only to get our mom off my case.

"I got this for you." He's holding a large box with a ribbon on top.

"What is that?" I ask warily.

"Life's too short to drink terrible coffee." He shrugs. "I thought it might make teacher life easier if you all had access to decent coffee. Or tea. Or cocoa. I think they even make soup in pods. I subscribed you to a delivery service. There's a flyer in the box with the login info. You can select what you want. Otherwise, they'll just automatically choose some stuff for you."

"I'm sure the staff will really appreciate that," I say.

"So have you talked to Dean lately?" Jackson asks.

"Not really. Not since he went back to LA." I flip through the menu, as if I have not essentially memorized it after eating here a thousand times.

"Why?" Jackson asks. "Did something happen? Do you want to talk about it?"

"Nothing happened. I've just been really busy. I've had a lot to do at school, and I've been putting more energy into my own art."

"You're doing your own art again?" Jackson seems surprised and genuinely interested. "Good for you, Chelsea. What are you working on?"

"I'm not ready to share it yet," I tell him. "But maybe soon."

"What's the medium?"

"It's a combination of paint and photography," I say. "You know what? Here's a bit I can show you." I pull up my latest piece on my phone and zoom in on the detail of the dog.

"Murphy!" Jackson says. "He's an angel. That's just perfect. God, I miss that dog. He was such a good boy."

"He really was," I agree.

"Why the fuck was he even in the car with Dad that night?" Jackson is looking down at his hand, tears in his eyes.

"Who knows. He probably just wanted Dad to take him for a walk and followed him out the door," I say. I've had the same thought a thousand times over the years. "He really loved Dad, despite everything." So had I, I think. But it seemed nobler on the dog.

"I really let you down, Chelsea." Jackson is staring down at his hands again. "I shouldn't have left you alone in that house with Mom and Dad when Dad was such a mess. I should have gone to college somewhere closer to home so I could be there for you and look out for you more."

"Like you looked out for me with prom? No thanks. Let's face it, when you intervened on my behalf, you didn't exactly knock it out of the park."

Jackson flinches, and I ease up. "I absolve you from that particular guilt, Jackson. You were a kid too. There's not much you could have done to change things."

"Yeah, well things might have gone down differently if you and Dean had been honest with me. How was I supposed to know you were in love with each other if neither of you bothered to mention it?"

"Love is a big, four-letter word, Jackson. We were kids. I don't know that I'd go that far."

"I may be a dumbass, but I know most people aren't still pining over a trivial high school crush more than a decade later," Jackson says. "Actually, I'm kind of jealous. I've never been in love. What's it like?"

He's looking at me like he wants to take notes for his AI.

"Well," I say, rolling my eyes, "I imagine it's similar to the way you feel when you look at yourself in the mirror every day."

Jackson balls up his napkin and throws it at me.

"You should get back to Dean already," he says. "He told me that you're not taking his calls. What's up with that? If anything, you should feel vindicated. He didn't stand you up. He was totally into you, Chels. What's the issue now?"

I've been asking myself that same question. Again and again. It's like chasing my tail. It's my new favorite pastime. That and looking for signs that he might be coming home soon. Except every time I search his name online, I end up seeing photos of Dean and Zara out together, which isn't exactly reassuring. I believed him when he said they weren't a couple, but they look so good together, I can't help but feel jealous. He isn't having lunch at The Ivy with me.

"I'd rather wait and talk to him in person," I tell Jackson. "If he ever decides to grace us with his presence again."

Now that the days are longer and warmer, I've taken to walking to school daily so I can spy on the work in progress at the amphitheater. I can hardly believe how quickly things are coming together. The paths down to the seating areas have all been paved. Planters have been installed and filled with thousands of begonias. Hanging baskets dripping with colorful fuchsia plants are dangling from the lampposts of all the vintage-style lamps lighting the pathways. The seating areas have also been regraded and terraced. And last week, the covered seating areas got fitted with new seats.

This morning, when I passed, there were trucks and a crane setting up to deliver something big. I wonder if it is the mechanism that will allow the stage to rotate. The Riley teams have been working so hard, at this point, it doesn't seem like there's much more that needs to be done.

But Dean's still in LA.

"The fact that Dean was totally into me doesn't actually make me feel better." I stare into the glass of soda that Kenna has just placed in front of me, watching the bubbles rise. "In some ways, it makes it worse."

"Makes what worse?"

"The fact that he just left. He walked away, and he never really looked back, you know? If he really cared, why didn't he stick around? Why didn't he come back?"

"He went to college ... he didn't ship off with Space Corp. And after that, he was just in LA, Chelsea. He could have come back, or you could have gone to him," Jackson points out. "I mean, I've managed to stay in touch with him all this time."

"Yeah, but I didn't want to be his anchor, you know. I didn't want to hold him back."

"Like Mom did to Dad?" Jackson says, quickly making the connection. Ball and chain.

"Yeah, maybe," I say, taking a swig of the Dr. Pepper. It's so sweet and fizzy and still feels like a treat. Our mom never let us have it at home. I don't want to cop to my father's influence over me. I hate having it pointed out that his baggage left a dent in my foundation. How many times had I heard him blame my mom for his band's failure?

"You know it wasn't Mom's fault, right?" Jackson touches my hand. "Any more than it was yours or mine. Our father was a miserable piece of shit to make us feel like we were responsible for his failure."

"Well, I imagine it's hard to be a rock star when you've got a baby," I theorize.

"Bullshit. It's harder to do anything when you've got a baby," Jackson argues, "but plenty of people make it work. You know, I used to be obsessed with the offspring of successful rock stars."

"I had no idea," I say, taking another sip of my drink and thinking, *that's so Jackson*. He probably did statistical analysis on them.

"I once put together a photo album and sent it to Dad, just to point out how fucked up it was that he blamed his failure on having me."

"Seriously?" I look at Jackson. "You did that?"

"Yeah." He laughs. "But the joke's on me because most of those kids of rockers are actually pretty fucked up after all. But the point is, you and I are lucky. Somehow, we came out okay. We're normal."

"You think?" I ask, wondering if Jackson would say the same thing if he saw my art.

"Well, I mean, I know that I'm good. You seem a bit hung up on sweet romance novels and your high school crush."

"Yeah, I was thinking about all that when I made this," I say, zooming back out from the detail of Murphy to show him the entire piece.

It's worth it for the spit take.

dean

. . .

"SHE HASN'T EXACTLY FORGIVEN ME," Jackson brings me up to speed. "But at least she's speaking to me again." We are meeting at the tux shop to pick up my suit and go over the plan. "Don't worry. It's all going to work out," Jackson says confidently. "I ran some—"

"Shh. Zip it!" I hold up a finger to silence him and give him a warning look, then pull my jacket off the hook on the fitting room door.

"It better fit," I say. "There's no more time for alterations now." I eye the tired, old tailor in the corner. He's already gone back to watching a game on his phone, his ear pods at maximum volume.

"It will fit," Jackson says. "I gave him the exact measurements you sent and paid him extra for the rush job."

"And you didn't make my legs two inches shorter or my arms two inches longer?" I check the fit. In retrospect, I probably should have kept the tux I bought to wear for the Academy Awards. But I'd thought it would be bad luck to assume I'd have an opportunity to wear it again. I didn't want to tempt fate, so I'd donated it to charity.

"It was kind of tough not to mess with the measurements," Jackson admits.

Thankfully, the tux fits perfectly. Even better than the one I wore to my brother's wedding. Just to be safe, I check the seam in the rear.

"Jesus, what do you take me for?" Jackson looks wounded.

"The reason for this whole mess," I say.

Jackson pouts. "One day, the two of you will thank me. If you'd simply look at all the data, you'd understand—"

"You really need to shut it." I cut him off. "You're still on probation. I'm calling a friend. I need a second opinion."

I dial Zara, hitting the FaceTime button so I can show her the tux. She picks up right away.

"What do you think, Z? Is this going to work?"

"Of course it will work," says Zara. She's sitting in bed, eating a salad.

"I'm glad you're taking it easy," I say. Her bump is just starting to show.

"Holy shit!" Jackson says, peering over my shoulder. "I still can't believe you're actually friends with Jaguar Woman. That's really her. Like live and in person."

"Cool your jets, Jackson." Zara stares him down. "We are not friends yet."

I stifle a laugh. The last time I saw Jackson this starstruck was when we went to a comic-con together in high school and he met the son of the DND creator.

"You two will be friends," I say confidently, "eventually. You'll have no other choice. I guess I can skip the intros."

"You look good, Dean," Zara says. "Show me your shoes? And tell me how you feel."

"A little nervous," I admit.

"He's got this," Jackson says to Zara.

"Where are we on the dress, Jackson?" Zara asks.

"I've got it here." Jackson holds up a big, white box. "My mom had it cleaned, and she said since the fabric is a knit, it should fit her fine, even if she isn't exactly the same size she was in high school."

"Take the top off. I want to see it," Zara demands.

"Yes, ma'am." Jackson nods. I turn to look as well. I'm dying to see the dress that seventeen-year-old Chelsea selected to wear to senior prom.

"Dean, don't look. It's bad luck to look," Zara says.

"I think that's wedding dresses," I argue.

"I still think you shouldn't look." Jackson takes Zara's side, grabs my phone, and waits for me to close my eyes before opening the box.

"Oh, it's gorgeous!" Zara exclaims.

"My sister sewed all the sparkly beads on herself," Jackson says. "My mom told me it took her hours."

"I bet it did," Zara comments. "I sure hope that made you feel like shit."

"Pretty much," Jackson admits.

"Good. Lean in." She laughs, a little wickedly.

"You're mean," Jackson says as he packs up the dress again. "I like that. Dean didn't tell me you were mean. You can open your eyes now, Dean." He hands the phone back to me.

"We're going to head over to the community center now," I say. "Eli and my dad are already there with the prom committee. They should have everything set up in the amphitheater in the next half hour."

"Great. Looks like 'Operation Rewind' is a go," Zara says. She's clearly enjoying her remote role in this drama. "Now, go get your girl. I hope she knows how lucky she is."

"Thanks for all your encouragement, Zara," I say.

"Are you kidding? I live for this shit," she scoffs, tossing her long braids back over her shoulder. "And I owe you. You've always been there for me."

Jackson cocks his head, scrutinizing my face before commenting, in typical, straightforward Jackson fashion, "Okay, just to be clear, though, you two are definitely not an item, past or present?"

"No," I say. "We've never been an 'item.' We're good friends."

"Besties." Zara nods.

"Uh … I don't think so." Jackson looks offended. He raises his brows and folds his hands across his chest. "I've known him longer."

"And you think that means something?" Zara's brows come together and her face turns ferocious, similar to the look Jaguar Woman makes before pouncing.

I clear my throat. "As fun as it is to watch you two fight over me," I say, "Jackson and Chelsea should probably know the whole truth about our relationship, Z." I'm done with keeping secrets from my two oldest friends. "Can I tell them?"

"Okay." She nods.

I check to make sure that the tailor is still otherwise engaged before I go on. "Zara is my silent partner in the theater. That's

283

why we've been spending so much time together. We've been working out a lot of the details. I purchased the property and have paid for most of the renovations, but a theater like ours needs working capital."

"Okay, that's cool, but why keep it silent?" Jackson looks confused.

"Because this isn't my story. It's Dean's," Zara says. "I'm working on my own production at the moment"—she points down at her proto-bump—"and my significant other and I are private people. I'm happy to be playing the role of fairy godmother."

"Wow." Jackson shakes his head with admiration. "I think you just got even cooler, if that's possible."

"Don't even think about telling anyone this info, or I'll make what you did to Bryce Holm seem like child's play," Zara warns. "You'll probably see more of me later this summer. I'm just trying to stay in one place till I make it through my first trimester, but I'll be there for opening night."

"*If* the doctor says it's okay," I say.

It feels so good to finally have all my cards on the table. I'm just ending the call when the bell trills again, announcing a new arrival.

"Oh." Noah looks startled as he rolls in through the door, aided by a knee scooter. "It's you. You're back. Just in time for the prom." He looks from me and Jackson and over at the tailor, who is still so fully engrossed in his game, we could probably walk out with half the items in the shop before he noticed.

"Hey, Noah," I greet him.

"Nice tux," he comments, looking me over. "You going to be at prom? I hear from the committee that it's really coming together over at the amphitheater."

"Better than a stinky, old gym," I say.

"Yes, well, I'm sure it would have been fine in the gym, but it's really great of you to step it up for the kids."

"Of course," I say.

"And thanks for picking up the bill for The Shepherds Hut and sending my mom the Titanium Man swag. She's a real fan of the franchise."

"The Shepherds Hut?" Jackson asks.

"Long story." I dismiss the question.

"Do you think one of you could get that man's attention for me? I'm just here for a cummerbund. I'm chaperoning tonight, and I thought I'd add a little flair to my suit." Noah shifts uncomfortably on the knee scooter.

"Of course," Jackson says, tapping the tailor on the shoulder while I gather my things to go.

"Do me a favor, Noah?" I ask. "If you happen to see Chelsea, maybe don't mention to her that you ran into me? She doesn't know I'm back. I was hoping to surprise her."

"She's a really special woman." Noah scrutinizes me.

"Don't I know it." I nod.

"Well then, good luck tonight." Noah's lip quirks in a wistful half smile. "Or maybe I should tell you to 'break a leg'?"

chelsea

. . .

I POP a pod into the new coffeemaker in the teacher's lounge and make myself a coffee. I have to hand it to Jackson. This is a vast improvement. It's also made me the staff hero.

"Hard to believe it's prom already, huh?" Noah rolls in on his knee scooter. His recovery is going well, and his doctors are saying that he should be able to walk without crutches by the summer. Mara has gone home to Buffalo, and Noah's been able to resume most of his normal activities. Not that any of us are launching educational initiatives at this point.

The month of May is the hardest time of year to teach. Nobody wants to be stuck in a classroom anymore, including the teachers. One minute your students are studying for midterms, and the next, they're staring out the window, wondering if they should change the spelling of their name or dye their hair. There's an overwhelming sense that big changes are coming, and the anticipation is killing. We've all got our seatbacks in the upright position and our tray tables locked. We just have to get through finals, prom, and graduation before we taxi to the gates of summer.

"Is that a cummerbund?" I point at the festive, multicolored sash tied around Noah's waist.

"Yeah, I thought I'd jazz things up for tonight," he says. "And then I thought, why not wear it to class? Some of my students aren't going to the prom, and I'd hate to waste the opportunity to show off a perfectly good cummerbund."

"Very practical." I smile, thinking that the cummerbund over his school outfit is not unlike streamers in the gym. So Noah. But in an endearing way.

"Will I see you at prom tonight?" Noah takes a sip of his coffee before placing it in the cup holder on the scooter.

"Of course. There's no getting out of it once you're signed up to be a chaperone. I mean, they wouldn't even let you off the hook, and you broke your leg." I gesture to the scooter.

"Oh no, I don't want to get out of it. I'm a total drama junkie. It's like a night at the theater for me." Noah smiles chummily. "And I can't believe what they've done with the place. I drove by during lunch. I had no idea."

"So, it's better than the gym after all?" I tease.

"So much better." Noah smiles and studies me for a moment. "I hope you enjoy it, Chelsea. I don't think any of it would have happened without you. You're the star of the show."

"Don't be silly, Noah." I feel myself blushing. "I'd like to take the credit, but Dean Riley's the one who actually came to the rescue. He's the one who fixed the sets and offered up the community center."

I take my coffee back to the art studio. During the next block, I direct my students to wash brushes and clean out their cubbies. Their conversations all seem to be revolving around corsages, limos, and party buses. Good.

I wait a few minutes, and once they are settled into their tasks, I check out Dean's Facebook page again.

Nothing. He hasn't posted anything new since he first got home and shared about the theater. I can't believe it's been three weeks and Dean still isn't back. Not even for prom.

Where the hell is he? Prom is the first event to be held at the community center since the renovation. They're setting it up in *his* building. Doesn't he need to be here? Doesn't he *want* to be here to see it?

I wish Dean would just come home already. I have so much to say to him.

dean

· · ·

MY LAST TASK before going to Chelsea's place is stopping by the amphitheater to make sure everything for tonight is perfect. Jackson follows me in his car, parking around the corner, while I head down the slope to survey the scene.

The last-minute decision to move the prom outside to the newly renovated theater was a lot to pull off in just over two days, but when I called my dad and Eli, they were both totally on board.

"Are you kidding me? How sick would it be to go to prom in a theater with a rotating dance floor?" Eli enthused.

"Maybe you should bring Brittany," I suggested, thinking my sister-in-law would probably appreciate the do-over.

When my dad heard the suggestion, he even offered to babysit Braden so they could make it happen.

"Wow," Jackson says, jogging down the hill to join me. "This is really happening."

"What do you think?" I ask.

"It puts all the other proms held here in the past to shame." Jackson whistles. "This is like prom 2.0."

The path down to the amphitheater stage has been outfitted with a red carpet. Inside the tented terraces, round tables have been set up. They are all dressed with gold lamé table-cloths and floral centerpieces topped with playbills. Carnival lights are strung back and forth overhead, which will make the entire place glow tonight. Space heaters have been set up at intervals, but the forecast is looking like we won't even need them.

Every table is themed to match a different musical theater production that the high school has staged in the last fifteen years. There's everything from *Annie*, to *West Side Story*, *Fiddler on the Roof*, *Guys and Dolls* and, of course, my favorite, *Little Shop of Horrors*. Refurbished sets from each of these shows are lining the stage, providing the backdrop and flanking a DJ stand on an elevated podium.

A large, lit marquee on the front of the podium reads "Theater Lovers." My dad custom-made it himself, building the box, drilling the holes, and fitting them with lights.

I snap a few photos to send to Zara. She's the one who sprang for the tents and table dressing, insisting it was all good PR for the theater.

She responds immediately with hearts and lightning bolts. She's clearly reveling in the role of fairy godmother/patron of the arts. I'm just about to send another text thanking her, but I see my father and Eli coming down the hill toward us. I quickly slip my phone into my breast pocket.

"It's okay. Don't let me interrupt your message," my dad says.

"I was just thanking my friend Zara for her help with the decor," I say. I pull out the phone briefly to tap send while my dad waits patiently.

"Nice tux," my dad comments. "It suits you. Fits you better than the one you wore to Eli's wedding."

"Thanks," I say. "I thought maybe you were going to tell me I was a little overdressed for a jobsite."

"Nah, I was just about to tell this one here"—he tilts his head toward Eli—"that he needs to go home, take a shower, and get changed. He can't expect to take his wife to prom smelling like that."

"I smell great," Eli says. "I should probably check on the limo, though."

"I hope you bought the insurance policy." Jackson snorts. "Otherwise, you'd better keep your date away from the peach schnapps."

"Yeah, I got the insurance," Eli says. "Brittany won't be drinking, but I can't guarantee she won't puke at some point. Her stomach is always a little funky till she gets into the second trimester."

"Seriously?" I high-five my brother. "Congrats!"

"We weren't going to tell anyone yet, but she's already poppin, and the dress she's wearing tonight totally shows off her bump, so …"

"You two don't feel weird crashing the high school prom at your age?" Jackson asks.

"Wait till you're married with kids." Eli laughs. "We'll probably barely last till ten, but we don't get a lot of chances to get dressed up and get out these days."

"They'll probably spend the night doing it in the limo." My dad rolls his eyes.

"Dad!" Eli and I both yell at the same time, while Jackson and my dad chuckle.

"With that, I'm out." Eli shakes his head and turns to go.

"You should get out of here too," my dad says to me. "You've done enough." He surveys the scene with a look of satisfaction. "I don't think any of the kids are going to forget what you've pulled off here tonight. You're doing a lot of good for this town, Dean. I'm so glad you came back. And I want you to know I'm proud of you. I can't wait for opening night. I'm even reading *A Midsummer Night's Dream* to get into the story."

When he meets my gaze, I can see he has tears in his eyes. He shoves his big hands into his pockets and shuffles his feet. I am momentarily rendered speechless. I sneak a glance sideways at Jackson, who appears to be examining the hanging flower baskets.

"So, what do you think, Jackson?" my dad booms. "You okay with my son taking your little sister to prom? Does he have your approval?"

"Well, sir, it's not up to me." Jackson shrugs his shoulders and turns his palms skyward. "Turns out, it never was."

chelsea

. . .

THERE IT IS AGAIN. I heard it when I was washing my face, and I'm hearing it again now, as I'm changing into a simple, black, sheath dress to wear as a prom chaperone tonight.

That damned motorcycle. Every time I hear it, my hopeful heart accelerates. But it's just a phantom noise. A trick. I don't know what I was thinking would happen tonight. I guess I just really thought he'd be here. I assumed that he'd want to see how it all came out.

Apparently, Dean Riley has bigger fish to fry. California fish. Because he isn't here, and I'm assuming he's still down there.

My door buzzer sounds, and I buzz the take-out delivery person into the building. I already know it won't be Donovan tonight because he's busy getting ready to take his date to prom. Madison is probably putting the final touches on her contouring, documenting her signature "prom eye" for her YouTube channel followers.

I should have just enough time to scarf my burger and chili fries before walking over to the community center.

"You can just leave it out there," I call out through the door, remembering the last time I ordered chili fries from The Onion. What had Dean's story been? Porch pirates?

A moment later, the buzzer rings again. That's weird. Maybe the door got stuck? I push the buzzer again and go back to wait by the door. This time, I open it, checking the hallway for the delivery person. There's no sign of the guy, but my food is already sitting there in a bag on the floor outside the door. That's strange. Someone else must have rung my apartment by accident right after the delivery. I hope I didn't let a murderer into the building.

I bend to retrieve the bag and turn to go back inside. That's when I hear the elevator. The doors are opening, and someone is calling my name.

"Chels! Wait! Hang on a minute!"

———

10 Reasons to Go to Prom with Dean Riley: A List by Chelsea Porter

1. He's put up with all my bullshit for the last ten years and three weeks. Dean doesn't seem to care what anyone thinks.
2. He's wearing a tux, and he's standing in front of my door.
3. With flowers. Is that an orchid in that corsage?
4. Is that a C on that red helmet? I knew I wasn't imagining that motorcycle.

5. Is that my prom dress in the box? He got my mom to give him the dress?
6. Oh, God. His eyes.
7. And his hair.
8. And his body.
9. And his lips. He's such a great kisser.
10. Do we really need to go anywhere?

By the time we stop kissing and I catch my breath, the chili fries are cold. I don't even care. I pull Dean into my apartment.

"Is that a yes?" Dean traces my jawline with one finger as he gazes into my eyes, waiting for my answer.

"Ten years is a long time to wait for a prom date," I point out.

"Thirteen for me," he says.

"Better late than never," I whisper.

"Will you put on the dress? I'd really like to see you in it."

"You can look at this while I change." I hand him an oversize envelope with his name on it. Inside, there's a print of the image we created together. I was going to send it to him if I didn't hear from him. Suddenly, I feel shy. I don't want to watch him when he looks at it. What if he doesn't like it?

I duck out of the room, taking the dress with me. I can't believe my mother kept it all these years. It's packed in tissue and still looks brand new. I sit on the edge of my bed, examining it, this dress I so carefully selected all those years ago. It is a slinky, iridescent, silk knit, sheath-style dress. Sleeveless, with a deep V neck. The bottom edge is slightly flared. From the knee down, the dress has a pink ombre effect, reminiscent of a sunset-lit sky. It's much longer than the prom dresses girls are wearing these days. But it's not overly chaste. There's a slit to midthigh on one side. Tiny, iridescent, crystal beads are scattered across the bottom and along the bodice. I touch the color-washed area near the hem. The choice of dress had been so intentional, I'd imagined the night as some sort of symbolic sunset on my childhood.

"Here goes nothing," I say to myself, pulling the dress over my head and saying a silent prayer that it will still work. My boobs are bigger than they were at seventeen, and so is my ass.

But somehow, it still fits. In fact, I think it fits me better now than it did then. My grown-up body fills the dress out better. I'm so glad the dress was saved.

————

"May I have this dance?"

Dean is leading me down the garden path toward the amphitheater stage. The grounds have been dramatically transformed. Fresh paint and strategic lighting have elevated the high school theater sets, turning them into professional-looking masterpieces.

But the pièce de résistance is the slowly rotating dance floor at the center of the amphitheater stage.

"You got your turntable." I smile.

"I got a lot more than that." Dean squeezes my hand as we step onto the platform. The DJ is playing Coldplay's "Us Against the World," and Dean pulls me so close, I feel like I could melt into him.

"I'm sorry I missed your prom," he says. "But I don't really want to turn back time. I want to slow it down. I want to make the most of every moment. I want to be here, in it, in the moment with you."

I close my eyes and nuzzle my head into his neck, breathing in the clean, familiar scent of his warm skin. "I want that too, Dean." I inhale again. I can't seem to get my fill of him. "I hate when you leave. Please tell me that spending that much time in LA is not going to be a regular thing."

"No." He laughs. "A friend of mine pointed out that I can't call LA home anymore if I'm parking my bike in Ephron."

"Zara?" I ask, tentatively.

"She's my partner in the theater," Dean explains. "Nothing else. I swear. She's got a partner, and they've been doing fertility stuff. They were trying to keep a low profile while that was going on. She's dying to meet you. I promise there was never anything else going on there."

"I believe you." I smile wryly. "After all, Jackson's AI said that there was no hope for the two of you to date."

"His infallible AI." Dean laughs.

"You should have seen his face when I showed him my art." I smile recalling it.

"I hope he told you it was incredible," Dean says protectively. "Because it is incredible. You are fire."

"He was actually very complimentary," I say. "Once he recovered from the shock."

"Speaking of brothers," Dean says, "it just occurred to me that I haven't seen Eli and Brittany yet, have you?"

I glance around. The dance floor is crowded, but at our age, we aren't exactly blending in with the students. But it's not like they care. A few of them have even given us high fives. It should be easy to spy a couple in their mid-thirties, but I'm not seeing them.

"You looking for Eli?" Donovan asks as he and Madison cross our path, taking their place on the dance floor.

"Have you seen him?" I ask.

"We just saw them getting into a limo." Madison bites her perfectly painted lip and flutters her butterfly lashes. "It's still parked in the back of the lot, but the windows are pretty steamy."

Dean laughs as the song changes, and he spins me away to the other side of the platform. "I hope they're both getting the prom they really wanted."

"I know I am," I say. "What about you?"

"I am enjoying this do-over quite a bit." Dean cocks his head at me. "It wasn't Brittany I really wanted to take to prom."

"I know she's your sister-in-law, but honestly, I always wondered what you saw in her," I say. "She's way too conventional for you."

"You think?" Dean slides his hand over my rib cage, slowly stroking to the rhythm of the beat.

"Would she play the color game with you? Let you paint her body?" I ask.

"It's true, she never asked me to press her button," Dean whispers against my ear, sending chills through my whole body. "If she had, I might have had to admit I was just using her. Trying to get over you."

"I really tried," I admit. "I really tried to get over you. But nobody else is you. I think I just imprinted on you, or something."

"Does that mean you are team Jacob?" Dean snorts.

"I'm team *Dean*," I say emphatically, attempting to fit myself still closer to him. I need more of me touching more of him, and I need it now.

"That's fortunate"—he kisses me gently—"because I'm team Chelsea. It was always you. Do you think you can forgive me for taking so long to come back?"

There are other people on the dance floor. I know there are. But I can't feel them there. I can't see them. For me, right now, there's only the two of us, slowly spinning in the actual, starry night, staring at the stars in each other's eyes.

"I can try." I smile.

"Thanks for waiting for me, Chelsea."

"Thanks for finally taking me to prom, Dean."

"There's something else I should probably tell you." He holds my face in his hands, cupping it gently.

"What's that?" I ask.

"No pressure, but I got us a hotel room."

I turn my head to kiss the center of his palm before reaching up to take his hand in mine. We're both shaking a little now, vibrating with anticipation.

"In that case, Dean, I think I've had enough of prom. Why don't we get out of here?"

chelsea

. . .

"I DON'T WANT to hurt you," Dean says, peeling the dress off my body.

"You won't," I assure him.

He's reserved a suite at a cozy inn a few towns away. There's a fire burning in the fireplace and music playing on the sound system. Champagne is chilling in a cooler, and there's a plate of fruit on the table near the balcony. Nice touches, but neither of us has an interest in anything other than getting naked. Quickly.

I slide his shirt off his shoulders with two hands and hook my thumbs in his boxers, anxious to get them off so I can finally see all of him in the firelight. No brushes, no paint. Just the friction of bare skin on skin. I want to experiment with color on his body using my breath, my lips, and my tongue. I want to see him transform like a mood ring, powered only by my touch.

His skin is hot and silken. He smells clean and tastes like rivers. I work my way down, pausing for him to step out of his shorts. Finally, we are both naked. I press my lips to his root and roll my head from side to side, loving the way he pulses against my cheeks, my nose, my eyelids. He is purple and he is gold, shining in the firelight.

"You need to slow down." He moans. "I don't think you understand what you're doing to me."

"I don't think *you* understand." I rise slowly and press his hand between my legs, making the effect he has on me clear. "I want you. I want to feel you. I want you to paint me from the inside."

"What color shall I paint you with?"

Dean lifts me by the hips, and I wrap my legs around him as we make our way to the bed.

"All of the colors," I say.

He sits me down on the foot of the bed. "Let's start with the warm tones," he says, kneeling between my legs. He's backlit by the fire, and the skin on his back is warm from the heat radiating behind. "Lie back now." He tucks a pillow beneath my head.

"You're not too hot?" I ask.

"I'm good," he says.

"I can feel the heat from the fireplace," I say. "I felt it between my legs, when you just moved for a minute."

"And how did that feel?" he asks, breathing hotly against me.

"Like rust and dragonfire," I answer.

"And this?" His tongue darts out, to tease and flicker against me, finally daring to plunge when I moan.

"Oh, God," I say. "That's a whole other shade of desire. Slow down. Please. Or hurry up. I don't want to run out of colors."

He works his way up to my breasts, dragging his lips like a palette knife, scraping lightly with his teeth. "We will never run out of colors, Chelsea. We'll invent our own."

"Keep going," I say as his tongue moves in slow circles around my areola.

"Copper, folly, conch," he whispers, slipping one long finger inside of me. Then two. I feel myself contract against the hot, slippery tightness, almost to the point of pain, and then back to pleasure as he bends down to kiss my bud again.

"Please," I say. "Please, can we try? I want you. I want to feel all of you."

Dean positions himself above me, and I am arching toward him, my body issuing its own invitation, begging for him to push past the doorway and come inside.

"Once we do this," Dean murmurs against my lips, "once we go there, there's no turning back."

"Lust, ruby-colored lust," I say, raising my hips to meet him, feeling the shallow penetration of his tip. I'm straining against an insatiable desire to thrust higher, pull him deeper. I don't even care if it hurts at this point. Not feeling all of him inside me hurts.

But Dean holds steady above me, waiting for me to calm and relax a bit more.

"That's not lust," he says. "Kiss me and feel my heartbeat."

I lay a hand on his chest as his lips move against mine. It's fast but steady. His tongue parts my lips and slips inside to meet mine, and at that same moment, he pushes deeper into me. Only slightly. I buck up toward him, dying to meet him in the middle, to feel the entire length of him filling me.

"Your heart just sped up," I point out.

"It's matching yours," he says, pushing infinitesimally deeper. "Do you feel it?"

"I do," I say. I feel both our hearts, throbbing together.

"You know what I think that color is?" Dean asks.

"I'm hoping you'll tell me," I say breathlessly. "Or better yet, show me."

"Do you trust me?" Dean asks.

"Completely." I nod.

"Could you hold still for a moment?"

"Do you have any idea how difficult that is?"

Dean raises his eyebrows at me. "Are you kidding me?" He threads his fingers through mine, bracing his hands against the mattress as he continues to hold still for another moment. And then just when I'm sure I cannot take it anymore, he kisses me and thrusts fully, deeply, completely into my lush core. It's supposed to hurt when you lose your virginity. Everybody says this. Except it doesn't hurt when I finally lose mine. What I feel is more like expansion. Like a stretch. The good kind of stretch. The kind where you slowly lean in, taking your time and sinking deeper.

Dean doesn't stop there. Now that he's found his place, he begins to move again, slowly making that space his own. He moves against me, inside of me, recharging and rearranging my molecules with every charge.

"Are you going to tell me the color now?" I ask, waiting to hear his color word, wanting this game to go on and on forever.

"This is the color of love, Chelsea. It's the color of me inside of you, loving you, and making love to you."

That's all it takes to push me over the edge, and I take him with me as I go, but not before I manage to tell him that I love him, too, and confirm something that I think I've always suspected.

This is my favorite color.

epilogue: chelsea

We wrap the latest episode of Lit Lovers with a discussion about prom. Alexis and I think it should count as a trope, but Jackson disagrees.

"Is prom really even a trope?" Jackson argues. "It's more of a vehicle to explore tropes. I mean, everyone from Shakespeare to Jane Austen has included a big dance in their rom-coms, but it's not really a trope in its own right, is it?"

"There have been so many great movies about proms," I say.

"I loved *Pretty in Pink*," says Emily.

"I loved *Blockers*," says Jackson.

"You would love that one." I snort.

"I didn't go to prom," Emily admits. "I think that's why I like any opportunity for fancy dress parties now. I was robbed."

"I just want to hear all about Chelsea's decade-late prom date with Dean Riley. How was it? Did you guys slow-dance? Did anyone twerk? Did you guys get a hotel room after?"

"Ugh, no! No, we don't need to hear about that." Jackson moans. "In fact, we're done with this whole topic. We're not talking about prom anymore. All further talk about prom on this podcast has been canceled."

"What? That's not fair!" Emily protests.

"Canceling prom is kind of my brother's specialty." I laugh. "You'll have to forgive him. His date came out at his prom, dumping him for her best friend."

"Is that so?" Alexis perks up. "How did that make you feel, Jackson?"

"That was right around when you started developing your relationship AI, wasn't it?" I tease my brother.

"So how about that theater that's coming to town." Jackson attempts to change the subject again.

"Dean Riley's theater," Emily says. "I am so excited that they are staging *A Midsummer Night's Dream* here in Ephron.

"With Rafe Barzilay," Alexis gushes. "I need to get everything waxed and *Summer Stock* ready, stat."

"Don't you think that's a little presumptuous?" Jackson sounds doubtful. "I'm sure a superstar like him isn't looking for a small-town hookup."

"I mean, you never know, he might date local." Alexis is hopeful. "Sometimes celebrities date regular people."

"I think that's a whole different trope," I mention. "One where he'd need a safe place to hide out, and you'd need to be a grumpy innkeeper with a garden that needs tending."

"I can absolutely run with that scenario," Alexis enthuses. "And in that case, maybe I should skip the waxing?"

"The cast will be arriving next week to start rehearsals," I point out. "And there are a couple of surprises that have yet to be announced about who's coming. I guess that means people will just have to follow the Turning Table Theater of

Ephron on Facebook, Instagram, and TikTok if they want to find out more about Rafe and the rest of the cast."

"You little shit. I see how you did that." Jackson snarls. "You can tell your *boyfriend* if he wants a plug on my podcast, he can pay like all the other sponsors."

"How about you tell your *best friend* that you'll be happy to plug his theater, and promise that you'll never meddle with his love life ever again," I say as sweetly as I can. "But seriously, performances are scheduled for a limited run in July, and seats are sure to sell out. It's a can't miss, so make sure to buy those tickets as soon as possible."

"Enough!" Jackson throws a pillow at me.

"Well, folks, sounds like this episode is about done." Alexis sighs. "I'm not sure what else to say besides, 'Lord, what fools these mortals be!'"

THE END

author's note

I have a confession. I never went to my own prom. I graduated a year early, and more to the point, nobody asked me to go with them. It made writing this story bittersweet. I could imagine how Chelsea felt.

The house I grew up in was in a cul-de-sac, and my bedroom windows looked out onto the street. I recall sitting in my room and spying on my neighbors as they loaded into their limos, dressed to the nines. I told myself I didn't care, and that prom was a "stupid provincial ritual" that didn't matter. What did I care if a bunch of people who liked to get drunk in basements had a party without me? Wasn't that the whole reason I'd chosen to graduate early? So I would be free to do cooler stuff?

Yeah, right. I wasn't fooling anyone. Not even myself. Where was my Jake Ryan?

As a teenager, I was like Dean, in a hurry to get out of the town that I grew up in. I couldn't wait to live in a city with clubs and galleries, theaters and museums. I wanted to travel and meet people who were more like me—dissatisfied with the status quo, too sensitive, too smart, too young, too much of everything.

But also had the fear that I would never be enough.

As an adult, I am sad that I didn't go to my prom. I am sad I was in such a rush to leave so much of my childhood behind. I love following my high school friends on Facebook. We have history. Now I wish I'd paused long enough to make that memory, and found someone to go to prom with me, even if it wasn't a Jake Ryan situation.

There are a few other things I had in common with the main characters in this book. Like Dean, I have always struggled with feeling like I had my parents' approval. And like Chelsea, I am a little sister, well acquainted with the teasing and torture that older brothers can dish out.

The thing I related to most in this book was Chelsea's need to express herself artistically, even if she was not being acknowledged for it. My creativity has to come out, one way or another. Although I have yet to experiment with trompe l'oeil painting, I do feel a bit like I'm getting naked in public every time I release a new book.

I'd love to hear what you thought of this book. You can email me any time: Author@CiaraBlume.com.

If you enjoyed this book, I hope you will take a moment to leave a review on Amazon, BookBub, Goodreads, or wherever you buy and/or share book recommendations. Your reviews help other readers find what they are looking for, and they also mean the world to me.

Here's all the places you can find me:

Facebook https://www.facebook.com/ciarablumeauthor

Instagram: https://www.instagram.com/xociarablume/

Goodreads: https://www.goodreads.com/ciarablume

Book Bub: https://www.bookbub.com/authors/ciara-blume

If you'd like to enjoy bonus chapters, fun giveaways, and a heads up about the latest books in the Lit Lovers Series, sign up for the Ciara Blume Playlist on https://www.ciarablume.com

xo,

Ciara Blume

26851712R00194